ATHANIA

ATHANIA

J. Peter Barragan

LEONINE PUBLISHERS
PHOENIX, ARIZONA

Published by

Leonine Publishers LLC
Phoenix, Arizona, USA

ISBN-13: 978-1-942190-55-4

Library of Congress Control Number: 2019920401

Visit us online at www.leoninepublishers.com
For more information: info@leoninepublishers.com

Dedication

To my wonderful mother, Isabel B. Barragan.
Her prayers, love, and encouragement
made this book possible.

Contents

Chapter 1

Unwelcome Visitor

The reader stared intently at the paper, rereading it, hoping it would be different. Tearing through the first paragraph, she willed the letters to form different words and those words to create different sentences. A sigh escaped her lips, and her eyes closed.

Not again!

A sudden chill penetrated to her core—she was no longer alone. Her eyes opened, but she didn't look up; the overwhelming presence filled the room. The door was still closed and had never opened; this visitor didn't need doors.

He's watching me, she thought. *If I ignore him, he'll go.*

The reading resumed, her attention never leaving the newsprint. The presence enveloped her like heavy fog. He had promised to return, and true to his nature, it was always when she was least prepared to deal with him. He would not be greeted, not this time. She reached the end of the story, but her eyes never left the paper. Her gaze quickly returned to the beginning.

If he is ignored, he will go away, she hoped.

His eyes did not look at her, but peripherally, they recognized her attempt to pay him no attention. The intruder willed its presence upon her, but acknowledgment was not needed — she knew he was there. Motionless in the chair, he was a statue. They'd played this game before; the first to speak lost. The intruder always won. Patience was his strong suit. He so wanted to see those eyes — it had been too long.

"My eyes are pleased...I've missed you so." He shifted in the chair and crossed his legs. Her indifference amused him.

Always playing this game, he thought.

She kept reading, her only movement the turning of a page. The visitor stared directly at her downcast eyes.

He continued: "Much time has passed. I never expected you'd end up somewhere like this. Someone of your quality deserves better."

A well-manicured hand swept dramatically around the room, hoping she'd respond. Looking at the sparse office, he noticed that the only item of prominence was a neatly arranged bookcase, firmly attached to the wall.

"These many books, you of all people know they are filled with lies — especially that one." His gaze settled on the largest book on the shelves; a space of nearly a foot on either side separated it from the others. Its significance was clear.

2

"Every time I hear of it or see it, I fear for the naive souls that will be enticed by its falsehoods. It is a work of fiction, pure fiction. How can so many be fooled by the written words of a mortal?"

"I know the truth, something you've never spoken." The reader broke her silence, but did not look up. The game and its outcome were known to her. Unlike the past, she was now prepared.

"I don't lie; I've never lied, especially not to you." He turned from the bookcase and their eyes locked.

"So beautiful." He sighed heavily. "Your eyes…so stunning…I've missed them so."

Her stare bored into cobalt irises, his contrasting dark hair making them as bright as a clear night moon. He wore an expensive black suit, dark shirt, and red tie. Their eyes remained locked as both waited for the silence to break. He was something she never wished to see again, but she knew why he was here now. Not looking at him was impossible; his gaze was magnetic.

"You are here, why? I told you your presence was something my life needs not." The lips moved, but her face was stone.

"You desire my presence. That is why I am here."

A faint smile softened his face. Hers remained firm. The more he stared, the more he thought of Greek statuary.

"It has been a long time, I'd wager four or five…" He stopped when her gaze flickered downward.

Slowly reaching across the desk, a long-fingered hand drew the paper toward him, but he did not turn it around. His eyes moved from right to left as he read upside down.

"You think I had something to do with this? Why?" A pained expression crossed his face. "As logical as you are, you can't connect this to me. I've been wronged many times, but this is…"

He continued reading, eyes darting back and forth. When finished, he sat back and let out a long breath. His head tilted upward, and then in the direction of the bookcase.

"You know He's never coming back." When he returned his attention to her, she was not looking at him—she was looking at the book.

"He will, and you know it—that is why you worry so."

He saw a faint expression of satisfaction appear on her lovely face. Focusing back on him, her expression returned to stone.

"That…that…subversive 'self-help' book has been the cause of so much chaos and confusion. I hoped once the 'magician' had gone back to His master, everyone would forget Him and things would return to normal. I didn't think His 'talking heads' would spread His lies so effectively." He grimaced as if he tasted something sour.

"Things would be much different, worse for all of us, if He hadn't opened people's eyes. Those who

4

keep them closed will wander aimlessly." She gazed wistfully out the window.

"You believe this because of what? A few parlor tricks and mass-hypnosis? I offered the truth, but instead, they believed Him. You remember that saying: 'Greatness inspires envy, envy inspires spite, and spite spawns lies.'" He shook his head. "You were young and impressionable, seeking answers. You wanted to believe His soothing words. I showed the reality, but you refused it. The hysteria enveloped you, and blindly you followed His band of liars. I provided a key, yet you refused to open the door." He shook his head. "You'd be in a much better state if you'd followed my instructions."

"I was there—saw what He did. There was no deception." She watched a small bird fly from a nearby tree. "A key? That wasn't a key—it was a curse. And if that portal opened...even poor Pandora could not fathom the terror that would be unleashed." She looked around the room, as if seeking something.

"If you only use the power inside you...one little step." His fingers made a walking motion on his palm.

"That's akin to infecting an innocent person with a deadly disease." She rubbed her hands as if washing them.

A long silence followed. The reader looked back down at the paper and he stared out the window.

He took a deep breath. "You have been missed. It's been too long. I do love you so. I merely wanted

5

to share my good fortune with you, and the world. In the short time we were together, you taught me more than my many years of study. You're truly a special being."

He talked, and she stared at the newspaper.

"After all this time, the falsities, the deception, you were the one person who I thought would be able to see through it. I was the victim of a smear campaign. He is the one who truly hates me, not the other way around. I was my Father's favorite, and deservedly so. Michael and I were like brothers, but his jealously clouded his mind and he betrayed me. I simply questioned our Father and he banished me from the community. Michael used his influence to turn the others against me. I had my allies, but we were outnumbered. Because they raised the same questions, they were banished too. Michael's army could not destroy me, so they decided to murder my reputation with false hopes. I know not what saddens me more; the loss of my family or the awful things they said about me."

He lowered his head and looked at his hands. She looked up from the paper and was about to speak.

"You needn't say it. I will leave you now." With that, he left in the same manner he arrived.

When he vanished, she got up from her desk and removed the large book from the shelf. Opening it, she removed a small card. Looking upon the face on the front, she whispered, "Please come back! The world needs you."

Chapter 2

Learning to Not Believe

"There is no God."

His conviction was unquestionable.

"For that matter, there is no Jehovah, Jesus, Buddha, Mohammed, Allah, no creator of the universe, no higher omnipotent being, no saints, no angels, no Holy Spirit, no ghosts, no anything like that. Air is the only thing we can't see, but know it truly exists."

Using the chuckles as a pause, the speaker sipped water. He scanned the crowd over the top of the glass; his satisfaction swelled — the hook had worked.

"Some believe fairy tales, and want you to believe them too. They've been fooled and want you to be fooled too. Those who accept the made-up stories to be true, think it will 'save' their non-existent souls. The leaders deceive you because they want to control you, control your mind, and take your possessions and money. The believers of these fables follow the leaders like brainless sheep."

Stepping away from the podium, he surveyed the audience again. They hung on every word, and he thrived on it. The skeptics—he'd work on them later.

"When man evolved from the ape, he also developed an intellect—a blank slate. Without teachers or books, he alone created explanations for his world. The first thinkers wondered much: 'What was that big yellow ball above? Why does it go up and down? What is the smaller blue ball up above and why does it come out after the big hot one leaves? Why are they not side by side? Why is one big and one smaller? What are the little lights up there near the blue sphere? And why are they seen when the hot ball is not there? Why are they there at all? Why are some easier to see than others? Why can't they be touched?'"

On a large screen behind the lectern, an image of the sun, moon, and stars appeared. The speaker strolled to the opposite side of the stage.

"Without the truths of modern science, early man could only guess. Everything was 'magic' and must be where it was for an inexplicable reason. Tribes and clans formed, and talk and questioning began. The talking produced theories and explanations. Somewhere in all these 'caveman klatches,' the fable was born; the story of a 'higher power.'"

The screen behind the speaker went from blank to an image of cavemen, sitting around a fire. Their hands were wildly gesticulating. Some appeared awed, some looked skeptical, but they were all focused on the one who was talking.

"When early man discovered fire, he was astonished. The flame's essence was mystifying; it was painful when touched, gave warmth at a distance and allowed him to see at night. Animal flesh tasted better when the fire touched it. He reasoned fire was a good thing, even though it was an unknown. Group discussions led to the belief that all the things in his environment were somehow interconnected."

He strolled back to the podium and drank more water. Glancing at the audience, he saw that some were taking notes. He was pleased.

"As early men talked, some noticed that explanations caused others to pay attention. The 'explainers' realized they could use their stories to manipulate fellow tribe members. The more fanciful the explanations were, the more people relied on them for information. This 'Pied Piper' approach eventually led to the concept of religion. These first priests convinced the gullible that they had the ability to intercede with the higher powers. All the clerics asked for was unquestioned obedience. In the early days of civilization, devoid of science, the masses fell for the scheme, hook, line, and sinker. These original con artists planted the seeds of the worldwide epidemic we now have in the concept of organized religion."

A new image appeared on the screen; it depicted an early human, wearing an elaborate headdress. His outfit was festooned with feathers, bones, and leaves.

"The first hucksters spun their tales into convoluted doctrines and gospels, complete with ceremonies, rituals, and rites. The harder the rules became, the more power the priests wielded. The masses of fools grew to unimaginable proportions."

Upon the utterance of the word "masses," a new image appeared on the screen: a packed church. A religious service was underway; it was a Catholic Mass.

"As you see, things have not changed much in the last few millennia. Early man can be forgiven for his gullibility, but modern man has no excuse. With all we know today—the idea that thinking people still believe in religion! It would appear that all we've gained from evolution is the ability to talk and walk upright. The ninety percent of the world that believes in religion are no better off than the first cavemen." The speaker smiled inwardly when the crowd chuckled.

"In spite of all this idiocy, there is hope for the future—your presence here proves that. Some of you are probably under the 'God Spell,' but my hope is that you will come over to the side of logic and science. When you learn to see the world without the blinders of religion, things will become clear and you will regain control of your own life."

As he uttered the last word, he saw the crowd's demeanor change ever so slightly. *The hook is set*, he thought. Things were on schedule.

"There is evidence that God does not exist. The tricksters have no evidence that He does. They use words like 'faith' and refer to the writings of their predecessors as 'proof.' They point to books like the Bible, Torah, Talmud, Vedas, and Koran as evidence. These collections of 'fairy tales' are nothing but the scribbles of earlier storytellers and liars. They point to this collection of scratches as proof of their version of 'God.' They try to convince you that if you do not follow these creeds, you will suffer in agony. They try to convince people that if you adhere to their rules, and contribute to their cause, you will find salvation, peace, nirvana, and paradise."

A new image appeared: a group of preachers, swimming in a pool filled with gold coins.

"We will take a short break; when we reconvene, we will move on."

Another drink and a glance at the group. Some pointed to the screen image and chuckled. He was about to reel them in.

Chapter 3

Dreading Discovery

Ania stared out the window at the cloud-shrouded skyline. She used all her mental energy to erase the memory of the visitor. Her mind's grip was strong and she feared it would trigger his return; he was not wanted or welcome.

A sudden brightness parted the clouds, forcing her to adjust her gaze. The winter dreariness was tiresome, and she hoped the sun's surprise appearance foretold warmer days ahead.

"Doctor?" The voice followed a gentle knock from the doorway behind her.

Her reverie broken, she turned. The door was ajar, but the speaker was not visible.

"Please, come in." She turned over the morning's newspaper.

"Hello, Doctor, I'm early for our appointment, but your assistant said it would be alright to come in." The door opened the rest of the way and her newest visitor walked in. "Your Greek is near-perfect. Sounds like you studied in Crete, but also spent some time in Athens." She smiled as he approached.

"Good call. I did learn it initially in Crete — and a few years later spent time in Athens."

He stood in front of her desk, and rising, Ania extended her hand. Shifting a briefcase from his right to his left, he firmly shook hers. The room started to spin and Ania felt as if she were losing her balance. The guest's hand was released, and the doctor used both of hers to steady herself on the desk.

"Are you all right?" He reached to catch her, but she waved him off and quickly sat down.

"I'm fine — stood up too fast. I have occasional bouts of vertigo. Please, have a seat." She motioned to the chair next to him.

He presented a card.

"I've been expecting you, I'm always glad to help. Please make yourself comfortable. May I offer you something to drink? Water? Tea? Coffee?"

"Tea would be great. Very cold out, something warm would help." He smiled sincerely at her.

Looking at the card, she said, "A pleasure to make your acquaintance, Mr. Airaldi. Excuse me one moment." She picked up the telephone. "Grace? Would you please be so kind as to bring some tea for our guest? Thank you." She gently set down the handset.

"Please, Doctor, call me Ben." He set down his attaché. "Is something burning?" Ben sniffed the air. "Smells like an entire matchbook was just lit."

"I had a scented candle burning for a spell, took a few matches to keep it going." Ania slid open the window, hoping the sulfuric odor of the last visitor would finally dissipate. "Some tea will be here shortly. Excuse the clutter; I need a bigger office or fewer books." She motioned toward the bookcase.

The doctor was trying not to stare, but her new visitor looked faintly familiar. She'd never actually seen him before, but something about his persona felt comfortably familiar, as if she'd known him for years.

"I'd vote for the bigger office—can't have enough books. My own office looks like a library, no bookcase though." He chuckled. "Doctor Socratatos, we appreciate your taking time out of your schedule to help. You've done so much already." He spread his hands wide.

"Please, it's Ania only, the students call me 'Doctor.' From your credentials, won't we be calling you doctor eventually?" She nodded approvingly in his direction.

The doctor's compliment was significant to Ben; he'd never met her before, but her reputation was renowned in the realm of Western civilization studies. She had no equal.

"Someday—but aren't we all students? Your PhD is one of my ultimate destinations, the master's

degrees are just mile markers—learning is a passion."
He let out a breath. "On another note, thank you for
your work on the Ron Black matter. Your analysis
cleared the air once and for all." He shook his head
as if relieved. He didn't want to gush, but her body
of work was the most impressive thing he'd ever
studied. Athania Socratatos was about his own age,
but she wrote about Ancient Greece like she'd seen it
firsthand.

"Mr. Black claimed that his work was fiction, but
during his junkets and interviews, he presented it as
fact." Her thumb motioned dismissively at the bottom
of the bookcase. "Having a copy here troubles me, but
now and then a student or colleague challenges my
critique and I need to refer to it."

Ben looked at the book, sitting unceremoniously
between two volumes entitled *Telling Lies* and *Fiction
Is Better than Fact*. The top of the book revealed
numerous yellow sticky notes pointing out. They and
the novel were dog-eared. It was obvious she'd been
through the work many times. Her reputation as a
scholar was well-known; he was glad she'd "chewed
it up." He detested the book like nothing else. He
laughed to conceal his disgust and said, "A 'liar's
sandwich'?"

"Precisely; it's a disgrace. His reasons were
mercenary, and he didn't care if it would be used
as a weapon. A weapon in the never-ending war
against…"

She was interrupted by the sudden entrance of a lithe young woman wearing a bulky gray sweater and matching slacks. She carried a tray with a teapot and two cups.

"Thank you so much, Grace—I appreciate it. Leave for lunch early." Ania turned the tray so that one of the cups was closer to Ben.

Grace looked at Ben and he smiled, causing her to blush. The doctor had already noted how handsome Ben was, but she was much older than Grace, and could control her outward tells better than the younger woman.

The girl's complexion returned to its natural color when she turned to her boss and protested, "Doctor, it's only ten and there are things to finish before lunch."

"I understand, but you've got a thesis due soon. I can review those term papers myself. Take the extra hour and go work on it—somewhere away from here. You need quiet." Ania smiled and made a gesture of plugging her ears.

"Thank you, Doctor, be back by noon." She turned to leave.

"Make it one. I need some..." Ania exaggeratedly looked around the room as if searching for something. "I need some multicolored note cards; they have them at that new bookstore on Stone Peak Way. The java is good, too." She winked at her.

"Thank you!" Grace squeaked, and made a quick exit.

"Hard worker?" Ben said after she left.

"Very hard—too hard. She's writing her master's thesis and needs to finish soon. I promised her I'd review it. She loves books, too. Grace lives across town, and that new bookstore is too far from her home." Ania poured hot water into his cup.

"I love books. Problem is finding them in other languages." He lowered a bag of tea into his cup.

"Really? What languages?" She looked up from her mug.

"My goal is to have at least one book in every known language; it's a hobby." Ben sipped his tea.

"What other languages do you speak? Greek is clearly your strong suit," she said in Greek.

"I can read and write Italian, French, German, Portuguese, Spanish, and some Russian. I'm learning Dutch and Welsh. Japanese, Mandarin, and Cantonese will follow soon." He took another sip.

"Quite an impressive course of study. I understand why you work where you do. You must be very busy." She cradled her cup with both hands, and blew the steam away.

"Always been a dream to be in the one place where all the world's languages are spoken, sometimes shouted. I listen in on the discussions, very rewarding. There's something about hearing a native speaker talking with other native speakers on neutral ground." He set the cup down.

"That's something. I've sat in on some sessions, hearing the representatives from the various countries, and trying to guess what region they're from. That's my hobby."

She looked at Ben; as learned as he was, Ania was relieved he spoke plainly and didn't put on airs. He didn't have the "I know more than you do" aura that many of her colleagues did. He probably knew more than most university teachers, but he had the humility of a student. He was likable and she was curious about his experiences.

"Doctor, I mean, Ania, do you think in Greek or English?" He sipped from his cup; the hot liquid didn't faze him.

No one had ever asked her that question; his curiosity intrigued her. "Well, Ben, what do you think?" She raised an eyebrow, playfully putting him on the spot. Class was now in session.

"Greek's your native language, but your English is flawless. You have no accent, yet your pronunciation tells me that you learned English later in life. I guess you first learned in the United Kingdom and perfected your English skills in the States. You have the ability to think in both languages." He set down his cup and waited for her reply. A wisp of confidence flashed across his face.

"That is very good — you are correct. Any thoughts on what region of the United States my

English-speaking abilities were polished?" Her expression encouraged him to continue.

"My estimation is you learned by listening to English speakers from various regions of the States, but that's based on your writings. Your spoken words lead me to Maryland, St. James?" His words were said uncertainly, but his expression said he knew he was correct.

"Very good! Your linguistic skills are excellent. Which writings of mine were you referring to?" She looked at him, concealing a growing admiration.

"The writings on Black's book. I'd read his 'hit piece,' though solely for scholarly reasons. Every word was a slap in the face. Your response made his book look like the tabloid rag that it was. His lies were exposed and the issue settled." Ben gazed at Ania with gratitude.

"I just told the facts, and countered him line by line, chapter by chapter. He didn't have an agenda, other than his desire to make money. His backers, the ones with the agendas, were pulling his strings."

As he listened, Ania surmised that Ben was her apparent age. Her professorship made an impression and he showed the right amount of respect. She saw his admiration, and it embarrassed her. *If he only knew the truth*, she thought.

"You know his book sales dropped by fifty percent the day after you released your critique?" He laughed.

"That was not my intent. He had a right to earn his living, but the minute I heard of the book, my reaction was obvious. My goal was strictly scholarly. If his bottom line suffered, well... He actually contacted me recently. Believe it or not, he wished to collaborate with me on a new work." She ruefully shook her head.

"You turned him down?" The answer was already known.

"I graciously declined on ethical grounds; he was politely informed I do not write fiction, especially his kind, that which deceives."

"Let me guess...aliens?" Ben snorted.

"Unfortunately, yes. He wanted to write about how ancient space visitors arrived during the BC to AD epoch and..." She couldn't finish.

"Let me guess; He was an alien and the Twelve Apostles too." Ben snorted again.

"Actually, half-human, an alien for a father and a human mother." Ania showed a flash of anger.

"His Father was not of this Earth, but He was the Son of God, not a martian." Ben said seriously.

"The unfortunate truth is that if his efforts bear fruit, people will buy into it even more than his last piece of 'airport lounge literature.'" She sighed.

"The current heroes today are vampires, wizards, witches, werewolves, and zombies. This trend troubles me. Evil is being glamorized and even exalted. It's as if we're all being conditioned to accept it." Ben scrunched his face, like a young child trying to figure something out.

Ania reflected on what Ben had said for a few moments before speaking; her second visitor was the antithesis of her first that morning. She wondered how Ben would feel if he knew who'd been sitting in the very same chair an hour earlier.

"Well, you didn't come here to discuss the rantings of a delusional mercenary. What may I do for you…and the mission?" Ania took out a pen and pad of yellow paper. As was her habit, she noted the date, time, location, and name of the person with whom she was speaking. Weeks, sometimes months later, it was much easier to identify an errant piece of paper if she knew with whom and when she had spoken.

"Well, it's about a recent discovery in Germany." As he spoke, Ben leaned over his briefcase, not looking at her.

She was relieved, for if he had been watching, he would have seen her reaction to the word "Germany" — she broke the metal tip of her pen on the paper.

Not now! she thought.

Looking back at her, Ben saw her expression dissipate. It was fleeting, and he quickly forgot it.

Ania maintained a neutral, scholarly look. It masked a waking worry.

Not there! she thought, as she picked up another writing instrument, and resumed. Focusing on writing allowed her to conceal her concerns.

21

Chapter 4

The Numbers Game

"Thus far, we've discussed the theory and history of organized religion. Let's shift gears, and I'll show you something amazing. During this morning's registration, you were given a notepad and pen, please take them out; as you do so, every one of you think of a number between 1 and 999."

Sipping strong, hot black java, he studied the audience.

"All have a number in mind?"

Most in the audience nodded their heads in unison. Some were still looking for their paper and pen.

"Now, what I would like you to do is write that number down on your notepads. Please make the numbers large enough so that you may read them from the pad as it sits on your lap. Concentrate on the written numbers and burn them into your mind."

The audience did as instructed and signaled that they were finished by looking at him.

"You all have the number written and can you see it in your mind's eye?"

They nodded.

"Okay. Here you go…catch!" From the podium, he forcefully threw a large foam ball to an audience member about five rows back.

The surprised man looked to the speaker after catching it.

"Sir, you with the ball. Have you visualized the number written on your paper?"

He slowly nodded.

"Sir, I look at you, and you have the number in your mind's eye. Your number is written on the pad on your lap. Is there any way I can see that number?"

The man shook his head.

The speaker closed his eyes for a moment, looked up at the ceiling, and gesticulated with his hands as if in a trance. After a few seconds, he looked directly at the man. "Sir, your number is 777." He said it with confidence, and the man looked down in amazement at the number on his pad.

The pad was displayed to those around; they all saw the number 777.

"Kind sir; please throw the ball to someone else in the audience, but do not look where you throw. Toss it like a bride would hurl a bouquet, over the shoulder."

The man launched the ball seven rows back and a long-armed woman caught it.

"Ma'am, you are now holding the ball, please do as the gentleman before you did. Look up at me and visualize your written number in your mind." He focused on her like a laser. Quiet murmurs emanated from the crowd. He closed his eyes again and looked at the ceiling as if he were searching for the answer.

"Your number is 457." This was said with the same level of confidence.

The woman looked quickly down and up; she was shocked.

"Please show your notepad to those around you." As she did so, looks of awe were cast at the speaker, and the murmuring grew louder.

"My gentle lady, please throw the ball to someone else, just like the man before you did."

She wildly tossed the ball still looking at the speaker. The ball bounced off a few grasping hands and landed in the lap of an elderly gentleman several rows behind her. The octogenarian with the ball was given the same set of instructions. Once again, the correct number was announced. The man was amazed, and he looked at those nearby.

The murmurs grew louder yet. Every time the ball was thrown, eager hands reached for it, their owners hoping to make the speaker guess incorrectly.

For fifteen more minutes, the ball was randomly tossed, and each time the speaker successfully reported the number. By the thirtieth time, the audience was abuzz, and suspicious glances were cast about. Every time a number was announced and the catcher showed the crowd the same number on his notepad, gasps and wide eyes abounded.

"By my count, I have correctly told thirty out of thirty random people the number they thought of and wrote on their notepad. All thirty were in random positions in this auditorium, and have come from varied backgrounds. They do not know one another. You have all seen that there was no way this could have been staged or preplanned. The tossing of the ball was completely subject to chance. If you think this was a trick, will you at least acknowledge that the selection of the 'guesses' was in no way predetermined?"

Most of the audience nodded their heads, some hesitantly and some forcefully.

"You are all charged up, and now would be a good time for a break. We will continue afterwards."

With that, the lights were turned up, and people got up from their seats.

The speaker walked off stage and quickly disappeared. As the audience stood, there was loud chatter about the demonstration and people were trying to guess how he did it. The words "trick," "magic," and "psychic," were uttered. The word "witchcraft" was even heard once.

Chapter 5

As Bright as the Dark

The darkness was impenetrable. It had never seen the light of day or any other illumination. It was total and complete darkness, devoid of any semblance of illumination.

"What is thy bidding, my liege?" a penitent voice prayed.

"Your task, what comes of that?" A growling, baritone voice echoed within the darkness.

"She has held out for much time; I presumed she would have already submitted to the lure of your power and glory." The penitent voice paused. "Her resolve surprised me."

"Her sire taught her well. She clings to his ministrations, despite all that has transpired. He could not have known what was to come, but his fortified spirit crossed and was passed to her." The baritone was tinged with anger.

"Convincing her to make the right choice was a challenge I accepted. Stronger souls have already come to your light. An opportunity to awaken the anger she once felt, that will push her across," Penitent's voice proclaimed.

"It was unfortunate she looked up at that moment, and saw that beacon, for she not only knows of Him, she knows of His power. That may prove an insurmountable barrier." The baritone cracked when it said "Him."

"She clings to what she believes her eyes saw. She may have her father's conviction, but that is mere faith, and faith can be tested. I can convince her to bring others to our cause... One soul is all she needs, that will topple the rest." Penitent's voice was arrogant.

"Had she succumbed, we would not have wasted time with lesser converts. We would rule, and He would be cast aside in shame." The baritone became a rumble.

"It is unfortunate she has delayed your plans—our plans, but my other endeavors are bearing fruit. You see how a passing whisper can cause someone to destroy those he says he loves," Penitent said triumphantly.

"Yes...that was a partial success; unfortunately he was the only one we claimed. Those he destroyed go to Him." Baritone said "Him" with contempt.

"I find that mere whispers into the unthinking mind start ripples that grow into tidal waves. If I can start one large enough, it would end this silly game now. Unfortunately, many waves dissipate," Penitent said with sorrow.

"This game is useless. I warned Him so long ago. He has the power to bend all to his will, yet he lets them decide. It is as if he is trying to prove something. I asked Him why he gave these creatures the choice, but His explanation made no sense. He thought that by the power of His good graces, they would follow Him willingly. I warned Him that these talking primates were not worthy of his efforts, yet He constantly referred to them as His 'children.' This troubled me, for I thought we were His only family," Baritone said with anger.

"His confidence in the intellectual powers of these creatures will be His undoing. I have proven that many times. He gives them silly rules to follow; all I need to do is say things in their ears and their response is base. The rest is their own doing," the penitent voice answered.

"Be wary my son…something is coming, I know not what, but I have sensed it." Baritone's voice quaked.

"He is not going to return now!" Penitent protested.

"No, He is biding his time. I believe He is going to give the primates a symbol—something to strengthen their misguided beliefs. I know not what, but it is coming." The baritone was certain.

"I too sensed something, after seeing my protégé. Almost as if a presence was…following me. I could not see it, but it was near," Penitent offered.

"Continue your efforts. You whisper, then a primate listens and is brought to our cause." The baritone's statement concluded the meeting.

"Your words are my command, Father."

Chapter 6

Uncomfortable Facts

Ben rifled through his briefcase. His attention diverted temporarily from her, Ania used the opportunity to set her expression.

"Doc...Ania, I'll start at the beginning—it will make the most sense, and place the discovery in its historical perspective. With your background, you'll certainly catch things we've missed. I have a report from a colleague who documented the find. I'm sure you know Doctor O'Toole. It's current as of three days ago."

Once he'd straightened his papers, his gaze returned to Ania. She was sipping her tea, deep in thought. Ben noticed her demeanor was different, but his excitement about the information pushed this observation aside.

"Very well...proceed." Ania set the teacup down. A slight tremor in her hand caused the cup to tinkle on the saucer. The sound echoed in her ears; Ben did not notice.

He read from a sheet of paper with a scholarly voice: "In the seven decades since the conclusion of the Second World War, countless artifacts have been recovered in the former European theater of hostilities. A significant number of finds were in the long-silent battlefields, all across the continent. Most artifacts have been small in size, such as metal fragments, weapons, and personal items of the belligerents. Some finds have been larger; a prime example was a German tank found in a rural Russian bog. The larger items included jeeps, trucks, and motorcycles. Many were found in rivers and lakes and small bodies of water. The discovery of these items has reinforced conventional wisdom regarding where specific land battles occurred. Most of the artifacts were discovered accidentally, during excavations related to construction projects. When something of historical significance is found, the excavation stops and archaeologists are brought in to recover the item. Construction work is never delayed more than a few days."

Ben looked up from his papers; Ania was listening with rapt attention. She nodded slightly, prompting Ben to continue.

"The large European cities, especially in Germany, were the locations of the fiercest battles, and consequently, many were reduced to rubble. In the postwar years, the cities were rebuilt. During this reconstruction period, large quantities of unexploded ordnance, or UXO, were found, mostly without incident. The Allied forces kept thorough records of all bombing campaigns, and, as part of the effort to rebuild Europe, the majority of hazardous items were removed and rendered safe."

Ben handed Ania a glossy black-and-white photograph. Looking at it, she saw a depiction of an excavation. Based on its appearance, the photo looked to be from the late 1940s. In the center of the photo was a large bomb, sitting at the bottom of a pit. Several men in American military uniforms stood nearby.

"Over the years, explosives occasionally surfaced, but they were removed safely. While many were duds, some were dangerous. In one case a construction worker was killed when his bulldozer unearthed and detonated a live shell. Military experts took control of the situation and searched the area, unearthing five more large bombs. The explosive devices were deactivated and removed without further incident. Since this tragic occurrence, historical experts are consulted and review all proposed construction plans. They determine if there is any record of the location being the site of a battle or bombing campaign. If no archival evidence is found, the project is approved. Until recently, no more live ordnance has been accidentally found."

Ben unfolded a map and set it on the desk in front of Ania. The map was of Germany and showed the country's current topography. Red notations identified areas where bombing operations had been conducted and where major skirmishes had taken place. Ania noticed some handwritten notes in the lower right corner of the map; they indicated that it had been drawn five years earlier. The map was printed in blue ink, on white paper, and the majority of the country was shaded in red. The names and dates of countless battles were noted. The earliest dates were from 1938 and the latest 1945.

"I understand that as of now, most of the country has been searched for bombs?" She used the tip of her pen to point to various spots on the map.

"Yes. During the twenty or so years during which cities like Frankfurt, Dresden, Cologne, Stuttgart, and Berlin were rebuilt, thousands of Allied bombs were found and safely removed. It wasn't very difficult, as most of the shells never fully penetrated the ground. A lot were just sticking out. As you know, many of the buildings in these cities were built after 1945."

Ania thought for a moment and carefully chose her words. "Were bombs found outside the major city centers? Such as in rural areas or farm lands?" She looked down at the map in an effort to hide the expression she knew her face was showing.

"They were. Most of the Allied bombing campaigns launched from Great Britain, and concentrated on northern Germany. The southernmost major city to be targeted was Cologne. All the bombs loaded onto departing planes were dropped, but if for some reason a mission was aborted prior to arrival at the target location, the bombs were ejected over unpopulated land as the plane returned to the UK. The practice was to jettison the bombs as soon as possible. Most of these 'dump' locations were in the north-western section of the country." Ben pointed to the area.

"Bombs discarded over nonstrategic areas? Wasn't that a waste of resources?" Ania knew the answer as she asked it, but she wanted Ben to remain oblivious to what she actually knew.

"Taking off with a load of bombs was hazardous enough, but landing with even one onboard was suicide. The most common reason planes aborted missions was damage from the Luftwaffe. The bombers limped back to safety, and many were targeted as they left. The crews dropped the bombs in order to prevent them from detonating while the planes were still in flight." Ben was still looking at the map and his papers.

"Were these areas checked for bombs after the war?" Ania looked up as if remembering something.

"Yes, quite thoroughly; the Allied forces, especially the United States, went to extreme lengths to ensure all ordnance was recovered after the war."

Ben pulled out another map, this one printed on a single sheet of paper. This map of Germany was broken down into grids. In about every other grid area was a notation about bomb recovery efforts.

There were notes on almost every section of the country.

"Quite the task," Ania remarked as Ben showed her the map.

"It was. After President Eisenhower took office, one of the first things he did was order a comprehensive study of all bombing sorties and recovery efforts. Immediately after the war, there were sporadic reports of European farmers being killed or injured when their tractors rolled over buried bombs."

Ben handed Ania a copy of a document bearing the seal of the president of the United States. The word "DECLASSIFIED" was stamped along the side of the page. The document was a written order, addressed to the Department of the Army, and signed by President Dwight D. Eisenhower.

"To this day, unexploded ordnance or UXO as it is now called is still occasionally found in the former European theatre of World War II. In June of 2008, a five-hundred-pound German bomb was dredged up in an East London river. Not only was it still active, it actually started 'ticking' as Ministry of Defense personnel began to diffuse it. It was the largest bomb ever recovered in the United Kingdom."

Ben pulled out another photograph and showed it to her.

"Was this near 'Bromley-by-Bow'?" she asked, examining the photograph.

"Yes—that's right! BBC?" Ben was surprised she knew.

"London Press. I read it every week," she said, studying the photo.

Ben was impressed.

"I know World War II is not your area of expertise, but I'm about to get to the part you will find extremely interesting." He pulled out more papers.

"Actually, this fascinates me. I have been all over Europe since the war ended, and it chills me to think we might have trudged over live bombs. Please go on." She looked at the map of Europe.

Looking at the papers, he thought her statement odd: *I have been all over Europe since the war ended.*

The way she said it implied that she had been in Europe prior to World War II. That was impossible; she was in her late thirties. His job was to listen to what people said and what they didn't say. He was good at his work, and many a negotiation turned on verbal slips. He pondered for a moment and quickly dismissed it, reasoning that it was a minor error in her diction. She spoke the most perfect English he'd ever heard, but he knew it was not her native tongue. Chalking it up to a rare translation error, he gave it no further thought.

"As mentioned earlier, Cologne was the southernmost major city to be targeted. Several miles southwest of Cologne is Aachen…" Ben looked up, seeking a sign of recognition.

Upon hearing "Aachen," Ania felt a chill. Despite many, many years of practice, her face could still reveal her true feelings, and to hide them, she reached for her now-empty teacup. She pretended to take a sip as Ben looked at her.

"Starting to pique your interest?" He said it with a look that convinced her he could read minds.

"Aachen?" She feigned ignorance. "You're pulling my leg." Ben was incredulous.

Chapter 7

Tricks and Whispers

The speaker was already at the podium when the audience filtered back in.

"As you take your seats, you'll see a questionnaire on your seat. We would appreciate it if you would complete those before the end of this session. The forms may be deposited in the boxes by the doors when you leave for the next break. All I ask is that you fill them out by yourselves, without discussing your responses with others. After they have been completed and submitted, please feel free to discuss the questions with others during the break."

The speaker pressed a button on the remote he was holding. The projector turned on and an image of several religious icons appeared on the screen. They were sitting on a pile of money.

"Organized religion is about making money, pure and simple. If you do not believe me, go to any organized religious service and see if you can get through it without being asked for a contribution. Of course,

you will be told your 'gifts' are for 'good works' or
'the poor.' These snake-oil salesmen will gladly tell
you that as you empty your wallets. They will appeal
to your sense of charity and guilt. If they were really
honest, they would tell you it was to line their own
pockets. Of course if you knew the truth, you'd not be
so generous."

The screen changed and the next image was a
list of several Fortune 500 companies. Next to each
were dollar amounts, listed as "Yearly Profits." They
all showed profits in the millions. A new screen
appeared and a list of the major religions appeared
alongside the businesses; the religions showed profits
in the billions. A collective gasp flashed across the
audience.

"Organized religion uses an independent business
model. What this means is that each church operates
as a sole proprietorship. The Catholic, Episcopal,
Lutheran, and Methodist churches are franchises. The
Catholic Church leads these in pure profit. Not only
is this organization a business, it is also recognized as
a sovereign nation-state. Unlike other governments,
it is allowed to operate with impunity within the
borders of this country. Most of the money it 'earns'
goes straight back to Rome. I'll delve into this scam
later."

"What do you think?" the co-ed whispered to her
friend.

"About what?" her friend replied.

"You know, how he did that trick with the numbers," the co-ed whispered back.

"It's a parlor trick; you don't really think he's psychic, do you?" It was said mockingly.

"How could it be a trick? I mean he told like thirty people their numbers. I think he might have ESP or something," the co-ed whispered, looking sideways at her friend.

"There's no such thing. It's all tricks and subterfuge. He's making some kind of point." Her friend shook her head in annoyance.

"I don't think so: one of my professors said clairvoyance has an empirical scientific basis. I believe it exists." The co-ed looked admiringly at the speaker as he talked.

Her friend continued to shake her head in disbelief.

"Unlike other legitimate businesses, religious organizations have an unfair advantage; they pay no taxes." A new image appeared; it showed a man in a clerical outfit driving an expensive car and smoking a cigar.

"Why is it that any person or entity that makes money in this country has to pay income taxes, except for churches? Why is it that we all work and pay our fair share of taxes, yet people who trick and spread lies don't do the same?" He looked disgusted.

The next image to appear was a scene in which a religious figure was toasting a man who looked to be a politician.

"The real power in this country is wielded by the hucksters in the long robes. A follow-up session will talk about the naive national leaders who willingly subordinate their will to the grifters. What I want to talk about now is the evolution of the religious con."

A new image was projected on the screen; this showed a group of people, wearing clothing that appeared to be from ancient times. Standing before them was a lone man, holding a set of stone tablets.

"The pre-historic con men were able to use their explanations of natural phenomena to trick the masses. As civilization's knowledge base increased, these simple explanations no longer held power. The tricksters were forced to show 'miracles' or 'gifts' from a higher power. These physical manifestations, supposedly from the 'creator,' were called 'miracles' and coerced compliance."

The speaker walked away from the podium and stood at the foot of the stage. He held his palms up toward the ceiling and looked down at the floor.

"Oh divine creator, give us a sign," he said in an exaggerated tone.

The lights in the auditorium dimmed, and sounds of thunder shook the room. There were flashes of lightning, and everyone felt a rumble. There were murmurs and shrieks. Just as quickly as the sounds and lights appeared, the house lights came back up, the speaker was gone from the stage. More murmurs were heard, and heads whipped about in search of him. A disembodied voice dismissed the audience for another break. As the crowd filed out, they all dropped their questionnaires in the box as instructed.

· · · · · · · ·

Bel walked down the busy street crowded with late-morning commuters. Pedestrians shuffled along in cold-weather clothing. Bel's sleek dark suit and red tie stood out amongst the bulky trench coats and down jackets. He walked easily, as if he had all the time on earth. His breath gave off enough heat that it formed a cloud about his face. A young woman, wearing an expensive overcoat and matching shoes, passed him and briefly glanced up at his face. Their eyes met and locked for an imperceptible moment. He smiled seductively, then looked down at her stomach. He looked back up at her as if disappointed, and his smile faded quickly. He glanced away, as if she was no longer there.

Something about his attractive face, and his sudden aversion, pushed her over a mental edge. Her mind changed from where it was a second earlier and she gave in to what she believed was her only decision, and hers alone. She continued on her way, albeit with a more purposeful gait. After a few blocks, she entered the lobby of a gray steel building and checked in with a guard. He directed her to the elevators, and picked up his radio: "One coming up. Female in tan overcoat, looks about six months along."

A few seconds later, a voice replied on the walkie-talkie and said, "We'll be expecting her."

After riding alone to the thirteenth floor, she left the elevator and encountered another guard; this one was standing in the foyer.

"You have an appointment?" he asked. She responded with a simple, guilty nod.

He extended his arm and pointed down the freshly-carpeted hallway.

The woman walked down the corridor and stopped before a closed door. A surveillance camera was mounted overhead. Next to the door was a call button. She pressed it and waited.

"New Woman Clinic, may I help you?" a voice crackled from the small speaker.

"I'm here for my procedure," she said with a shaky voice.

The lock buzzed and the woman pushed open the door. She forgot about her protruding stomach as she opened it, bumping into it. She stopped, and stepped around the door.

I won't have to worry about this thing much longer, she said to herself as she looked up and saw the receptionist.

Chapter 8
Close to Her Secrets

"*Touché*, Charlemagne. That's why you are here."

She smiled at him with a knowing look and pointed to a nearby set of books. Ben's eyes followed hers. He saw no less than four books with the name of the ancient ruler printed on the spine.

"We're getting close." Ben pulled out more papers.

Ania's mind drifted, remembering things from long ago. *Too close! I can't believe this is happening*, she thought.

"As you know, Aachen is very rural, and there was no major settlement there until the nineteenth century. During the war though, this was the site of the first American skirmish on German soil. After the D-Day invasion, Aachen was the first German city captured by Allied forces. This occurred in late 1944. There was considerable aerial shelling that took place during the fighting."

He showed a photograph to Ania; it showed a city in ruins.

"So I gather from what you've told me so far that live bombs have been found in rural Aachen?" She looked at him.

"Understatement of the millennium." Ben's raised right eyebrow emphasized his point.

"So, shells from the Battle of Aachen?" she asked, looking back at the photo.

"Well, the discovery of these devices is puzzling on two counts. First, aerial bombing back then was not as accurate as it is today. During the war, dropping one was like pitching horseshoes from a moving train; you might get close to the target, but the possible impact area was about a half-mile square. Neither the Luftwaffe, nor the RAF, nor the Army Air Corps intentionally dropped bombs anywhere near their own troops. The second thing is that the bombs were dropped over a period of several years, long before the Battle of Aachen." Ben's hazel eyes bore into Ania's for emphasis.

"Several years before?" She looked at the photo and saw piles upon piles of bombs.

As Ben took out another photograph, he said, "The bombs were found in layers, like a well-crafted lasagna. The ones found near the surface were all made during 1945. The next layer down had bombs from 1944. The ones below them were from 1943, and so on. The earliest bombs were from 1938."

He handed the photograph to her. In the picture, she saw neatly arranged rows of the destructive devices, segregated into groups. Small numbered, yellow cards were next to them.

"Why did the Allies bomb this particular area? Was there something of strategic importance there?" She already knew the answer to her own question.

"They weren't dropped by the Allies, they were dropped by Axis air powers."

The last word sent a chill down her spine.

"They were dropped by German planes?" She was curious, but deep in her subconscious, the answer materialized.

"Yes, and these were not just ordinary explosive devices, these were 'super-duper' ones." He said it like a ten-year-old child talking about a new toy. His use of the word 'super-duper' showed that although he was in his late-thirties, he still held a boyish sense of wonder.

"'Super-duper'?" she said with a mocking smile.

"Yes — most bombs the Luftwaffe dropped, especially those dropped on Great Britain, were designed to cause fire and topple buildings. These 'super-dupers' were specially developed. They were deep-concussion bombs. Think of the current 'bunker-buster' ones in use around the world."

He took out a grainy black-and-white photo. It looked like it had been taken by a crude camera, and in a hurry. The words "CLASSIFIED, 1937" were printed in an old, typewritten font. Next to it, in a more recent font, were the words "DECLASSIFIED,

1987." The photo showed what Ania surmised was
a bomb, but it didn't look like anything she'd seen
before. This particular explosive device looked like a
small rocket, complete with oddly-shaped fins and a
sharply-pointed nose.

"These bombs were called *tief schaden*, which
means 'deep damage' in English. They were designed
to penetrate the ground and then detonate several
minutes later."

He brought out another photo, this one taken
recently and in color. It showed a similar device, only
this one appeared to be in a museum of some kind.
The image was of professional quality.

"There was a bunker at this location?" Ania
steeled herself, fearful that her thoughts were not
buried deep enough.

"No, not here. The only real bunkers were near the
city centers. Also, these early 'bunker busters' were in
short supply. They were developed specifically to be
dropped on London. The Wehrmacht knew the Brits
sought refuge in the subway tunnels. They hoped
these bombs could penetrate the ground and detonate inside the 'tubes' as they call them." Ben took a
relieved breath. "Thank heaven they did not use them
on that city, they would have killed thousands. Those
humble *'tubes'* were the only reason there weren't
more casualties in England."

"Were any actually used on the subway tunnels?"
She took a deep breath, feigning fear of the answer.

"No, that's the thing. It appears that every one of these bombs was dropped on that site in Aachen." Ben shook his head in confusion.

"Every one? How is that known?" She knitted her brows.

"These were designed by many of the same scientists that designed and built the V-2 rockets. After the war, they were brought to the States and extensively debriefed. They talked at length about these bombs."

He pulled out a modern color photo of the ubiquitous V-2 or "vengeance weapon," complete with black-and-yellow livery. The missile looked like a rocket from a 1950s science fiction movie.

"Do the scientists know why the bombs were dropped there?" She cocked her head as she looked at the photo.

"They had no clue. The minute they were built, they were whisked away and the scientists were never told." He shook his head.

"How is all this known?" Her head shifted in the other direction.

"I read through all the declassified debriefing reports. After the scientists were settled at White Sands Proving Grounds, they were debriefed for months on end. The focus of the interviews was the V-2 rocket, but the *tief schadens* kept coming up. The scientists were puzzled as to why so much effort was diverted from the V-2 to the *tiefs*. The Reich high command called the shots, and they were told to make these bombs their number-one priority. They did not know why, as the only 'bunkers' within range were those obstinate English tunnels. They protested that the effort being placed on these bombs was slowing the V-2's development. In retrospect, it was a good thing. Had they developed a better guidance system, London would be no more." Ben looked relieved.

Ania made some notes on her pad and spent a few moments pondering what she wrote.

"How do they determine the year the bombs were dropped?" She looked at the photo and tried to discern any differences. They all looked identical.

"Germans are fanatical about their manufacturing. After the Industrial Revolution, everything made in Germany had a date on it, whether it was a watch, a car, a tool or…a bomb. The date codes document the month and year in which the item was made. The Wehrmacht did the same with every tank, plane, vehicle, rifle, pistol, uniform, helmet, and mess canteen. If it was German made, it had a date on it. Not only did the Wehrmacht note the date, they also noted the factory that made it."

He took out yet another photo.

"They did this with bombs?" She looked at the next photo; it was a close-up of German inscriptions and a date.

"They did, that's how the bombs were identified as being made between 1938 and 1945. The dates and the layering indicate that the bombs were dropped year by year." He brought out several more photographs, each one showing a different device and date.

"There's a common denominator." She arranged the photos like playing cards, so that the dates were next to one another.

"Knew you'd see it. Isn't the month coincidental?" His eye gleamed. She had noted that every month was April.

"Though the year changed, the month didn't. But do you know if they were actually dropped around that time? It looks like they had an issue with Lent." She looked closely at the photos. She knew the Nazis didn't so much have an issue with the Easter Season, they had an issue with whatever was in that part of Aachen.

"Well, we know when the bomb was made; when it was dropped could be anytime later. I can guarantee you though that the bombs never stayed around long after they were made." He took out yet another photograph.

"Why is that?" She waited for the next image.

"After a bomb is made, it's quickly removed from the factory and sent to an ammunition dump. The fear in the factory is that if an explosive device goes off as it's being made, it will set off the whole works. Within hours of manufacture, it's sent to a collection point and carted off to an airfield or train depot for loading. Conceivably, a bomb could sit around a few months after manufacture, but it's almost a certainty that all these things, made during the same month, were dropped almost immediately."

He showed her the photo. She looked at it and saw several bombs, cut into pieces like cucumber slices.

"How do they cut these open? Won't they explode?" Her eyes went wide.

"An aerial bomb is a very simple device. It's a big container full of gunpowder. The detonator is in the tip. When the bomb hits the earth, it goes off. If for some reason it doesn't land on the tip, the impact of hitting the ground hard enough does the same thing. When the ordnance disposal personnel find a live bomb, they unscrew the detonator from the tip. Then they cut a big hole in the top and remove the 'guts.' It's now as harmless as a metal trash can."

He used the tip of a pencil to point out the components.

"We have here bombs all made in the same month, dropped in 1938, 1939, 1940, 1941, 1942, 1943, 1944, and 1945, by the German Luftwaffe, in the same spot, in a place that had no strategic value."

Ania looked at her bookcase, searching for an answer. "What is the connection with Charlemagne?" She thought of the ancient king and remembered details about his face no one would believe she'd seen.

"This is why I'm here. The countryside near Aachen is tranquil and some of the most beautiful in Germany. About six months ago, a retired doctor decided to build a house there. He wanted a sub-basement wine cellar and they dug deeper than usual for a house. As the construction crew began the excavation, they found an unexploded, World War II era bomb. As per protocol, the local authorities called in the military, and they rendered the bomb safe. As part of the recovery, they checked the area for other UXO and found several tons of unexploded devices."

Ben took out another photograph and showed it to her. She saw another excavation site, but this one had bombs too numerous to count.

"And is there something more unusual than that?" She looked at him, hoping internally the digging wasn't too deep.

"Yes, they didn't detonate. Every single one was live." He looked back down at the photo. "Ordnance back then had about a thirty percent failure rate. This means that one out of every three bombs was a dud or didn't 'go boom' on impact. Statistically though, some of these should have exploded, but they didn't. The German military are still scratching their heads over this. I mean, every one they found was live, but for some unknown reason, they didn't function as planned." Ben made an "explosion gesture" with his hands.

"I know little about military ordnance, but from what I gather, the German air powers dropped several thousand tons of bombs on their own soil, and not one detonated?" She was astonished.

"That's right. Aside from 'divine intervention,' there is no reason why not even one bomb exploded. Until recently, I knew little about military explosives myself. In the last week, I've learned more than I ever wanted to know. It's what was found after the bombs were all removed."

Ania sat bolt upright in her chair, as if struck by lightning. "Ben, I just realized I have to get something from a colleague a few doors down before her next class. Would you excuse me for a few minutes?" She moved from behind her desk and toward the door.

"Oh, of course — no worries." Ben looked back down at the papers in his hands as she walked by.

Ania barely made it out into the hallway. She thought she would pass out, if that were possible.

After all these years? They've found it? It can't be! she thought to herself, rushing down the hallway toward the ladies' room. Fortunately, Grace was gone; because if she had been sitting at her desk, she would have seen Ania speed by with a look of horror on her face.

She made it to the ladies' room and locked the door. She stared into the mirror and began quietly reciting something in Greek.

Not now, not now, not now! she said quietly to herself in her native language and then in English.

53

Chapter 9

Bad News

Ania stood before the mirror in a trance. Opening her eyes, she calculated she'd been gone five minutes. There was no doubt in her mind where this was leading, and no avoiding it any longer. She took a deep breath, opened the door to the ladies' room, and walked back to her office. She entered and took a seat. Ben was concentrating on a document.

"Ready for the good stuff?" he said excitedly.

Ania hoped there would be something good; all the talk of bombs and destruction left her with a feeling of death.

"Yes, your reference to Charlemagne has piqued my interest." Picking up her pen, she leaned forward eagerly.

"As I was saying earlier, after all the UXOs were cleared, the German military double-checked the area. The officer in charge ordered that the site be dug down another two meters, wanting to ensure that there were no more explosives. When the first 'scrape' was heard, the soldier operating the backhoe stopped. He later said he thought he'd found yet another bomb. The area was cleared of nonessential personnel, and the UXO team went in. At this point the excavation site was twenty meters deep. While the team was in the hole, the perimeter personnel couldn't see them. After what seemed like an eternity, the first UXO technician emerged from the pit. His protective armor was off, and he was gently cradling something in his arms. The people standing nearby watched as he stood there, staring at the object he held." Ben lit up.

"What was it?" Ania was about to explode.

"It was a crucifix," he said simply.

"A crucifix?" she asked, cocking her head.

"Yes, a crucifix. As the military personnel approached the first UXO technician, the other two UXO technicians emerged. Their protective gear was off too and they were also cradling crucifixes."

With a broad grin, Ben handed Ania a photo. Centered in the picture were three crucifixes, laid on a white cloth. A ruler was placed at the edge of the sheet to show their relative size. The center crucifix was nearly six inches tall and appeared to be made of gold. The other two were smaller and looked like bronze.

Ania peered at the photo.

"Why were they there? Have they been brought here?" She knew the answer but feigned curiosity.

"No. The three UXO technicians found them at the bottom of the dig. They found them buried just as they were depicted in the photo: side by side with the gold one in the middle. That's not the end of it." He produced another photo and handed it to her.

"What?" It was an exclamation, not a question.

"In addition to the military personnel, an archaeologist was there. As the three soldiers emerged from the dig, they called him over. He went down into the dig and found these." Ben pointed to the photo. It showed numerous crucifixes, some still partially buried, some free of dirt. A small shovel and an archaeologist's brush were next to them.

Ania looked up at Ben. Her expression told him he'd made her day.

"They found the first three crucifixes a week ago. As of this morning, they have recovered over one hundred. They're finding more every day." Ben's level of excitement rose. "The belief is that there may be thousands!"

"Have they been dated?" She held the photo up to the light and studied it closely.

Ben pulled a single sheet of paper from the sheaf he'd been holding and handed it to her. "They are estimating that the crosses are five hundred years to... two thousand years old."

"When were they buried there?" Ania read the paper with an urgent fury.

"The crosses are 'layered' in the same way the bombs were. The two-thousand-year-old cross has been buried there for..." Ben looked up at her.

She looked directly back at him.

"It has been there for close to two thousand years," Ben said triumphantly.

"That is not possible. That area was largely uninhabited until at least the sixth century AD. They believe the Romans were the first to travel to that area. But if that crucifix was buried there two millennia ago, this would place it at the time of..."

They both looked up in unison at the largest book in Ania's bookcase, the book with the obvious place of prominence.

"Yes, Doctor Socratatos: that crucifix was buried there, a thousand miles from the Holy Land, at the time of Christ." Ben's boyish and affable expression turned deadly serious.

Chapter 10

The Gravity Of

They stared at each other for several moments.
Ben watched the gravity of the information settle into
Ania's acute mind. Ania stared back at Ben; his excitement over the information was obvious. She thought
quickly, knowing that the more she was silent, the
more her face would reveal her secrets.

"How is it known that the oldest crosses are two
thousand years old?" She wrote something down.

"The first three specimens were carbon dated. The
testing showed them to be between five hundred and
seven hundred years old. The process being used
is extremely accurate. The lab is estimating that the
oldest were placed twenty-one hundred years ago."

Ben gave a sheet of paper to Ania.

Ania took it and studied it. She knew the testing
was accurate—the crosses were close to two millennia
old. Though she was holding the paper in front of
her, she was not reading it. Her eyes were looking at
the text, but she wasn't seeing it. She remembered a

time that seemed like yesterday, although it was long
before that. She had never in her life anticipated being
in this situation. Ben's eagerness was the exact opposite of what she felt: dread.

"If we accept the fact that the crosses are that old,
how do we know when they were actually placed
where they were found?" Ania wrote more notes.

Ben recognized the Socratic method again; he
enjoyed it. Always strong in his convictions, he found
that the exercise had the benefit of answering questions about his beliefs that he never thought to ask.

"That's a good question. As I mentioned earlier,
the site was layered, and it's beyond certain the
bombs were first dropped in 1938. The time period
between 1937 and the first century AD... They've
stratified the layers of burial and are aging the crosses
found the deepest. These were most likely the first
ones buried, and they've been dated to the first
century AD."

Ben watched while Ania pulled a book from the
case and reviewed several pages. He reached into his
pocket and removed a vibrating cell phone.

"I am afraid I must leave; they are calling an
emergency session of the Security Council and the
ambassador needs my assistance."

He returned the phone to his pocket and quickly
put his papers and photos back in his briefcase.

"May I have copies of these documents?" Ania
asked, as she gathered the papers off her desk.

"Those are all for you. May I call you in a day or so to get some initial theories? We know this is a large volume of information, but anything I can relay to the on-site team would help put things in perspective." Ben set his briefcase on his lap.

"There will be information for you by tomorrow. This is a major archaeological find; the sooner we develop some theories, the better." She stood with Ben.

Ania stepped around her desk and offered her hand to Ben; as she did, her hip knocked a large textbook off her desk and onto the floor. The newspaper underneath it fluttered down after it. Both bent down to pick them up; Ania picked up the book and Ben the newspaper.

"It's unbelievable what that madman in West Virginia did; his entire family and his coworkers." He looked at an above-the-fold story on the front page. "'Fifty innocent lives taken.'" Ben shook his head.

"It truly was," Ania said grimly.

"Human life is sacred. I can understand someone being mentally troubled enough to take their own life; but his co-workers, his wife, his children." Ben shook his head again.

"The only thing is, with the poison he used, they lost consciousness immediately..." Ania looked at the headline as Ben placed the paper back on her desk.

"It's like Satan was whispering into his ear and urged him to do it." Ben sighed.

Ania remembered Bel's denial a few hours earlier — Bel really did talk into that killer's ear.

Ben walked to the door and Ania followed him. He turned and they shook hands, causing the same dizzy sensation to envelop her. She was able to hide it this time.

"The cell phone number on my card is the best one to reach me at. I'm rarely in my office." Ben looked up at her.

"Thank you for sharing this extraordinary find with me, and give my regards to the ambassador." Ania waved him out.

"Thank you again for your time. You have been extremely generous," Ben said in Latin.

"Latin too?" she replied in the ancient tongue.

"It may be a dead language, but it feels very comfortable to me." Ben turned and waved as he walked down the hall.

She didn't know why he spoke in Latin, and it surprised her. Fluent Latin was not something she'd heard in many, many years. It brought back memories for her. Latin was the third language she learned to speak, Aramaic and Greek prior. While Greek was her native tongue, Latin was her favorite.

Ania gently closed her office door and turned back toward the window, watching clouds roll by. Taking a deep breath, she recited something to herself in Greek. She looked down at Ben's business card and read the title: "Ben Airaldi, Special Assistant to the Holy See's Mission to the United Nations."

Chapter 11

The U.N.

Ania had been to the United Nations building
several times since arriving in the States. The edifice's
exterior exuded a sense of glamor and international
intrigue, yet the inside was nothing more than bland
austerity. The tall glass building contained the admin-
istrative offices, and the plain, squat one housed
the general assembly. While the Vatican was not an
actual member of the United Nations, it had representatives who were assigned there. The Vatican staff
worked out of offices belonging to the Italian dele-
gation. Though a sovereign nation-state, the Vatican
did not have an embassy in the United States or an
ambassador. There was an Apostolic Nunciature that
maintained "official" diplomatic ties with the US
government. With almost eighty million Catholics in
the United States, there was very good reason for the
government to maintain good relations with the small
Roman nation.

Ania's last visit here was scholarly in purpose; she spoke countless languages and frequent visits allowed her to assess her competence. Knowing a language was not enough for her; she wanted to learn the regional dialects as well. Most people were familiar with the different accents of their native language, but a great many polylingual persons were ignorant of those other languages. Although she considered her "curse" a negative, having lived so long allowed her mind to reach a level of knowledge and cognition unknown since the time of the Old Testament. Her mental abilities were far beyond the collective level of her colleagues; something only she would ever know.

Ben's office was on an upper floor at the east side of the tower. She greeted the receptionist in Italian and noted that the woman's accent was Northern, close to the Swiss border. In addition to Italian and English, she had traces of German, Romanish, and French in her speech patterns.

Ben came out promptly to meet Ania in the reception area. He appeared excited — something that troubled her.

"Welcome, Doctor...Ania...good to see you." Ben was about to offer his hand but hesitated, waiting for her to offer hers first.

Ania realized that Ben had old-world manners. "And you too."

When her hand met his, she felt the identical dizzying jolt she'd experienced the first time they met. This time, she was able to mask her reaction.

What is this? she thought. In her time on earth, a time span not possible for mortals, she'd seen many things and learned even more. This physical reaction she had to Ben was nothing she'd ever experienced before. The only thing remotely similar was when she was with Marcus, and those memories were two thousand years old. She would reflect on it later.

He motioned to her to follow him, clearly excited at what he wanted to show her. "Please follow me."

They walked down a hallway toward a series of offices. They entered one about the size of Ania's, but it was crammed with twice as many books as hers. The books occupied most of the space, and there were almost as many photos, maps, and sketches on the walls, shelves, and desk.

"Your love of books exceeds mine," Ania said admiringly.

"I mentioned there could not be enough books to satisfy me."

Rather than leading her to a seat, he pointed to a large map of Germany tacked to a wall. "Look familiar?"

Ania knew that Ben knew she'd been in Deutschland, although he had no idea, and could not even fathom that it was long before he was born, before his parents, grandparents, and much further back.

"Looks very different from this vantage point."
The terrain of southwestern Germany was probably
unchanged from when she was last there. She pointed
to a large red symbol where the excavation site was.
It was not lost on her that the mark was in the shape
of a cross. "Looks to be just north of Charlemagne's
cathedral."

Ben took a pen and pointed to the shape. "This
cross denotes the location of the dig. It is almost
exactly two thousand meters from the northern end
of the structure. We've gone through the historical
records, and this spot has no known significance."

Ania knew what that significance was, but she
could never tell him. How could anyone imagine that
actions she'd taken so long ago may have altered the
course of Western civilization?

"The crosses; could they have been from cem-
eteries?" She threw the question out to mask her
knowledge.

"Not these. These crosses were handmade, and not
consistent with a grave marker. Some were as large
as three feet tall, others as small as an inch. Some
were of gold, some of iron, stone, marble, wood, jade,
bamboo and just about any imaginable material. The
on-site personnel have identified materials from as
far away as Asia and as close as Germany itself. There
is evidence that some of the crosses are made from
materials found only in North America."

He handed her a printed list. As she scanned it, she saw that nearly 3,000 crosses had been logged so far. The list described the size, weight, material, and possible origin of each artifact. She'd suspected the crucifixes might end up where they did, but not in those numbers and especially not made of materials from thousands of miles away.

"How is the radiocarbon dating progressing?" she asked.

"That's taking the longest. In a lab, it can be done in hours. Out there, it's taking days. The newest cross is from about the time of the Crusades. The oldest, as I mentioned yesterday, is from the time of His death... resurrection." Ben's affability suddenly became solemn reverence. "Those crosses are being looked at most closely. They are made of iron and marble and many of gold, and these materials have been traced directly to the Holy Land."

They looked at each other for what felt like minutes; the two scholars, on accepting the scientific evidence, knew that these crosses were from the time of the Crucifixion; they were made at the time of Christ's death and were now being found, over two millennia later, 1,800 miles away. They silently acknowledged that this find was the most significant in the history of Western civilization.

"How did they determine when these oldest crosses were actually placed there?" She focused on the list. "Have they correlated the soil layers to a time period?"

"Based on rough estimates, the working theory is that the soil layers span the first to seventeenth century AD."

He looked into her eyes as she digested the information. He couldn't help but notice that the color in her eyes seemed to flicker. For the first time, it dawned on him that she was the most beautiful woman he'd ever seen. He might have noticed it sooner, had it not been for his attention to the work at hand.

Ania noticed Ben's pupils dilate slightly. She realized he saw something in her eyes; she could control her facial expressions, but her eyes always did what they wanted. She looked down to hide them from him.

"How do they identify the different time periods?" She kept looking down, willing her eyes to behave.

"That's a little out of my field of expertise, but the analysis has something to do with soil compression. When the soil is disturbed, it settles differently than the surrounding earth. It's the same process they use to locate forgotten graves; they use ground-penetrating radar, which shows differing densities in the geological composition. Undisturbed soil is very dense, any disturbance is less so." He shoveled some more papers.

There was silence for several minutes as they became lost in the information.

They are right—I know, I buried them, she thought to herself.

"There were no migration routes at that time. Are they sure about the dating?" She threw out this red herring to hide her real knowledge.

"After the first team dated the crosses, a second team double-checked the results. Both groups concurred the earliest crosses were placed around the first to second century AD. Carbon dating is not an exact science, but the margin of error is about fifty years. There's no doubt the earliest crosses were from the first few decades after Christ."

Ben looked up to the wall above his desk and Ania followed his gaze; Ben was looking at a simple, yet beautiful wooden crucifix. He looked back at her with a smile on his face.

For the next few hours, Ben and Ania reviewed maps, reports, photographs, and reams of handwritten notes. Ben elaborated on the information he'd given her previously and she listened intently, taking copious notes on her folio. She kept her face down as much as possible, hoping Ben would not read her reactions; in two millennia, she'd learned to control her outward display of emotions quite well, but Ben seemed to have innate ability to read facial "tells." She knew the history of the crosses, and how they got there; she had seen it happen. Ania hoped Ben could not read that on her face.

Athania Socratatos remembered the Christian pilgrims well; the first ones had arrived barely a year after she and Marcus found the hiding place. The sudden appearance of strangers alarmed her and she'd feared they'd been followed. Although they traveled under the cover of darkness, they still encountered other travelers, and occasional troublemakers. Ania had no difficulty fending off small groups of attackers, but her concern was always for the treasure. A large number could be problematic, and she knew His enemies moved in bulk, like most hordes did. Thankfully, the only foes they had dealt with were the criminals who saw the woman and young boy as an easy target. In the five years it had taken her and Marcus to reach Aachen, they'd overcome many threats. Marcus's bravery never faltered, but they were usually outnumbered and he was only a boy. Ania's abilities always tipped things in their favor. She never took another human life, but many a would-be robber or rapist limped or had been carried away by accomplices.

When she and Marcus had reached the cave, they hid the treasure and Ania remained on constant guard. Marcus stayed with her for a few years, and she'd used the time to pass along her father's teaching. When he was of age, she sent him on his way, and admonished him to "Do good." He left reluctantly, but she assured him she would be alright. Armed with the knowledge she imparted on him, there was no doubt he would thrive. He swore to never reveal the location of the cave, and she had no doubt he would protect the secret with his life; considering who'd healed him in Capernia, Marcus's life was like few others—he'd been saved by the faith of his father.

Thoughts returned to the pilgrims; they'd wander into the clearing, directly over the cave. No sooner would they reach the spot, then they'd drop to their knees, as if paying homage to something they felt, but could not see. She surmised they had seen an invisible light, not with their eyes, but rather souls.

Ania had seen it happen thousands of times, and it was always the same: a mournful collapse, weeping, then composure and a straightening of posture. Some that limped to the site walked away, carrying their crutches. They came with a light in their eyes, and as they silently walked away, it looked as if an aura of illumination surrounded them.

Ania knew they had found what they came for. They didn't know that they were in the presence of the original symbol of their faith, but they felt it. They also didn't know that Ania, the daughter of the philosopher Socrates, was guarding the very thing that drew them to that spot. The moment they left, she made sure the next pilgrim was unaware that a fellow visitor had been there just hours earlier. She was the reason the crosses were buried so deep. She knew that if His enemies discovered them, they would know to start looking deeper. She would have given her life, if that were possible in order to keep these enemies from taking what they knew they needed to take. She'd traveled very far from home to keep it from them, and keeping it safe was her sole purpose.

At the time of her original travels, the world was much bigger and she hoped His enemies would never stumble this far, unless they knew pilgrims were drawn here. They didn't believe in Him, but that was not their concern. They thought that by extinguishing His mortal life, they would regain control, but they never imagined that in leaving earthly form, He saved the world, even for those who rejected Him.

With an empty tomb, they were baffled, and this confusion gave her the opportunity to do what the angel told her to. By the time the fools came to their senses, she and the thing they now sought to destroy were far away. They failed, but she knew they would never stop. They just didn't know that the protector of what they sought to destroy was the daughter of someone who understood logic and reason in ways their rote learning could never match. She was the daughter of the philosopher, one of the founders of Western civilization. In moments of pain and anguish, when she was much younger, she imagined that those who condemned Him to death were related to those who condemned her father.

Immediately, when logic, reason, and intuition regained control of her mind, she knew the real answer—those who fear losing false power will silence any person or any concept that questions their legitimacy. Athens and the Holy Land were far apart, but ignorance and evil were not anchored to any one location.

As Ben shared information with her, information she already possessed, Ania realized the treasure was in jeopardy once again. She would continue to protect it from His enemies and those who in their quest for truth, would unknowingly hand it to them.

Chapter 12

Insatiable

Seth Steinbeck had met many women in his life, but none was like Bella. She was not only attractive — he was drawn to her beauty. Seth could not take his eyes or attention off her. Her gaze reached into his soul and held him fast.

"So tell me, Seth, how did you come to your beliefs about religion?" Bella's eyebrow raised slightly, emphasizing her interest.

"I'd say it was an 'evolution.'" He smiled at her.

When she smiled back, he lost any remaining sense of himself. All he could think of was her. The deep blue-eyed gaze was mesmerizing; he'd been hypnotized before, but this was something different. His attention was on her and her alone. An explosion could go off near him and he wouldn't have noticed.

"Were you *ever* religious?" she asked as they entered the diner.

There were people waiting, but upon seeing Bella, the host left his station and immediately ushered them to a table. Bella winked at the young man and he smiled.

"Friend of yours?" Seth asked with a twinge of jealousy, forgetting the question.

"I've seen him around. I figure he may want a favor." She demurely sat, never taking her eyes off him.

Seth took his seat across from her, still transfixed by her beauty. Only when she took up the menu and looked at it did he dare look away. He noticed a few other men watching her, too. A smugness washed over him as he reveled in the fact she was there with *him*. He wanted to gloat to the other admirers that his date was the prettiest in the place. When he looked back at her, she was looking at him, a serene smile on her face.

"You know what you want to order?" he asked, barely aware of the menu he was holding. Her facial reaction belied her real desires.

"I'm a creature of habit, always have the same thing. So tell me, what is your religious history?" Bella cocked her head slightly and raised her chin.

"My folks were Presbyterian, dragged me to church every Sunday. I bought into it for a while, but as I grew, my mind questioned the drivel. I needed to see proof, and there was none." He shook his head and grimaced.

"I too bought into all that, but only because I loved my father so much. Eventually it dawned on me, that it was all bunk. Father and I became estranged over his teachings, and I left home. Never looked back, never been back. I think for myself." A satisfied expression developed on her face.

"My folks aren't happy with the direction I've taken now. I don't see them much anyway." He smiled at her.

"My father's not happy with me either, but I'm all grown up and his beliefs are not mine. I originally bought into all his ministrations, but eventually it dawned on me that his doctrines made no sense. My love for him could no longer influence my thinking. I miss him, but being on my own is empowering. My destiny is mine not his." A slightly-smug smile crossed her face.

"I think that's all religion is; parents learning it from their parents, then blindly teaching their own kids the same garbage. If you think about it rationally, religion is simply a delusional balm, a way for people to deal with a world they do not understand. We all need beliefs, and a paternal, 'higher power' is easier to accept than the cold hard fact that we are a product of nature and nothing more. Waiting for a perfect afterlife is easier than dealing with the here and now."

Seth was able to regain his focus, his mind back on his learned lessons. He noticed that as he spoke, Bella hung on every word. He was going to elaborate, but the waitress interrupted them. After taking their order, the middle-aged woman left and Seth was eager to resume the conversation.

"So you like your meat rare?" Seth commented on her choice of a steak, extra rare, with a side of cold fruit.

"I'd eat it raw, but the health department would frown on that. Most places won't cook any less than medium." She sipped from her water glass.

"I took you for a vegetarian." He smiled.

"Oh no, my appetite for flesh is insatiable."

Bella's choice of words intrigued him. Her face remained pleasant, but he sensed she had a hunger for many things.

They continued their talk, Bella listening intently as Seth spoke. While she said little, her facial expressions revealed she was absorbing his every word. As he went on, the mysterious woman never took her eyes off him. He wanted to know all about her, but talking to people about his beliefs evoked a sense of pride that dominated any other interests.

The food came, and Steinbeck continued to talk. Bella still said very little, cutting her near-bloody meat into small, dainty bits. She chewed slowly, savoring every morsel. Seth liked how she listened, never interrupting him with so much as a question. The more he talked, the more intently she listened.

After nearly an hour and a half, they finished their meal. The lunch crowd had thinned out and there were only a few other patrons.

"I'm going to have to get back, I have another session at three." Seth reached for the bill, but Bella got it first and slowly drew it back toward her.

"This is my treat." She retrieved a small, black leather purse, no bigger than a cell phone.

Seth would have normally fought her for the check, but something about the way she looked at him said it was not a matter for debate. "Well thank you. I did all the talking, never gave you a chance to speak."

"I should thank you; I've never had someone explain things so clearly. Your reasoning would reach even the most deluded, religious zealot. You have a gift and I hope more people listen to your words."

She retrieved a single bill from her purse and left it with the check. The check was for much less than the hundred-dollar bill she left.

"Shall we get back?" Bella made a motion to leave.

"Are you coming to the next session?" Seth could barely hide his excitement.

"I'm not letting this opportunity get away; I've learned more from you in the last hour than in my entire life. I want to hear more." She had a look of glee in her eyes.

"I'm flattered; the next session will be even better; I'm speaking about the 'unholy' connection between Big Religion and their elected stooges. It's timely, given current world events."

Seth stood as Bella did. She smiled at him and turned to leave with him.

"What about your change?" Seth protested.

"Oh, the waitress gave great service, she earned it." Bella smiled sweetly.

"That's almost a forty percent tip," he said.

"It's only money. Hopefully she will 'pay it forward.'" Bella's smile turned conspiratorial.

Seth was impressed by the generosity. He wasn't hurting for money, but he'd never left such a large tip. He followed her, and glanced back at the check and money. Later, he'd swear the bill glowed red for a fraction of a second.

Chapter 13

What to Do

Ania walked back to her office from the U.N. Her experienced mind was awash in fading memories and developing possibilities. She left the building not remembering the trip from Ben's office to the lobby. It had been well over one hundred years since she'd left Germany, but memories flooded back like she'd been there just yesterday. She had left Europe reluctantly in the late nineteenth century, intent on returning when she had the means to move the treasure to North America. While waiting for an opportunity, several wars, including two on a global scale, intervened. She had harbored concerns that the two world conflicts might lead to a discovery, but it never dawned on her that a war that had occurred seventy years earlier could unearth the treasure *now*.

Up until the 1960s, she had entertained ways of getting the treasure to the New World, but as logistical opportunities increased, so did this country's unworthiness to host it increase. By the 1980s, Ania determined that the treasure was safer where it was. He was going to return someday, and when he did, she knew He'd know what to do with the former object of His significance.

The other pedestrians around her were mildly bundled up for the eastern fall. She wore a light coat over her black turtleneck, but it was merely for show. In the last two thousand years, she'd never been cold. She'd never been hot for that matter, either. She sensed climates and temperatures, but they had no effect on her. Whether she was in a scorching desert, or a freezing blizzard, Ania felt no difference either way. She dressed to match the local populace, merely to blend in and not stand out. She felt as she did so long ago in the temperate Greek weather.

She had been cursed on a cool spring day, and since then, that's how she felt. That was also how she looked, too. In two millennia, Athania Socratatos had not aged one second. She appeared today exactly as she did in 399 BC. Nothing about her person had changed, not even the length of her hair and nails. The only thing that had aged was her mind, and that was merely in the way she saw and processed things. She surmised that her mind didn't actually change, it merely absorbed everything she'd seen in all these years. It was believed that a mind had a limitless ability to learn and absorb, and she knew she was proof of that.

As she walked onto the campus, she calculated she could remain there for another ten years or so. Ania moved around much, especially in the last hundred years. She found teaching to be a constructive way of passing along her father's teachings, especially at the university level. Her first teaching positions had been at small schools. She could only remain a few years, because if someone saw she didn't age, it might arouse suspicions. The longest she had ever remained at one educational institution was ten to fifteen years. The only thing anyone ever said was that she looked younger than her actual age. If they only knew the truth.

When she reached her office, she was mulling over her options. The excavation was far from the hiding place, at least vertically. The unexploded bombs posed no danger to the place, but inquiring minds did. She was wondering if she'd need to go to Aachen, to see for herself. A red light on her phone signaled a waiting phone message. As soon as she played it, she realized she was going to Germany. Ben's enthusiastic voice confirmed her travel plans:

"Doctor…Ania…it's Ben; how would you like to go to Germany, courtesy of the Holy See? I'm leaving in two days."

Chapter 14

The Encounter

Most American universities were intent on distancing themselves from anything even remotely connected to Christianity, loudly proclaiming neutrality and "inclusivity." The state schools were the worst offenders, but even many religiously-affiliated universities were following suit. The borderline hostility toward one of the world's oldest and most established religions was growing every year. The university where Doctor Athania X. Socratatos taught, while not religiously affiliated, had no plans underway to follow suit. As a smaller, private university, with generous alumni, it did not need any government funding. The school could have used such funds for the benefit of the students, but there were always webs of thick strings attached.

Hillside College was founded in the late 1800s by a small group of philosophers dissatisfied with the nepotism and elitism of the Ivy League schools. Beginning with a consortium of those wanting to teach, and those wishing to learn, Hillside was born. This group was grounded in the teachings of Socrates, Plato, Hypatia, and Aristotle. One and a half centuries later, Ania had found the student body to be comprised of highly eager pupils, willing to learn.

Invariably, there was also the occasional student who forgot that the school was a place of higher education, and so brought their activism and soapbox with them. These agitators rarely gained traction in their causes; the rest of the students focused on their studies instead of being caught up in movements. Most of the faculty were there to teach, not indoctrinate. The school had a reputation for encouraging free thought, but frowned upon lessons that bordered on counter-cultural anarchy. There had been a few teachers over the years who wanted to continue the chaos of the 1960s. These professors eventually realized that while willing to learn, the students would not bend to their wills or blindly accept their philosophies.

Most of the pupils came from varied religious backgrounds. If a professor gained a reputation as being antagonizing toward people of faith, they soon found their classrooms empty, which meant they either kept silent or went elsewhere. The faculty, staff, and student body were there to learn and teach, not to try and change the school and the world by walking out of classes or holding protests. The accepted wisdom was that an education needed to be completed before someone went off on an emotional tangent.

· · · · · · · ·

Ania called Ben back and he answered on the second ring. In the three hours since they had met in his office, there was no new information about the dig, however there was a new development stateside. After listening to Ben for a few moments, Ania sat back and pondered what he told her. She paused for a few moments and was about to respond. But he excitedly spoke first:

"Will two days' notice work?" he asked.

"That should suffice — the chancellor and I are on good terms; considering the source of the invitation, he'd be glad someone from the school would provide on-site assistance."

Leaving on such short notice wasn't an issue — what vexed her was that she hadn't been in Germany since 1895, and things were very different now. She wondered if going back might trigger an event she didn't want to happen. She paused for a second, and said, "I assume we are flying." She said it as a statement, not a question, but there was a trace of concern in her voice.

"Does flying cause you fear?" Ben asked, recognizing a hesitation in her voice.

"No, not in the least. Why do you ask?" She sensed a shift in his demeanor, realizing he'd picked up on something.

"It was just the way you asked. I'd prefer to take a boat, but getting there in twelve hours is better than twelve days." He joked.

"No, flying doesn't trouble me, but the frenetic activity of airports at the beginning and end of a journey are like two pieces of stale bread on an otherwise splendid sandwich."

She said it with mirth, causing Ben to chuckle. Ben didn't like airports, either.

"Speaking of that, I have a dinner engagement with a member of the German consulate in two hours, to discuss the excavation. Would you like to come? It would be a great opportunity to introduce you. Our future host country will be pleased to know we've recruited someone of your talent and standing to assist with this mystery."

It was an offer, but Ben's excitement permitted Ania only one answer. She had been planning to go home and plot out a course of action, but a meeting with someone from the German government would give her possible insight into prevailing theories about the discovery. "I would be delighted."

Ania made a call to the chancellor's office, requesting the time off to travel. Word had already spread about the find. It hadn't made much of an impact in national news, but within the academic community, especially those who studied Western civilization, it was headline material. Not only was she given the go-ahead, she was also sent on full pay, and offered the assistance of a graduate student. She graciously declined the offer of help, explaining that the Holy See had sufficient personnel on-site. She was asked to report back regularly, sending as many pictures as possible. The school's website would note its involvement with the find, and up-close photos would generate more interest in the story. The chancellor gave her as much time as she needed on the condition that she update the school's blog as often as she could. Yes, the Vatican's invitation was a proverbial feather in the school's cap.

Later, Ben and Ania made plans to meet at the U.N., then walk to the meeting together. Ben was excited; Ania was worried.

"Dinner was splendid, thank you for inviting me," she commented as they left the restaurant. He held the door open for her, something she appreciated.

"You didn't eat much; the menu not to your liking?" He walked alongside her, stealing a glance at her profile as she looked ahead.

"I'm averse to large meals; I prefer smaller ones, spaced throughout the day." The real truth was she didn't need food to live; eating was only for the purpose of appearing normal.

"I imagine you are quite busy. The university doesn't mind you leaving on such short notice?" He stared ahead, focusing on something in the distance. He set the oddity aside, but kept it on his mind.

"Considering the significance of the find, the university is more than happy to join in on this endeavor." Ania stuffed her hands deep into the pockets of her coat. It was not very cold, but a wind-blown chill had come over the waterfront as soon as the sun went down. Ania wasn't chilled, but as with eating, she had to keep up the charade of being human. She wondered if she'd ever feel that way again.

Ania and Ben were alone in the middle of a deserted park. Many of the would-be strollers were driven inside by the chill. No one was in sight.

"I've heard a lot of stories of great historical finds," said Ania, "but I did not believe there could ever be something of this magnitude, that is until we met yesterday. The information Doctor O'Toole sent you this morning removes any doubt from my mind. I know of his reputation — he is not given to exaggeration." She continued walking alongside Ben.

He didn't know that when he wasn't stealing glances at her, she was stealing them at him. In the brief time since they had met, they both sensed a kinship; in what, though, they couldn't quite place.

"I'm astonished. Although Charlemagne established his capital there, that was nearly a thousand years after the date Doctor O'Toole has proposed the crosses were buried. I am eager to go there and see for myself." Ben smiled.

As they walked, Ben couldn't shake the feeling that Ania was holding something back. He'd only met her the previous day, but he felt as if they'd known each other for years. Her educational achievements were impressive, but his admiration of her was rooted in something he could feel but not name. He too was working on his PhD, but she already had three. Normally, he might feel intimidated by her superior academic credentials; but she possessed a humble and demure demeanor.

When they talked he could see her transition from teacher to colleague to student. This change was predicated on Ben telling her something she didn't know. She might be arund his age, but she was a tenured professor with real-world experience. There was no question that she spent little time in the "ivory tower." She was known to spend as much time visiting historical locations as she did teaching classes. The fact that she was born in the country that gave the world Western civilization was not lost on him. It seemed like the ancient Greek culture was embedded in her DNA. Something about the way she spoke and acted gave others a sense of experience beyond her apparent years.

While she was extremely interested in what they were about to see, he suspected that she knew more than she was letting on. She had a quiet yet honest air about her. He thought about things in a linear fashion; he surmised that she could think not only laterally but also on multiple tracks. Like a computer, it was as if she had many other programs operating in the background. She was intriguing, but he did not desire to pry into her private life by asking personal questions. He knew they would be spending a lot of time together in the next few days, and he decided to just let her reveal herself as she saw fit.

As they walked in silence, he stole another glance at her profile. He was sure he had seen her some-where before, but he could not place these vague impressions. Her features were exquisite, and there was a beauty about her that was unworldly. Doctor Socratatos reminded him of some of the artwork he'd seen in Rome — ancient beauties, their expres-sions forever captured in marble and paint. He felt a comfort with her that he rarely felt with anyone, even those he'd known for years. He knew it was prema-ture, but he really enjoyed being near her, wondering if... He was about to entertain thoughts of something possibly developing in the future, but the thing that had grabbed his attention a few moments earlier squeezed harder.

Walking alongside him, Ania knew that he suspected she was holding something back. The brief silences amplified this feeling, making her wonder if he could ever comprehend who she truly was. These moments were uncomfortable, but being around him put her at ease. She couldn't place it, so she simply attributed it to the fact he was a devout believer. He had true faith; he didn't see, but believed. Unlike her, who'd seen, and knew. She was about to break the silence, but he spoke first.

"Doctor." He gently grasped her right arm. The way he said "doctor" and the way he held her elbow startled her. She saw nothing in the path ahead of them, but in her peripheral vision, something to her right stirred. She glanced up at Ben, reading his expression and watching as his demeanor changed drastically. The normally affable expression on his face became something fierce.

Ben looked as if he was staring straight ahead, but she saw his eyes drift to the left and to the right, his stride never breaking.

"Yo man, got a smoke?"

The question came from a man who suddenly appeared in front of them, moving so quickly from within a tree line that he seemed to materialize out of thin air. His figure was silhouetted by a light behind him, and all Ania could see was that he was wearing a hooded sweatshirt under a ratty leather jacket. A thug from *West Side Story* came to her mind. Ania watched the dark-clad figure moving forward as Ben was about to reply. It was at that moment that she saw another man approach from their right, his hands in his pockets. She was about to warn Ben, when he replied to the man in front of them.

"Sorry friend, we can't help you."

As Ben said this, he used his right arm to move Ania directly behind him, placing himself between her and the dark-clothed tough. What transpired next only took seconds, but seemed like an eternity.

The man on their right quickly drew near and the leather jacket closed the distance rapidly. The man to the right said, "Turn out yuh pockets!" As he spoke, a large knife appeared in his hand. The man in front of them also produced a knife, this one smaller, but he held it in a more menacing way.

Instinctively, she prepared to act, but Ben reacted faster; in one fluid move, he swept Ania farther behind him, putting himself between her and the two attackers. Drawing his right elbow straight up, Ben struck the man's chin, jolting his head back, felling him like a large tree. The man's body thumped to the ground. He did not move, the blow knocking him unconscious.

The other man, seeing his accomplice go down, lunged angrily at Ben with his larger knife. Ben's left leg swept the man's feet out from under him. As the man fell, he slashed wildly with the knife, missing Ben's neck by inches. Ben spun away from the falling man, and using the same elbow, struck the man's head as he fell; the blow put him on the ground faster than gravity could.

Ania heard a thud, and was not sure if the noise came from the blow to the head or the man hitting the ground. Unlike the first assailant, this one started to get back up, lunging again at Ben with the knife.

Ania felt her rage explode, and was about to finish what Ben started when she became aware of someone rushing up behind them. A third man, coming out of nowhere, ignored her and lunged at Ben's exposed back with his own knife. Ignoring the woman was his undoing. As he aimed the point of the blade, Ania grabbed the wrist of his free hand; the last thing the third assailant remembered was being jerked backward violently and spinning in the air like a Frisbee, then being slammed into the ground. Whatever grabbed his wrist had the pressure of a vise.

When his world stopped moving, he dizzily looked up, and all he could see was a blurry outline. He focused and recognized the woman he'd rushed by. His initial thought was that the man who dispatched his two friends had been the one who threw him to the ground, but before he could look for him, Ania leaned over, and her left hand clamped around his right, which was still holding the knife. Her right hand grabbed the blade and snapped it in half. As she did so, blood trickled from her palm and fell on his shirt.

As her eyes locked on his, something pierced his consciousness and seemed to squeeze the inside of his mind. She opened her hand and the broken blade dropped to the ground. Now the grievous gash on her hand poured blood onto his already reddening shirt.

For a moment, the man saw exposed bones within the bleeding wound. He tried to look closer, but she grabbed him by his leather jacket lapels and picked him up. His world spun as he felt himself being flung over Ania's shoulders and behind her.

The moment he landed, he scrambled to his feet and ran as fast as he could. His chest burned as he tried to recapture the wind that had been knocked from his lungs. He looked over his shoulder at the woman, and saw her eyes glow like fire. She smiled pleasantly at him and he realized that the smaller-statured woman had flipped him around like a wet towel. He looked forward again and kept running as if his life depended on it.

When he was a safe distance away, he stopped, dry heaved and tried to catch his breath. When he looked down, the blood from the woman's wounded hand was no longer on his clothes. He grabbed his shirt from the bottom and pulled it closer to his face; but he could find no evidence that she'd bled on him. The vision of the fire-glowing eyes, and the vanishing red stain, frightened him to his core. Unsure of what had just happened, he became too scared to remain still. He ran off as fast as he could, still trying to breathe.

As Ben straightened up, Ania came up behind him. The two attackers lay on the ground, both unconscious. Ben stepped over one of them and gently took her by the arm.

"Are you all right?"

There was a tone of concern in his voice. He was not aware that Ania had fended off the third attacker. He looked over her shoulder and saw her attacker scrambling off.

She looked in the fleeing man's direction. "I think your martial arts demonstration scared him off." Then she looked back at Ben with a grateful smile. As she spoke, she buried her hands deep in her pockets. She did not want to risk Ben's seeing what had happened to her palm and fingers.

As quickly as the fierce expression had come over his face, it dissipated and returned to its normally affable state.

"Big cities stateside. I know why I prefer Rome." He dusted his hands off, and smiled at her. His expression contained no evidence that he'd just defused a deadly situation. They stood staring at each other for a few moments; they knew there was not much to be said. Then they walked off quietly together.

Chapter 15

The Flight

Ben and Ania arrived at the airport in the dark hours of the early morning. They had agreed to show up several hours before the flight and use the extra time to review the plethora of information they had thus far.

After checking their baggage and clearing security, they settled in the private lounge for business and first-class passengers. There were no other people in the club at this hour, and they used the quiet to their full advantage. The plane would not leave for three hours. They availed themselves of fresh tea and coffee from the breakfast bar.

"Doctor...Ania, I appreciate your upgrading us to first class. That was generous of you. Business class would have sufficed." Ben lifted his cup slightly for emphasis.

"Considering that your employer paid for the trip, it was the least I could do. This expedition is a high-light in my professional academic life. I'm excited beyond words." She gently tapped his cup with hers as a toast to their upcoming journey.

As their eyes met, both suddenly felt as if they were on a first date. Ben was slightly giddy, and so was Ania. An awkward silence would have followed, but it was interrupted by the ringing of Ben's cell phone. The first few notes of Mozart's "Ode to Joy" played on his phone before he answered it. "Rome calling—excuse me for a moment."

Ben got up and walked into the foyer to take the call. He was speaking perfectly-accented, fluent Italian as he walked away. Ania smiled and stared out the window at the darkness. Her mind drifted.

She visualized what Aachen might look like now. The astute scholar knew the world had changed considerably in the century and a quarter since she'd last been to Germany. When she last saw Aachen, it was rural and seldom traveled. She remembered standing on the deck of a steamer leaving Bremen, headed for the new world. She had felt the pangs of loneliness, realizing she would be an ocean away from the only thing that had ever brought solace to her troubled soul.

Ania assumed she still had a soul, but didn't think it was hers anymore. Since evacuating the treasure from the Holy Land, and until leaving on that ship, she'd never been more than a mile from it. When not reflecting in the cave with it, she was always nearby. Merely knowing it was nearby brought her a comfort beyond imagination. Her initial idea had been to bring

it with her to the New World — get it as far away from
the persecutors as possible and put an entire ocean
between it and those who would destroy it.

But prudence had convinced her that it was safe
where it was. Trying to bring it to an unknown world
could be perilous, not for her, but for it. She had
decided to travel to America alone, and later determine if ferrying it across the Atlantic was feasible.

The world was so different since she had first
found refuge in the cave; technology, industry, trans-
portation, national boundaries, world events, literature, and music — everything had vastly changed. The
new developments were exciting and troublesome at
the same time. The world, particularly Europe, was
not ready for it, or her. The nascent and free America
had been her only hope. The republic, created as it
was by people who recognized the stagnation of the
old world, was not consistent with what she knew
needed to be done. The writings of those in the new
nation were things she'd never contemplated. Its
Founders and those that followed were different;
they did not hold that a people were bound by their
lineage to stay in one place, station, or way of thinking. America was a blank page and it had presented
opportunities for her to reveal the treasure and hope
the world was ready to accept its promise.

Europe was in a constant state of turmoil, which
seemingly began when she had first arrived and was
still so when she left. She wondered if the forces of

darkness were so active on the continent because the treasure was hidden there. America was different; its founding documents evidenced that the people of this new country might be receptive, or so she'd hoped. Ania once thought the persecutors had died off after the first millennia, but realized their descendants had simply evolved into more sinister versions of their ancestors.

Ben returned fifteen minutes later, bringing two fresh cups of coffee. Although she didn't need it, Athania graciously accepted it. The brewed bean had no effect on her, but Ben's politeness required her to accept it with a grateful smile, as if the caffeine was needed to wake up.

"Arriving early and using this time to study was an inspired idea," Ania said, reviewing new information which Ben had provided her that morning.

"Flying has never been my preferred method of travel. I'd have gladly paid for the gas if we could have driven." Ben chuckled, studying an updated list of the crosses and their ages.

The truth was, Ania had never flown. All her travels had been by foot, boat, carriage, or horse. Her current physical condition easily allowed her to deal with the dangers those modes of travel presented, but being in the sky, thousands of feet above the earth—she knew not what might happen. If a crash occurred, would she survive, or would it finally be the thing that destroyed her? Her lack of control concerned her as well. Horses had thrown her, boats sank, roads had predators, but a machine that moved high through the air, thousands upon thousands of feet above the ground...

"What do you not like about flying?" she asked.

"The drudgery; all you see is air passing by — there's no scenery. In a car or train, there are things to admire. On a ship, you can move around. A plane is like a big aluminum coffin."

Ania's mind drifted back to the refuge; when she had left, she knew that no mere human could find it, let alone get to it. But with modern technology there was no telling what could be done. The bombs and crosses had been recovered fifty feet down. Her expansive mind remembered: that was about where she'd concealed them. The bedrock was two hundred feet beyond that. The refuge was just below that.

The bombs had been a feeble attempt by an evil maniac to destroy something he feared, but couldn't find. The force that called the faithful drew destruction as well. Its light had drawn the darkness that ravaged the area in the first half of the twentieth century. In the madness of the Second Great War, evil manifested itself in many ways. This juggernaut of doom sought the symbol of light in its midst, and while it could not destroy it directly, it used the weak-minded for its bidding. Fortunately, the human forces of darkness allowed themselves to become blinded by ambition, and in their quest, they stirred the forces of good to action. She had known that the United States would eventually take arms, and they most certainly did. The descendants of this fledgling nation—a nation that had not only acknowledged His existence but revered Him and allowed its citizens to do so—had freely sought out the evil and vanquished it before it enveloped humanity.

Looking at Ben, Ania remembered where she had been in December of 1941. On Friday, the fifth, her classes had been full of young men, whose lives were full of promise and hope. On the eighth, they were gone. Some had filtered back in during the following weeks. These were the ones who were still waiting to be processed or who had not been accepted into the military, for health or family reasons. She recognized their sadness; it was something she'd felt for so long.

"May I get you anything? I need to relax my eyes." Ben got up, rubbing his temples as he set down the document he was studying; it was a sheaf of papers, listing everything recovered at the dig so far.

"No thank you, Ben." She glanced up at him. He was bursting with excitement. If he only knew what he might find.

"I will be back shortly; I need to take a little walk." Ben stretched his arms above his head like a child just waking up. He smiled at her as he turned away.

Ania returned the smile. She felt something toward him, something she hadn't felt since she was a teenage girl. *Am I capable of that still?* she wondered to herself. Staring out the window, the first traces of daybreak came up over the tarmac.

Chapter 16

In the Air

Ben returned to the lounge after an hour, and they decided to head for the gate. Their non-stop flight to Stuttgart was only half full, and they had first class almost to themselves. After several hours in the air, the flight attendant brought them two mimosas.

As they drank, they made small talk, getting to know each other more. They took a break from the subject of the dig, focusing more on where they'd studied, and recent books they'd read. Ben was more comfortable around Ania, feeling less intimidated by her title of "Doctor." He was still years from earning his PhD, whereas this was something Ania had earned years earlier and three times over. Despite this, she treated him as an academic equal. The accomplished professor had the rare quality of humility, something in short supply nowadays.

The attendant walked by and topped off Ben's half-full and Ania's nearly-full flute. Realizing she'd barely touched her glass, Ania decided to continue her charade as a human and took an unusually large sip.

Ben was noticing a subtle change in Ania. Up to now, she simply appeared to be an accomplished, educated, soft-spoken woman. She now suddenly seemed younger not so much in age but in spirit. He thought it was the drink, but she'd consumed no more than an ounce of it. She wasn't drunk; she was… *free?* The concept lodged in his brain.

Ania remembered the last time she'd experienced this sensation — in London, after a performance. The man had been a playwright, a brilliant man, with a seeking mind. *The wine? It must be!* she thought to herself as she reclined her seat and rubbed her temples.

"Ben, I'm going to rest for a bit." His travelling companion smiled somewhat drowsily.

"Go ahead, no one will disturb you." He smiled and began reading a book he bought during his airport walk.

With closed eyes, she concluded it must be the drink. Not the alcohol, but the underlying essence of the nectar — the grapes, they were from Greece, they had to be. She should have asked first, but her mind was elsewhere. She feigned sleep, not wanting Ben to see her in this state. He was inquisitive, and she knew he sensed the change. The last time she'd been like this, Ania revealed her secrets to Bram. He had been drunk too, and fortunately he remembered her words as a fable.

Doctor Socratatos knew the effects would dissipate in a few hours; all she needed to do was refrain from speaking. She meditated, focusing on her earliest teaching days. Her mind drifted, not to a land of dreams, but to a state of much deeper relaxation. To a casual observer, she looked to be in REM sleep; in reality, the woman was going back in time.

Sitting under a tree, she was with father. His toga was threadbare, but clean. Hers was brilliant white. He smiled and sought her observations about all she saw. The curious daughter commented on the nearby stream, the tree, the sky, and the grass. He asked her questions about her perceptions. Assessing her observations, he asked her to provide facts to support them. For every given fact, he told her to contradict herself, and to find reasons why her observations were false. The exercise was difficult at first, but in questioning her beliefs, she found supporting ideas from an unseen source. She explained why the grass was green, the water dark, and the sky blue. When finished, the eager student not only knew she was right, she was also able to articulate the reasons why they were as they were, to a degree unknown even to her when they began. After several of these long discussions, she realized he was teaching her his method — the *Socratic method.*

• • • • • • •

They stared into each other's eyes. "This was a splendid day. I've never had such a wonderful time," Seth said, sipping his drink.

"Did you ever date religious girls?" she asked coyly, rubbing her finger around the rim of her glass.

"I dated a Jewish girl for a while. She took me to a bar mitzvah once. That was as boring as a Mass, only now some pimply teenager read out loud in Hebrew from a book. The 'after party' was great." He swirled the amber liquid in his glass, indicating what he meant.

"Any idea why people follow religions? There are millions around the world who do." She cocked her head slightly. She continued: "What finally freed your mind of the religion trap?" Bella drew a long fingernail along the stem of her glass.

"I must see things for myself. I asked questions, and the only reply was sermons and songs. If there really was a 'God,' where was He? Why did He let bad things happen randomly as they do? He never shows Himself. Never even shows a sign." Seth raised his hands in the air, as if conjuring a spell.

Bella giggled; "You are quite the entertainer!" She ran her hand across the top of his.

"It gets the point across better with the rubes." He finished his drink.

"I wonder about that too; I've never seen a 'miracle.'" She mimicked Seth's gesture.

"The only 'miracle' I saw was the ability of organized religion to convince people to give up their
money and lives for a 'cause.'" He rubbed his fingers
together as if counting money.

"What about these apparitions that appear every
now and then?" She drew her finger along the
tablecloth.

"Sure, some histrionic woman sees an image of the
Virgin Mary in a crack on the sidewalk." He snorted.
"You ever notice it's always some person from the 'old
country' who sees it? If you look at a cloud and tell
me you see an elephant, I'll see one too. That's the
power of suggestion, like those 'hidden messages' in
songs played backward. It's ridiculous."

"Did you ever think someone would try to pull
off a grand hoax, say find the Ten Commandments,
the Holy Grail, or the Ark of the Covenant? I mean
they've made many a movie about them." She tilted
her head.

"That's it, they're just movies. If someone pops
up with the Holy Grail, how would you know it
really was the Grail? I mean, I can show this glass
to someone and claim it belonged to Albert Einstein.
They'd have to take my word for it." He sipped from
the tumbler.

"What about the burial shroud they found long
ago. They claimed 'you know who' was buried in it."
She draped her napkin over her hands.

"They found an old piece of cloth with an image on it. How do they know it wasn't some farmer who lived a long time ago? They claim it's Christ—does anyone actually know what He looked like? They believe it because they want to." He smirked.

"Belief is a powerful thing," she sneered.

"I had a friend who was into conspiracies. You name it, he believed it. He claimed a multinational group controlled the banks. This group was responsible for an assassination, that group covered it up, on and on and on. I tried to reason with him, but his mind was made up. Even when I showed him proof, he dismissed it and said it was fabricated. He was a true believer, as they say." Seth drained his glass.

"Let me tell you something I heard about recently." She looked into his eyes. He didn't know it, but what she was about to tell him would alter the course of his life in a way that would frighten him.

• • • • • • •

Ania woke up from her pseudo-sleep. Her watch said five hours had passed. The wine's effects were gone, but an unfamiliar feeling enveloped her—flight. She'd never been this high in the air.

Ben was asleep, and quietly she got up. Ania found an empty window seat, several rows back. Looking out the glass, she caught her breath—she was higher than the clouds. In her longer-than-usual lifespan, she'd seen things no one else had. Being in the sky was alien to her. Looking down, she saw the billowy clouds and beyond that, the Atlantic Ocean. Her thoughts of Germany were forgotten as she absorbed the view.

I'm above the highest mountain on earth! she whispered to herself.

In addition to the view, Ania sensed motion; she was moving faster than any creature on the earth. As a child, she had looked at birds and wondered what it would be like to be so high in the sky, looking down on the world. If she could shed tears, they would have been flowing.

• • • • • • •

Seth and Bella stood at the railing, looking down on the water. Bella looked at the moon, Seth at her.

She's beautiful, he thought, admiring her profile. Her jet-black hair reflected light, looking like a black fire. Her intensely blue eyes seemed to glow. Her ivory skin radiated something akin to the heat of a fire. The more he watched, the more Seth saw an aura about her he'd never acknowledged before.

"Seth, what do you think the world would be like without religion, without belief in a higher power?" Bella gazed beyond the moon, at the stars.

"The world would be wonderful. No strife, no wars, all societies would be in the current century by now. People would treat one another better." He looked at the same cluster of stars.

"If there were no fear of punishment in the afterlife, what would keep someone from hurting others — stealing, pillaging, killing?" She looked down at the ocean.

"That's why there are laws. People stop doing bad things because they don't want to go to jail, not because someone had a set of stone tablets with ten 'commandments,'" he snorted.

"What if they found those actual Commandments? Would that convince people that religion was true?" She looked down at her fingers, admiring the crimson nails.

Seth noticed that her nails dripped light, just like blood.

"It wouldn't mean a thing. Unless someone has a video of old Moses coming down from on high, there would be no way to prove they are authentic. Sure, fools would buy into it and 'mend their ways.' There's no way they could prove the tablets were made by God."

"What about science? What if scientists — objective, rational scholars — determined that the tablets were as old as the legend of Moses himself?" She ran her hand along the railing, stopping at his wrist.

"That would be interesting. If I trusted the scientist's objectivity and it was proven that the tablets were that old, well then we know someone took the time to inscribe ten rules on pieces of rock. It still wouldn't prove a thing." Seth looked off in the distance, deep in thought.

"Well, what if they could prove that the tablets were several thousand years old, and that the writing could not have been man-made with the tools available at the time? Wouldn't that convince people?" Her gaze went up to his face.

"Not possible, but if it were…it cannot happen. There is no God, no angels, nothing, just like I said before. It's all a sham." He turned to her and looked into her eyes. Something drew his consciousness into hers.

"Seth, there is something going on, a situation that could sway millions of people. It's a grand plan that might offer proof that a higher power exists. Its influence could…well, change the world." Her hand moved from the rail to his arm.

"That's impossible. It can't exist; if it does, it's a hoax, a way to dupe people." An electric tingle traveled from her fingers. And up his shoulder.

"Shall we go back to my room? I'm in the mood for a nightcap." Her expression told Seth that an evening libation wasn't the only thing on her mind.

I knew this trip would be a good one, he thought to himself, as they left the deck and made their way below to her cabin.

Chapter 17

Wheels Down

The remainder of the flight was uneventful. Ania spent most of it looking out the window, absorbing the commanding view from the sky. This was the first time she'd seen the tops of clouds. It was magnificent. When it turned dark, she returned to her own seat and was surprised to see that Ben was not reading. His seat was reclined and his eyes were aimed at the dark window. A set of headphones covered his ears and he appeared to be lost in thought. When she sat down, he removed the diminutive listening device.

"Enjoying the flight?" he said hopefully.

"Very much so. I've never—I mean it's been a long time since I last traveled by airplane. What are you listening to?" She nodded to the headphones, hoping he wouldn't realize she'd almost said she'd never flown before.

"It's a German talk show. I haven't been in Deutschland for a while; my mind needs to shift gears." He raised his seat back so he was at eye level with her.

Deutschland — that reminded Ania she would soon be somewhere she'd not been for over one hundred years. America had changed considerably in its own right, but Germany, let alone Europe, had changed beyond description. She was well versed in world history and knew all about Europe's current state of affairs. All that information was gleaned from intense study and monitoring current events. But until she actually returned to her former home and saw things in person, anything she'd learned before was just theory.

"That sounds like a good idea. What regional accents do you detect from the speech patterns?" She retrieved another set of earphones from the side of the seat.

"The host sounds to be from the northwest area. He studied in Austria. The guest, she's from the east. She may have even been born in Romania." Ben touched his hand to his ear, as if concentrating harder.

Not wanting to interrupt him, Ania mouthed, "What channel?"

Ben replied by holding up five fingers. She switched over to the same frequency and listened for a few moments.

Ben was correct. She made the appearance of listening to the talk, but that was merely a way to allow her to concentrate on other things. She enjoyed talking to Ben, but she needed to refresh her memory before they landed. Closing her eyes, she meditated and allowed her consciousness to drift to the past…

Ania had reluctantly left Europe for the United States near the end of the nineteenth century. She desperately wanted to bring her charge with her, but it was impossible to move it without drawing attention. With the treasure as large as it was, it did not easily lend itself to movement, let alone concealment. After much mental debate, Ania had decided to leave it in the safety of a cave, and journey to America alone. The hiding place was well beyond the reach of prying hands or curious eyes.

When she left in the late 1890s, science and technology were in their infancy. In less than fifty years afterwards, steam power had been replaced by electricity, fossil fuels, and the power of the atom. The proper equipment, in the hands of the right person, might find it, she feared. Thankfully, its location was impossible to stumble upon by random happenstance. In order to discover it, someone would have to be looking very hard. Technology had advanced exponentially in the last century, but the ability to see through solid rock had yet to be developed. Ground-penetrating radar was a possible concern, but that only worked with organic soil. The cave was deep underground, and the entrance was not discernible to human sight. It was safe for now.

The other possible danger was the fact that towns and cities had sprung up within a mile of the cave, and unfortunately a house was scheduled to be built directly over the refuge. Even so, the cave was hundreds of feet underground. Unless the structure's foundation was going to be dug into the bedrock, the cave would not be in any danger.

The gentle bump of the massive 747's landing gear ended Ania's reverie. She marveled that something so large could drop from the sky and land like a small bird. She wished she had flown years earlier. The experience was unlike anything she'd ever known. It was dawning on her that she was *here* – the place Ania had last been so long ago. A mixture of anticipation, laced with apprehension, washed over her.

As they disembarked, Ania suggested they speak in German for the rest of the trip, and Ben gladly agreed. His fondness for the study of languages rivaled even her own.

It was obvious to the college professor that Ben's interests were similar to hers. There was a significant difference – his was born of curiosity, hers of necessity. But with every passing moment, she felt a deepening kinship with this enthusiastic fellow scholar. Ben exuded a desire to learn and grow, to a level above that of her best and brightest students. As most persons approached mid-life, the desire to learn tended to wane. Ben Airaldi was just the opposite.

Ania wished more of her students could be infused with his hunger for knowledge; higher education would flourish. She wished her true nature could be revealed to him, and with that, the true explanation of the dig's origins.

Clearing customs was effortless, thanks to Ben's diplomatic status. Avoiding the regular routine process saved them almost an hour. They collected their luggage and made their way to the car-rental counter.

Barely three hours after landing, they were checked into the hotel. The excavation site was still a good distance away, and given the lateness of the day, they decided to get a good night's rest and leave early the next morning.

Ania was surprised that Ben was willing to wait, but he'd barely slept on the plane, and fatigue was showing on his eager face. They bid each other good night and retired to their respective rooms.

Ania was thankful she had a night to reflect and plan a course of action.

Chapter 18

On Hallowed Ground

Once settled in her room, Ania turned off the lights and approached the window. Opening it, she shut her eyes and felt cool air caress her face. Each wave of gentle wind stirred distant memories from so long ago. She opened her lids and looked at the dark forest below; the traveler could not believe two millennia had passed since she first set foot upon this ancient Teutonic land.

Settling into a chair, Ania listened to the pine branches moving with the air's gentle push. Her mind returned to the present, then toggled back and forth between AD 33 and AD 2014. She thought back to how she first came to be in Germany, then how she had returned.

Ania's first visit to the Rhineland was with Marcus, her apt pupil and ward. Her return was with Ben—an astute colleague. Marcus knew why they'd come there, but little about her. In contrast, Ben thought he knew why they were here now—though

he too knew nothing about her. She had always felt
at ease with Marcus, and was becoming more so with
Ben.

Ania reminded herself about the dangers of
becoming too familiar with others. Bel aside, who
had known her since the curse took hold, Marcus was
an eager young servant, following the orders of his
centurion father. Yes, Marcus knew she was no ordinary woman, but per his father's orders, he had kept
his mouth closed and ears open. He knew she was
different, and any other person might have feared
her powers. Marcus trusted his father, and if the wise
warrior told him to trust her, that was all that he
needed to know. The only time the boy asked probing
questions was when she introduced him to the study
of philosophy. He was her first true student, and
to this day her greatest. In the few years they were
together, he had absorbed every lesson she taught
and every word she said. By the time he set out on his
own, he knew almost as much as she did.

Knowing she'd passed along her father's teachings to a willing mind helped ease the pain of losing
him. Although her greatest teacher was dead, his
knowledge and wisdom would live on in Marcus. She
took further solace in the fact that her parent's teachings were passed on to someone healed by the Savior.
She was confident that her former pupil had willingly
passed on his knowledge to others. She missed him,
not only because he was so willing to learn, but also

because he had carried something within him, no doubt instilled by the One who saved his life.

Ania remembered the one and only time she had revealed herself completely to another person. That disclosure resulted in something unfathomable. The blurry revelation of her true self was captured by an imaginative mind that gave it life. This form mutated into a figurative and literal monster, and no doubt it negatively impacted the world to this day. The playwright had had no ill intentions — he simply wanted to tell a tale, and possibly earn a living. He'd had no idea his creation would endure and thrive for over a century. In the decades since the story was told, an obsession had festered and taken on a life of its own. She knew the quiet Irishman based his renowned character's traits squarely on her own. The difference between Ania and the fictional ghoul was that she wasn't the "living dead," nor did she "turn" mortals. There were countless times she should have died, but for some unnatural and cursed reason, and a curse it was, she hadn't passed from this earth.

Athania Socratatos cringed when the playwright's story was first published in 1897, realizing that during several hours of discussion, something had stirred the creative forces of the writer's mind. She was one of the first persons to read his tome, and was somewhat relieved the character was vastly different from her. Ania's secret was safe for the time being.

The world's oldest "human" had hoped the story would eventually fade into literary history. With the playwright's certain future passing, she had assumed her secret would pass with him. Even if he remembered the specific details of her revelations, no one would believe he'd actually met a being who "couldn't die." When the playwright did die in 1912, she rested easy. She'd left England years earlier, and hadn't seen him since that night. Upon learning of his death, she immediately made plans to return to Europe, and retrieve the treasure. In 1914, she planned to sail across the Atlantic, using the cover of a silent film production company. Sailing back from Europe with the treasure could be explained — it would be declared as a prop, to be used in an upcoming, American movie. Anyone who saw it would not believe its real nature.

Her plans were put on hold when she learned that another author, inspired by the original playwright's story, had written his own. In the two stories, symbolic replicas of the treasure were mentioned, but there was no direct reference to it. The playwright had been well into his second bottle of wine that night, and the details of her story were thankfully jumbled by his intoxicated mind.

Rather than a hasty trip to Europe, she decided to wait a few more years, until this new story was forgotten. World War I placed her plans on an indefinite hold. In the early 1920s, she was able to create another cover; but then in 1924, there was a play, and in 1931, a movie. Every few years after that, another book, movie, or play surfaced. It was as if every time she had the opportunity to retrieve the treasure, the story was reincarnated and interest grew.

The chances of people making a connection between the stories and the object weren't strong, but bringing it to the States would not be a simple task. Unlike the early years when she had fled the Holy Land, Europe was now more populated, and travelling unseen in the dark was nearly impossible. She would have to bide her time, and wait.

Another world war erupted, and after that, Germany became divided. Her concern now was not that someone would realize the value of the treasure, but that the oppressive forces of Communism might see the treasure as a symbol, and destroy it out of spite. She'd waited two thousand years…in contrast, a few more decades would be a short span of time.

Dovetailed into the global turmoil was the invention of television. With this new medium, the story of the "Taker of Souls" developed into an unstoppable juggernaut. By the twenty-first century, stories, movies, and plays surfaced daily. One movie even depicted Judas Iscariot as being the original monster, having sold his soul to Satan for thirty pieces of silver. In this story, the ultimate betrayer was unsuccessful in his attempt to take his own life, and was then cursed to walk the earth, searching for more souls to claim for evil.

This story came uncomfortably close to Ania's. She'd told the playwright that she actually saw the real Judas, in the first few hours after the betrayal. His identity was obvious, because Bel's twin sister was at his side. Seeing them together, she'd realized that the sister seduced the original traitor in the same way Bel had seduced her. The only difference between her and the Savior's betrayer was that she "sold" herself for vengeance. Judas was damned — what she was… she didn't know. Based on everything she'd learned over the years, she knew she was not in Hades, nor was she in the afterlife, or purgatory, for that matter. The only place she could loosely equate her situation with was that of being in an eternal, earth-bound limbo. What horrified her most about all these tales was the perpetual fascination with the damned. She knew evil was seductive — she'd succumbed to it once and now here she was. Bel had tricked her all by himself.

And now with these movies and stories, Bel had learned the true, secret power of mass media. He didn't need to tempt people in person; he could let film, computers, and papers do his work.

If she'd ever thought of revealing the treasure to the world someday, the idea had completely perished ten years earlier. One sad day, a bored and lonely housewife — a mother no less — wrote a series of love stories about a pale, brooding teenage monster, and a smitten young girl. The "love story's" allure had now invaded the lives of the young and impressionable; Bel was truly succeeding.

Ania blamed herself for this worldwide epidemic. Maybe she actually *had* put Bel's plans into motion. Had her awful mistake, born in tears and rage, led to the surrender of souls to the forces of evil? She wondered: if she'd kept her secret, might the playwright have used his talents in other areas? He'd already been fascinated with the ancient, blood-thirsty nobleman, telling her that night that he was working on a new play. Her story was now mixed with that of the ancient character, and a new tale born. She hoped that someday, the world would forget about the monster that hungered for human "fuel"; that it would vanish from the face of the earth entirely. Then things might be better.

Ania's mind returned to the present, knowing that the Savior would eventually reclaim his kingdom. This thought made her smile. She'd learned by now that evil was glamorous, and deceived easily — especially the weak-minded, but it was not more powerful than its antithesis.

The smile broadened at the thought that she was no longer separated from the hiding place by the entire Atlantic Ocean — she was on the same ground as it was. A relieving sense of peace enveloped her — something that had been absent from her life for nearly a century.

Chapter 19

The Arrival

The pair walked hand in hand down the gangway.

"Was the trip all you expected?" Bella asked coyly.

"It was heaven—if I believed in that sort of thing." Seth grinned slyly.

They traversed the concourse, swinging their clasped hands to and fro like children. The last three days onboard were like nothing Seth Steinbeck had ever experienced—it seemed as if they never left their cabin. This mysteriously alluring woman had showed him the most unearthly pleasures. Time stopped when they were together, and he wanted more. She was everything he wanted in a paramour; she hung on his every word and shared his atheistic beliefs. For the first time, he felt important and worthy of admiration.

"Seth, there is no proof that God exists, but what would you say to someone who claims to have seen a vision or some physical manifestation of a deity?" She looked at him with admiring eyes.

"They're delusions. People see what they want to see. It's no different than believers in Bigfoot, the Loch Ness Monster, or UFOs. The mind is powerful, and misguided beliefs cause otherwise normal and rational people to see all kinds of things." He snorted derisively.

"What about things like the Shroud of Turin and the Guadalupe Virgin? Those things are physical, and many believe they are the image of 'you know who' and his mother." She wrinkled her nose as she said this, as if tasting something sour.

"Man-made forgeries. The ancient bedsheet, I mean no one even knows what He looked like. All anyone knows is that the rag is really old, and that it looks like a guy with a beard and long hair was buried in it. As for that bad piece of art, which the Mexicans drool over, it's a bad painting of some woman no one knows. Yes, these objects exist, but they only have meaning because fools buy into them." Steinbeck shook his head.

"Those things all appeared in the previous centuries. What do you think would happen if someone found the Grail or the Ark of the Covenant?" She looked up at him.

"You know, I'm surprised someone hasn't produced those things and tried to cash in on it. The Jews would be hard to convince about the Ark, but the Catholics...they'd go into a tizzy and claim to have proof that that charlatan was the 'son of the almighty.'"

Seth became irritated, not by her questions, but at the mere thought of these things that people tried to present as proof. He'd not given much thought to these relics, but something stirred within him—base anger, a hatred of anything he saw as a physical manifestation of any organized religion. He fondly remembered being involved in a plan to get menorahs and nativity scenes removed from public displays. He and a group of like-minded friends had flooded a local municipality's application system for a limited number of spaces in a public display lottery. Of the twenty available, he and his group had won eighteen, leaving the other two to a Jewish and a Catholic group. They built a series of signs almost eight feet tall with sayings about how Christmas and the holiday season were merely a ploy by retailers to get people to spend their money on overpriced goods.

"Well, what would happen if they discovered something historical, something that could be proved to be really old, something that would show that the Hebrews and papists were right?" She looked concerned.

"They did that with the Dead Sea Scrolls. Sure they were old, but they didn't prove anything. They were simply ancient texts of the original Jewish teachings. Unless they could find something as significant as a lost city or something…ah, they never will." A smug look crossed his face.

"What about all the things the papists have in Rome? There are many relics and such in their vaults. They even claim to have the tomb of one of the 'apostles' under a church." She looked up at him again.

"That place—I wasn't a big supporter of the Axis in World War II, but I can't believe the German and Italian armies didn't simply march into the Vatican and loot it. They might have been able to win the war if they'd used the booty to buy more planes and tanks." He chuckled.

"Why didn't they? I mean that place was squarely in the middle of Rome; I never grasped why they stayed out of the Vatican." Bella said the last word with much difficulty, as if she couldn't pronounce it.

"The pope, I think his name was Pius or something—he claimed the Vatican was a neutral nation. There was a treaty in 1928 or 1929, 'Lateran' or something, it established the 'palace' as a sovereign nation and everyone left the place alone. Personally, I think the Italians were scared because they believed all the Church's fairy tales. The Germans—I heard old Adolf was superstitious and believed the place had magical powers. He had a Rasputin kind of guy who advised him on how to win the war. This adviser told him that disturbing the Vatican or the pope would curse him personally and bring about the end of the German race. That was the same reason he never messed much with the churches either — he was scared. That movie was true in the fact that he was looking for that confounded Ark. He actually believed all that Hebrew mumbo jumbo. He thought that golden crate would make the Reich invincible. He even tried to find the 'spear of destiny.'" His shook his head again.

"Wasn't that…" Bella didn't finish the sentence.

"Yeah, just like the Grail, they claimed the spear used to lance him as he was dying had magical powers because his blood was on it. Must be in the same place as the Grail and Ark. Maybe they are both in the Ark and the Ark is inside the Trojan Horse." He looked at Bella, and they both laughed.

"My my, Mr. Steinbeck, you are quite the learned man. It stirs a passion in me like…" She led him by the hand to a thickly wooded area a short distance from the docks.

"Where do you take me, my muse?" He cocked an eyebrow.

"Well, there is no heaven, but I can show you something like the Garden of Eden…" With her free hand, she tugged at the string on her peasant blouse, turning just as it fell open. They entered the trees and found a grassy clearing, far from the rest of the world.

Chapter 20

The Dig

Ben was up and ready to leave at seven. He'd slept fairly well, in spite of the excitement of being so close to the excavation site. He did wake, though, every few hours, eager for daylight. He was about to knock on Ania's door, but she opened it as if she knew he was there.

"I heard you come out of your room," she said with a soft smile.

"Ready to go, Doctor…Ania?" he asked enthusiastically.

Ben noticed that the green flecks in her irises appeared even brighter than the last time he saw them. His study of her eyes held his attention, until he realized he was staring. With all his excitement over the archeological find, it never registered with him that Ania was a truly beautiful woman. He noticed she was wearing glasses, something he'd not seen her don before. He couldn't tell if they were prescription, but they were slightly shaded. They looked like the type that darkens in sunlight. Even with the mild tint, her eyes seemed bright.

If the ever-present excitement over the dig wasn't competing for his attention, he might have noticed other subtle changes in her countenance. Earlier that morning, Ania had even noticed that something looked different in her own face. Studying herself in the mirror earlier, she saw something that had been missing for years: joy. She knew she was close to the thing she'd spent countless years guarding, and it awoke something in her soul — a soul the highly-rational woman believed was tainted with darkness. The treasure in the cave was showing its power, even from miles away.

Ben attributed the perceived changes to jet lag, knowing it could affect perception. He thought nothing more of it.

Ania self-consciously touched the frame of her gradient-lens glasses. She hoped the prop would effectively conceal her eyes. "Let us depart."

She knew Ben was studying her eyes, and used the statement as an excuse to check her door, breaking visual contact with him. Ben's demeanor was easygoing, but Ania was learning that it concealed a razor-sharp perception.

They went downstairs, reflexively stopping by a brightly-colored coffee cart. Ben ordered a large cup of strong German brew, and Ania opted for Earl Grey tea. Neither was hungry — Ben was too eager to get to the excavation site. Hunger was the last thing on his mind. In Ania's case, she did not need her nourishment from food.

Ben's hope that day was for answers; Ania's were that he didn't get them all.

"Not much of a coffee drinker?" Ben asked, as he singed his mouth with the steaming-hot liquid. His face grimaced in reaction to the singe.

"Not so much; I have an occasional cup now and then, but it makes me jittery — especially the kind they serve here." She gently shook her cup for emphasis. The truth was, by the time Ania first experienced the taste of the oft-cultivated bean, she was already in her current condition. Drinking anything, coffee, tea, water…even poison…had no effect whatsoever. She had the ability to differentiate tastes, but craved nothing and the concept of food and drink was meaningless. The only reason she ever drank tea was to keep up appearances…accomplished college professors were supposed to have cultured tastes. Most times she never even drank — she'd make the motion as if she was, simply to keep up the ruse of her mortality. Since sleep was something she'd not needed in two thousand years, drinking anything in an effort to wake up was a moot point.

They walked outside to the parking lot and Ania soaked in the bright morning sunlight; the rays of warmth stirred energy in the air. She knew the comfort she sensed came not from the sun, but rather from the treasure that was mere miles away. The unfortunate day she had met Bel, she ceased to be human. The word "immortal" crossed her consciousness, but she forbid the word from entering her mind. Most would consider living as long as she had a gift, but to her it was a curse.

Ania was the only "living" being who knew of the cave. While it was far away, its power was affected by distance. She'd felt traces of it in the US, but being so close to it now, it's power was profound. The level of warmth she felt at that moment had been absent from her senses for over a century. Her new feelings this morning were familiar, despite the years that had elapsed. A new feeling—apprehension—jockeyed for position in her astute mind.

Ben approached the passenger side of the car, and opened the door for his associate. This gesture was something no one had ever made for her before. At that moment, she realized Ben wasn't just amiable, he was polite. In anyone else, the act would have appeared pretentious, but Ben did it with ease, as if it were second nature. They were colleagues, equal in most perceptible respects, yet Ben made her feel special. He was a true gentleman—something that seemed to be in short supply.

Ben retrieved a compact paper map from his jacket pocket, unfolded it, and draped it over the steering wheel. He studied it for several moments, as if memorizing it. He offered it to Ania, who noted several red ink notations near the top.

Ben started the motor and the two were on their way.

"Let me know if I veer off course; I'm fairly good with maps, but this part of Germany is new to me."

He made the statement evenly, never taking his eyes, nor attention, off the road.

Ania had never driven a car herself, but from watching Ben, she opined he approached the practice with surgical precision. It was clear that Ben's focus was on the task at hand, and nothing else.

Ania decided to make small talk, hoping it might reveal Ben's state of mind. She set the map on her lap, and retrieved her paper cup from the center console. She thoughtfully pretended to sip her tea, then spoke.

"How does driving in Germany compare to the states?" She looked out the windshield, as if admiring the moving drapes of green.

Ben smiled. Before responding, he checked the speedometer, side view mirrors, and roadway in a smooth succession of eye movements.

"I don't drive much at home — that's an exercise in brinkmanship. Drivers in most cities are aggressive, but those in the major metropolitan areas are down-right brutal. I find driving in the states a chore, but here it's almost a pleasure."

Ben's posture softened, and he eased deeper into the seat. His demeanor looked relaxed, but his eyes were actively scanning the road.

Ania watched as Ben maneuvered the car along the gently-curving highway. His expression showed he was clearly enjoying himself. After their first meeting, she'd assessed her companion's personality as easy-going, affable, and maybe even lighthearted. The encounter in the park showed he had a much different side — all business — life and death business. When he'd dispatched the assailants, his abilities and inner-strength shone forth. He was a warrior, but not like any she'd ever known. She'd met many a fighter in her long life: Greek, Roman, Hebrew, Hessian, and more recently, American. Ben was very different from any of them. You knew a warrior when you saw him. Ben's status as such was subtle, maybe even hidden. Despite the circumstances of the violent encounter, he showed no anger or hostility as he dealt with the situation. His defensive actions moved like the passing trees: smooth, even, and calm. Ania recognized that Ben was a man in total control of himself. His actions were devoid of emotion; as suddenly as the incident had escalated and de-escalated, Ben reverted from formidable foe, and back to humble scholar. Despite the transformation, his breathing remained constant.

His driving mirrored his fighting ability, only as he drove, there was a look of serenity on his face and gentleness in his movements. When he'd "protected" her from the attackers, his face was firm, but not tense. The look reminded her of the night she had met the centurion. He too had the mask of calm, even as he leveled his sword at her.

Since the moment Bel had changed her, she'd had to rely on herself, using the ill-gotten powers for protection. Being with Ben allowed her to forget she was different, even if for only a moment or two. The man was not a typical person.

They didn't talk much for the remainder of the trip; Ben focused on the road, Ania looked for recognizable landmarks. The landscape looked vaguely familiar, but the passage of time had changed things considerably. She thought she recognized a nearby ridgeline, and was searching memories when Ben interrupted the silence.

"Looks like we've arrived," he said, as the car slowed gently to a crawl. A fresh-looking road sign in German announced:

CAUTION — SAFETY OPERATION AHEAD

Shortly beyond the warning, a traffic barricade appeared at a bend in the road. A dirt turn-off branched to the left, but was blocked by three police cars, fluorescent green traffic cones, and a large wooden barrier. Ben slowed from a crawl to a creep as he approached the scene. A uniformed police officer wearing a bright-green vest held up a flashing-red semaphore, resembling a large lollipop. When the car stopped, the officer gave the car a once-over and studied the two of them carefully. Three other officers, alerted to the new visitors, stopped their casual conversation and directed their attention toward the new arrivals. Two of them cradled long, menacing-looking arms.

Before the officer could speak, Ben produced a leather wallet, and displayed his diplomatic credentials. He greeted the officer in High German, and the lawman's stiff demeanor softened to comfortable ease, as if he already knew Ben. Ania theorized that the official was a fellow Catholic. He waved to the other officers and they, too, relaxed. One even waved to Ben.

"Have you been up to the site before today?" the officer asked Ben.

"No, we just arrived last night," he replied, closing his wallet and replacing it in his pocket.

"Most of the military personnel are gone, but one remains in the event that more bombs are to be found. I grew up here and never imagined that so many explosives could be buried here. I traveled through with my dog once when I was a boy." The officer retrieved a pack of gum from his pocket. He offered it to Ben, who graciously declined.

"Has there been any media attention?" Ben asked, looking in the rearview mirror for approaching traffic. Even with the car motionless, Ben was on guard.

"There were a few here at first, but the last ones left several days ago. That maniac up north captured their attention." The officer's hand casually grazed the butt of his *Sig Sauer* pistol, safely ensconced in a sturdy-looking holster.

"Maniac? What happened?" Ben recognized the officer's subconscious move as a sign that whatever the "maniac" had done wasn't pleasant.

"A radical extremist in Berlin took over a crowded cafe in Frankfurt; he had a fully-functional AK-47 and could have killed many persons. Fortunately GSG 9 acted quickly before the situation could become deadly. Munich still haunts us; that kind of thing will never happen again." The officer was referring to the 1972 Olympic massacre of the Israeli athletes.

"What happened at Frankfurt?" Ben asked with concern, shutting off the engine so he could hear better.

"A lone wolf, they think he was affiliated with those cowardly, pajama-clad clowns with the white sneakers, walked into a bustling cafe and pulled his weapon from beneath his tunic. He took the place hostage and demanded Germany publicly 'unrecognize' Israel. They were talking him down, and it seemed he was about to surrender, then something set him off and he started shooting." The officer unwrapped a stick of gum and slowly bit it off, in three pieces.

Ben, who was hanging on every word, took an uncomfortable sip from his coffee cup. He spoke with a gulp. "What stopped him?"

"The United States Army, of course!" The admiration in his voice was obvious.

A confused look on Ben's face prompted the officer to continue.

"Thankfully someone from your US forces was there and stopped him before he killed anyone. My cousin is with the county police there—he thinks the soldier was from one of your Special Forces teams." The officer smiled when he finished the sentence.

"How did it play out?" Ben was waiting with bated breath for the answer.

Ania remembered the recent mass murders in the US, and wondered if Bel had anything to do with it. He was always around when a tragedy occurred.

"The negotiator was talking him down via a telephone, and he was about to acquiesce. Someone in a nearby crowd yelled something, and he stiffened up and began to sweep the room with a stream of bullets. A portion of his robe became entangled in the gun and your Army Special Forces man used the distraction to spring into action. The weapon was ripped from his hands and used as a club to the head. The terrorist ran outside and pulled off his outer clothing—he was wearing a bomb vest. He paused long enough to praise his supposed deity, when a GSG 9 sniper dealt with him swiftly. Thankfully, no one was hurt. The only real casualty was an espresso machine when he first took the place over." A relieved look washed over the officer's face.

"I'm glad to hear it." A similar look of relief passed over Ben's face.

"You Americans are very brave—the Army man is a hero. Word is already out that our chancellor is going to award him the German Gold Cross," the officer said.

A questioning look from Ben prompted the officer to elaborate.

"It's the equivalent of your American Medal of Honor. It is the highest award a soldier in our Army can receive. It is rarely given, and has never been given to a non-German soldier. Given what the Army man did, it is well-deserved." He pronounced this confidently.

"All good news." Ben was pleased to hear the outcome was positive, but was ready to move on; he started the engine.

Taking the gentle cue, the officer spoke: "Follow the road about one kilometer and the signs will guide you."

The officer caught the attention of the other officers, and they moved the portable barricade blocking the newly-graded road.

"Be safe, my friend." The officer waved them on.

As the car passed by the other officers, they slung their weapons behind their backs, as a sign of respect—something about Ben resonated with them. This only added to Ania's growing comfort with him.

He cordially bid them a good day.

"They are very friendly — it's like they know you," Ania commented.

"Contrary to what most people think, the German people are very warm and open…that is, once they get to know you. I've always enjoyed being here — lots of culture." Ben smiled, looking ahead at the rough-ly-hewn road. It was clear a tractor had recently cleared a path through the trees.

Ania nodded in agreement; she remembered the hospitality she'd encountered when traveling across this country en route to America. Thankfully, she'd left before the turn of the century; two world wars and a series of poor choices had rendered Germany somewhat inhospitable to strangers. She knew she would have survived, but her continued presence could have revealed the cave's location to the forces of darkness.

The car wound its way up the tree-shrouded road. The pines on both sides knitted their branches together, like clasped, praying hands. The light was so dim within the tunnel of green that Ben had to turn on the car's headlights. The road was smooth; the moist dirt responded well to the grading. The speed was kept under ten miles per hour, even though the road could have handled twice that. An occasional rock was kicked up by the tires and thudded against the wheel wells. The noise reminded them that despite the path's pavement-like smoothness, it was still under nature's control.

About a half-mile ahead, they saw an opening of daylight, signaling an end to the forest trail. Ania recognized where she was now; this road was not a "road" when she left, but rather a simple footpath— one she'd used regularly. The trees were taller now and their branches much thicker. She recognized the shape of the terrain and it seemed like she'd been here only yesterday.

As they reached the end of the trees, a large and bright clearing suddenly materialized in front of them. The area was roughly the size of two football fields, and square in shape. Whereas the road they'd just traveled was thick with foliage, the clearing was just as thick with equipment and people. The scene was reminiscent of a military field hospital. As Ben slowed the rental car, looking for a spot to park, a flood of memories overwhelmed Ania's mind. Her thoughts went back to the time of her last visit here. All the modern equipment, tents, trailers, and vehicles were in the very same place ancient pilgrims once trod. Ania's mind erased evidence that it was the twenty-first century, and replaced it with visions of humble and penitent visitors. They were the ones responsible for the presence of the crosses.

Ania clearly remembered hiding in the tree line they'd just left. Camouflaged among the greenery, she'd watch as the pilgrims arrived. The first appearance of strangers alarmed her—her initial thought had been that they were looking for the treasure. In a sense they were, but they posed no threat. They were not there to steal it—they were there to feel its power. The visitors were drawn to the clearing like iron filings to a magnet. They knew not why they were drawn to this place, but something in their soul stirred and drew them to the clearing.

The area had been desolate when Ania was last there, but was now full of people—an inquiring group. These persons were scientists, and they had tools and technology. Two millennia prior, this place was empty, and science was limited to scales and abacuses.

Ben spoke, bringing Ania back to the present:

"Quite a production," he said, with a solemn, almost reverent tone. He knew they were close to these crosses, but Ania knew he was also close to something much more significant.

She thought to herself: *If you only knew...*

They parked next to an orderly row of vans, trucks, and miscellaneous equipment. The parking arrangement was organized, as if each vehicle was placed with typical Teutonic precision. In the distance, a tall chain-link fence encircled a gaping hole in the ground. Ania knew that that space was directly over the cave.

An army-green tent, the size of a small house, was perched at the edge of the parking area. A large sign, with foot-high letters, announced 'SECURITY.' It hung from a wooden post, sunk firmly into the

ground. A smaller sign below it directed visitors to
check in.

No sooner had they produced their IDs and given
them to the guard than a tall man in dirty coveralls
ran up to them.

"Ben! Doctor Socratatos!" The man vigorously
shook Ben's hand with both his. His excitement at
their arrival was barely contained.

Ben used his free arm to gesture toward Ania, as
the man continued to pump Ben's hand.

"Doctor Lawrence O'Toole, please meet Doctor
Athania Socratatos. I told you she wouldn't miss this
opportunity," Ben said as O'Toole released his hand
and turned to Ania.

"Doctor Socratatos, an honor to meet you."

She extended her hand and he gently shook it
with both of his.

"I am privileged to be here—and truly flattered.
It's an honor to be invited to assist." An external smile
masked internal dread.

"Considering what we've found, its significance to
Western civilization…someone of your experience…"
O'Toole was clearly smitten by the woman. He'd
heard she was beautiful, some describing her as a
Greek statue come to life, but in person…

Ania realized the archeologist was focused on
her eyes—they seemed to brighten a shade for every
mile that brought them closer to the site. Ben hadn't
noticed yet, but O'Toole certainly did. She blinked

quickly, feigning that something was under her lid.
She used a knuckle to gently swipe at her eyelids. The
ruse worked and the transfixed man returned his
attention to Ben.

Ben noticed O'Toole was staring at Ania's face,
and he knew her beauty was not lost on the myopic
scientist.

They were enthusiastically escorted toward
another tent. Ania was relieved at the interruption.
She knew her irises were several shades brighter
now than when they left the States. She'd never
realized until this moment that the closer she got to
the treasure, the brighter her peepers became. Marcus
had once told her that her eyes lit up like a fire when
she was in a heightened state of alertness, but she felt
calm at the moment. She wished there was a way to
completely conceal the new brilliance in them.

Ben and Ania were shown to another tent where
they encountered yet another checkpoint. This one
was white, and looked large enough to host a three-
ring circus. Upon entering, Ben and Ania saw rows
upon rows of tables, all covered with soft-looking
green cloth. They both gasped; every table had
numerous crucifixes on it. A quick calculation by
Ania estimated the number at over three thousand.
Ben was transfixed. He took something out of his
pocket, kissed it, and whispered a prayer in Latin.
He sensed something inside the shelter, akin to the
feeling he had while being in church.

"Doctor O'Toole, how many?" Ben's voice trembled.

"As of today, 3,202. Most were found in the first few days. More are being found daily." O'Toole donned a pair of blue rubber gloves and handed two more pairs to the visitors.

The tables were in rows a hundred feet in length. There were ten rows. The assembled variety was staggering: large, small, stone, metal, clay, bone — every imaginable material. Each cross was displayed with an attached bright-yellow tag. On each label was a number, a date, and the finder's name.

The normally verbose O'Toole fell silent. Although not a very religious man, he felt reverence for the presence of the crosses.

Ben's eyes grew wide, trying to absorb what he saw. The scores of photos he'd seen previously did not show the true magnitude of the collection. In his life of intense study, he'd never seen anything like it.

Ania was stunned by the sight. Personally, she'd handled and buried each one. During the centuries she'd hid them, this was the first time they were visible all at once. If she hadn't been the one to put them where they were in the first place, she would not believe what her eyes beheld.

I was here longer than I thought! she thought to herself.

The years had flown by when Ania first arrived here, but seeing the several-thousand crosses told her that she had truly been there a long time.

Ania Socratatos remembered each and every one, and when it was buried. Her hope was that they would never be found. She remembered waiting patiently for the visitors to leave, then emerging from the trees. Ania would gently pick up a cross, study it, and burn its image into her mind. She'd set the cross aside, then use her strength to dig a deep hole. The cross would be gently laid in the earth, and the soil replaced.

"Doctor O'Toole, may we see the first three that were brought up?" Ania asked quietly.

Though the tent was a makeshift laboratory, it had the ambience of a church. Fifteen people wearing lab coats worked nearby — they too respected the quiet.

O'Toole led them to a small table, apart from the others. It was covered by a purple cloth. The three crosses were under a glass dome. Among all the artifacts, these were unique; the largest was over a foot long and made from exotic wood. The material was dark brown with traces of red. Considering its age, it looked newly made. The smaller ones were half the size of the first. One was wood also, but severely decayed, looking as if it might crumble. The third looked like the largest. The wood was brown but with green traces.

144

"These are the oldest," Doctor O'Toole said quietly.

"Radiocarbon dated?" Ben asked, his eyes fixed upon the relics.

"Yes — two thousand years old." His voice sounded certain.

"The wood?" Ania asked.

"All olive wood. The large cross and one of the smaller ones do not look like olivewood, but the tests confirm the type, and that the original tree was from Jerusalem."

While O'Toole studied the crosses, Ben and Ania's eyes met. Ben had a theory — while Athania knew the true reason.

"Ben, will you excuse me?" She stepped away.

Ben's attention was squarely on the multitude of crosses. He nodded without looking up.

Ania walked outside, and took in a deep breath. Turning her eyes to the right, she saw the edge of the hole, and used that as a reference point. She scanned the countryside and looked for familiar landmarks. Looking over to the edge of the dig, she saw numerous persons actively climbing up and down ladders, some going down into it, while others were coming up. They were hundreds of feet above the actual cave, but the steady rhythm of the activity was troublesome.

Looking at some people standing near the hole's edge, she whispered to them: *You're on top of it.*

Ania turned her attention back to the tree line; her vision swept across the tree trunks, looking for something she'd just remembered. After a few minutes, a pattern emerged in the landscape and the undulation of the hills. Her internal compass found a bearing — the cave was straight ahead. She glanced over her shoulder, ensuring that no one was looking in her direction. Quietly and unobtrusively, Ania left the area.

Chapter 21

The Return

It took over thirty minutes to reach her initial destination. The path she'd taken from the camp to her present location awakened new memories with each step. The closer she got, the further back in time she traveled. If not for her modern clothes, it could be AD 1800 for all Ania knew. The terrain appeared unchanged, save for the thicker trees that encroached the path, and this narrowed it significantly.

Two hundred years ago, the pines were nearly twenty feet from the trail; now they were within inches. To Ania, it looked as if the trees were growing closer to the cave. The ensconcement had a life-giving object in it, and the greenery clearly knew it.

The term "path" was a misnomer: there was no actual path — no line of dirt carved into the soil. The trail would be unrecognizable to a casual observer, but Ania knew it well. The ground she used as a road was covered in fallen pine needles, seed cones, and a sparse scattering of rocks. In the early years of

"AD," the footpath was nothing more than a faint line, marked by slight gaps in the foliage. As far as she knew, no trees had been cleared to make this earthen corridor, but due to her better-than-human eyesight, she could see a definite line to follow.

When first finding the divide, she only followed it because her belief was that the object was guiding her. The path was almost a mile from the clearing to the ravine, and upon reaching the rocky fracture of earth, the trail dropped sharply to the small canyon's floor. From this cliff, the cave's entry was down thirty feet and slightly to the right. The same force that led her here, led her down to the opening.

Leaving Marcus with the treasure, along with an admonition to remain where he was, Ania had begun her very first descent down the sheer granite wall. From the cliff, the vertical stone surfaces appeared somewhat smooth, with only the occasional, small outcropping interrupting the striations in the stone.

As Ania descended, a slight indentation began to show itself. It was slight, and it wasn't until she was actually a few feet below it when she saw the opening. An overhang of rock, shaped like the prow of a ship, concealed the entry from almost any vantage point. It covered the actual opening so well that the only way to see the darkness was to be exactly where she was now. Even from the canyon floor, some fifty feet below, the entrance was invisible.

The new green cover, thickest on the side of the cave, gave the ravine the appearance of a torn loaf of bread. From a distance, the fissure looked minimal—only upon a very close inspection would the depth reveal itself. This divide in the earth was the width of a two-lane highway, but trees grew from the edges of both sides. The scene looked like a jagged knife slash that was knitting itself back together. The foliage growing from each side was trying to come together. The towering, nearby pines did their part too: from the air, the stony cleft was almost completely hidden.

Deftly using a series of stone handholds, Ania began her descent into the dark maw. Her cliff-scaling movements would have impressed even the most accomplished mountaineer; she moved downward, using handholds that were no more prominent than a coat button. A plethora of possible places to grip were present, but one had to know exactly which ones to use. Some outcroppings were loose rocks, merely resting on a miniscule shelf. Using the wrong one, most would fall to their death.

In Ania's case, death was not a concern—she'd fallen a great distance once, and it did much damage to her body. The fall had occurred immediately after she'd changed. She remembered lying on the ground, several of her bones protruding from bloody gashes in her flesh. Because no pain was felt, she assumed death was approaching. She'd always been told that when one died, all mortal sensations vanished, and one passed on to…but when the blood had vanished and the bones mended before her eyes, Ania realized that whatever Bel had done to her provided demi god-like strength—not the only thing she possessed. This incident had given her the confidence to do what she'd done that awful night.

As a spider-like crawl lowered her to a thirty-foot depth, shadows became long and light was barely a flicker above her head. Looking up, she could see patches of bright blue sky, contrasting with the green and brown walls. Lush growths of flowered vegetation now occupied every horizontal spot, giving the vertical cliffs the appearance of emerald-green theater drapes. Her last time here was very different—the ravine's walls were grainy brown and devoid of life. The only things on the rocks had been vertical striations as the differing colors of stone blended together. Two millennia gave things more than enough time to change, and they most certainly had. The flowers and small bushes concealed most traces of rock, and the occasional ledge was barely visible amongst the growth. This change pleased her, not only because it hid the treasure more effectively, but because it heralded life and growth. While she was the only sentient being that knew what was nearby, the seemingly non-thinking plant life knew it too; it flourished on the power of what Ania had concealed here so long ago.

Ania probed the green veil with her hands for
nearly an hour, moving gingerly from ledge to ledge.
After several minutes, she closed her eyes, and using
her other senses, pierced the branches and leaves,
feeling the hard rock beneath. Her fingers flowed
across the stone, as a blind person reads braille. She
realized she actually could interpret each and every
bump and striation, remembering where the "writing"
would eventually lead. When her hand reached a
familiar edge, she knew she'd found it. Using much
effort, a string of thorn-laden branches were parted.
As the vegetation yielded, wooden barbs tore into
her skin, and blood began dripping down her arms
and onto her feet; she bled so much that a small pool
developed on the ledge where she was standing. Ania
perceived the sensation of pain, yet it did not slow her
movements. As thorns tore into her flesh, she imagined what He must have endured.

In the beginning, she'd sensed injuries, but it
always felt like nothing more than a feather brushing
her skin. The wounds rarely impeded her movements,
unless a limb was broken. All she need do though
was wait a few seconds, until the bone repaired itself.
With her focus on reaching the cave, the thorns were
inconsequential. The sight of free-flowing blood
affected her little, but the liquid made her fingers
slip, and she compensated by digging harder into the
rock. Every few seconds, a fingernail was torn from
its bed and dropped to her feet, but thinking of Him

refocused her efforts on parting the branches. She was careful not to break any of the vines, lest evidence be left that something was here. Nature had done a good job of hiding this place, and she did not want to undo what Creation had made.

Ania squeezed in between the spiked branches, the naturally-sharp points cutting into her face, gouging her shoulders and side. Once inside, she paused behind the injurious screen and looked into a small clearing. She waited a few moments, allowing her wounds to heal and the blood to remove itself to wherever it normally went. As the red liquid vanished, she was enveloped by a sensation of soft warmth.

I'm so close, she whispered to the emptiness surrounding her.

Moving deeper within the void, a faint shape materialized ahead. The sight triggered a memory of when she and Marcus were first here. Getting to this location had been difficult for Ania, and was nearly impossible for Marcus. He was small and agile, as most young boys were, but getting into this refuge required abilities that only Ania possessed. She remembered leading him down here for the first time, holding the treasure with one arm, and using the other to keep the youngster from falling to his death. Even as heavy as the object was, it was not what had made it difficult to reach the cave—which had dimensions that were extremely problematic. The object was much taller and even wider than Ania was, and its unusual shape hung it up on many obstacles. Simply getting it down the ravine had been an exercise in balance and leverage. Moving it into the tight confines of this place had been nearly impossible.

While Ania and Marcus descended the ravine, she had almost struck Marcus several times with the object. One time, he'd started to fall, and she'd had no free hands to grasp him. Somehow, she had managed to grasp his arm with the same arm holding the treasure. She'd originally been tempted to have him remain on the cliff's top while she moved the object into the cave. She'd decided against it because he had been sent to help her, and she felt a responsibility for his well-being. Leaving him alone for long was not something she ever wanted to do.

Marcus had only been able to offer a modicum of assistance, but through no fault of his own. He had been merely ten years old when they left Jerusalem, and in her eyes, was still a child. His greatest contribution to their journey was his companionship. After being alone for several hundred years, the presence of her charge had given her comfort. She had also felt a duty to the child—he had been healed by someone she revered. A sense of duty bound Ania to his continued protection and guidance. Marcus had been quiet at first, but he was curious, and developed great interest in her teachings. His curiosity gave her hope that although certain members of Greek society had believed her father was corrupting the young and needed to be stopped, his teachings would not be lost to history. The same people who murdered her father would not be able to erase the evidence he existed.

Returning her attention to the present, Ania looked around. The space she occupied wasn't much of a cave—it was barely fifteen feet square. A casual examination of this hollow revealed nothing. Ania knew what was there, though. She stepped forward and placed her hands against the vertical surface. She curled her fingers and the tips dug into the granite like a cat on curtains. Using only her hands, her body was pulled up and slowly moved upwards. With every new grasp, her fingertips were rubbed raw, and bits of flesh and nail fell in bloody clumps. This progressive damage to her fingers, however, did not impede her progress. She knew the injuries would heal within minutes, but losing her fingertips had the potential to let her slide back down. With harder effort, she dug deeper, the exposed bones now punching into the rock. The climb continued and eventually she reached the top.

Once there, a ledge appeared at eye level. She paused, resting what was left of her hands on the horizontal edge of the ledge. Her fingertips were within inches of her eyes; the climb had ground her fingers to the first knuckle and they looked as if they'd been eaten off by wild animal. But within seconds, bone, flesh, and fingernails regenerated. This sight was nothing new to her, but still held her attention. She'd been "different" for centuries, seeing cuts and scratches heal. Seeing limbs regenerate was surreal. She remembered watching stop-motion photos of plants growing over a period of weeks, and that was the only thing it could equate. These substantial injuries were the worst she'd experienced in the last hundred or so years, and it still fascinated her. When the last finger returned to its former state, she closed her eyes and breathed deeply.

"It is here, I am here, and will I see it?" Ania said aloud to herself, the words filling her with hope and energy.

She stepped forward, and gently placed her palms against another wall directly in front of her. She pressed a cheek to the stone between her hands; a sensation of warmth permeated her hands and face. The cave itself was cold and damp, and the surrounding stone should have been cold to the touch. She never knew whether the stone really gave off heat, or if it was her proximity to the object that created the sensation.

Ania slowly tightened her core muscles, and the growing tension radiated up her arms and down her legs. With slowly-building pressure, Athania Socratatos summoned all her internal and external strength and pushed forward with everything she could. For a few seconds, nothing happened. The pressure between her hands and the stone was increasing exponentially, and by now could have been measured in thousands of pounds. She felt her blood grow hot and her face radiated heat, which she could feel on the backs of her hands. After a moment, an ear-splitting scrape pierced the air as stone ground on stone. The wall began to move away from her as it recoiled from the push. Keeping the pressure steady, the unassuming university professor moved a five-ton stone wall five feet from where it once stood. A narrow opening, barely a foot wide, appeared at the edge of the car-sized boulder she'd just relocated. Ania stepped gingerly into the gap, as she'd done a thousand times before. Once inside, she stepped to the rear of the enormous rock. Summoning the same strength she had moments earlier, it was pushed back into place. The entrance was now resealed and remained hidden from any outside view.

With eyes closed and ears open, the silence was absorbed; no one had been here since she left. Ania took a deep breath of air, and a feeling of energy radiated throughout her body. The feeling was reminiscent of stepping into a warm bath in a cold room. A vibrant sensation completely enveloped the woman and penetrated her skin. The feeling moved deeper within and eventually reached her spine, and flowed back out. She could never understand the sensation, but the word that always came to mind was "hope."

No natural light was to be found, and the space she now occupied was nothing but inky blackness.

After a moment, her eyes opened and she was able to see the long passageway ahead. No light was evident, but due to her current condition, her eyes could penetrate the dark. She hadn't seen it, but when she and Marcus had come here for the first time, he said her eyes glowed like fire. They cast enough light that he was able to see in the darkness.

As she walked, the walls and floor were clearly visible, as if there was actual light. She couldn't articulate what she actually "saw," but it was not with her eyes. Her 'affliction' somehow allowed her to see through the dark. When she had first discovered this ability, she realized she was no longer using her sense of sight—even if she shut her lids, she could still sense where she was going. When enveloped in darkness, her "sense of spacial awareness," as Ania called it, bypassed her eyes and things before her simply materialized in her brain. The closest thing she could equate the sensation to was sonar. Images became clear to her, even though her optic nerves were not in play. As she moved along, she felt the temperature in the passage rise. She was very, very close.

Ben and Doctor O'Toole went outside and walked toward the trailer that served as a kitchen and break room. The other people involved in the dig were moving to and fro, a low hum of frenetic activity filling the air.

The two moved into the trailer, and were pleased that it was unoccupied. The doctor removed a foam cup from a dispenser, and poured steaming coffee into it. He offered it to Ben.

"Doctor, were the Germans able to make sense of the bombs? I mean, they were on top of the crosses. What was the Wehrmacht trying to destroy? The crosses?" Ben asked as he looked down into the cup, wondering if it was typical Teutonic, extra-strength java.

"Though they recovered and deactivated them, they had little information. Anything prior to 1945 is something they'd rather forget. I do have a colleague in Maryland, an archivist, digging through records from the Allied forces. He said he would let me know what he finds. Honestly, the bombs pale in comparison with the crosses." He poured himself a cup and took a gentle sip, but grimaced at the taste. He was more of a tea drinker, but good Earl Grey was hard to find on this side of the Rhine. "During the 'troubles,' explosives were a constant source of worry. Northern Ireland was a war zone. If I never see another destructive device in my life, it will be too soon."

Ben knew the doctor had been torn between two worlds during the internecine war in Belfast. He grew up with an Irish father and an English mother — one Catholic, the other Anglican.

"German java is so strong. Maybe if they drank more tea..." O'Toole said, as he took another sip.

Ben saw the humor in the Irishman's unfinished sentence. The war had been over for decades, but hard feelings lingered. Ben knew the doctor had lost family in the fighting.

"It seems they sensed something was here and tried to destroy it. Maybe they knew the crosses were nearby and were trying to erase any symbol they considered contrary to the Reich's aim. I cannot fathom why so many failed to detonate—they were live, but they didn't go 'boom' like they should have." Ben shook his head.

"When I arrived they were still deactivating them. The ordnance specialists were baffled as to why they failed to explode. The explosives were live, the fuses were functional, and everything was assembled in 'good German order.' It was as if guardian angels caught them as they fell from the planes and gently set them on the ground." Doctor O'Toole made a gesture with his hands as if cradling an object.

Ben smiled.

"Doctor, you're onto something. I know my guardian angel is the only reason I'm standing here today."

The doctor observed Ben unconsciously rub the top of his arm, as if remembering a pain from long ago. Having carefully observed Ben's body language, the doctor realized that this learned young man possessed something he hadn't seen in his forty years of study and teaching: true intuition and curiosity. His innate curiosity was unmatched by any Oxford scholar. He knew what Ben had done before joining the Holy See. His title may have read "assistant," but he was much more. The doctor had known many civil servants in the United Kingdom, but none had Ben's skill. It wasn't frenetic energy of movement; rather his mind processed information faster than it could be absorbed. Doctor O'Toole was glad Ben was there. Perhaps he could solve the puzzle of the bombs and crosses — the explosives existed since the time of a madman, the icons since the time of the Savior.

Ania waited ten minutes before she entered the final chamber. She meditated, remembering that this had been her home for over two thousand years. That span of time had passed like hours.

The object brought comfort and peace. With a push stronger than the earlier one, the thousand-pound rock gave way, and a light brighter than the sun overwhelmed her.

Stepping around the obstacle, she averted her eyes and knelt on the ground. She refused to look directly at it, feeling unworthy. Ania had removed it from its initial resting place, guarding it like a newborn child. Prostrate before it, she remembered when her eyes had first beheld it. Its intended purpose horrified her. She would have destroyed it and saved Him, but the magnificent stranger had admonished her: "You must bear your own burden."

Remembering what he said, she drew a hand across her shoulder; the marks, similar to a birthmark, remained. Marcus had been the only person who saw them. Unlike other marks, these had never healed. Blades cut, stones bruised, falls broke limbs, and a sword had pierced her at one time. Those injuries healed before her eyes. But these unusual marks were unknown to her until after they had reached the cave. Marcus saw them first. To her, they were not scars or disfigurements; they were proof that there was hope for her.

Chapter 22

The Accident

Ania kept company with the treasure for only an hour, but she wished she could remain with it forever. The power it had was limitless, and she wondered if the world was ready for it yet. Maybe in another millennia…the amount of knowledge humanity now possessed was something not even her father could have fathomed. Advances in science, medicine, literature, art — it was something the Oracle could never have seen.

Unfortunately, wisdom had not kept pace. The power of the gift, in the wrong hands…when she was alone with it, its energy erased time. The two thousand years she'd guarded it had passed like mere seconds. The last hundred years, however, had felt like lifetimes. If another few centuries passed, maybe then…

Ania pondered what may actually happen if she actually abandoned the outside world.

She'd vanished from Athens shortly after her father's death. Her surviving family had missed her, but the rest of society gave her no regard. She was a mere citizen of Greece, one amongst thousands. Her prior life had been "off the grid," as a former student once put it. No written records existed of her birth, life, or disappearance. Even so-called experts on her father's work knew not of her existence. They thought the great philosopher had had a wife and two sons only. No one had ever known he'd had a daughter, Ania, in his later years.

In this current life, in the present, she had a birth certificate, a passport, a bank account and tenure — surely she would be missed, and many would look for her. The disappearance of a renowned American university professor and expert on Western civilization would mobilize significant resources. These resources would eventually find the earthen cleft, and assume she'd fallen in. The deep ravine would be searched with relentless fervor. This activity could very well reveal the cave — and what it held.

She returned to the present moment, and the remote possibility that the ensconcement would be found. The archeologists, scientists, and their staff were working a site fifty feet deep — directly above the cave. An impenetrable layer of prehistoric bedrock stood between the site and the stone cell. Trowels and shovels had little effect on granite, but heavy equipment could bore through it like a pencil through

a paper. There was a collection of heavy equipment
here, but thankfully, it had remained dormant. She
wondered if they would try to penetrate the bedrock,
in search of more artifacts — and while they might
not reach the cave, the pounding from above might
cause its collapse. The possible, theoretical eventual-
ities were endless, but she knew there was little real
chance the archeologists would find anything. Ania
would nonetheless remain close, and monitor the
activities.

As she journeyed through the woods, back toward
the encampment, she glanced at her watch — instead
of the watch, something else caught her attention:
her tattered coat. Her body showed no evidence of
her recent activity, but her clothing looked as if she'd
been attacked by an animal. Her lightweight field
jacket hung in tatters from her shoulders. The collar
was the only thing keeping it in one piece. She took
it off, and balled it up. Ania was relieved to see that
her long-sleeved shirt underneath was unharmed.
She did notice some small tears in her cargo pants,
but they were minor and difficult to see. She skirted
the main camp, and made her way to the rental car.
Luckily, the ever-prepared Ben had provided her
with an extra set of keys. He knew she didn't drive,
but had explained that it was a good idea for them
both to have a set, in case one was lost.

She too traveled prepared: she'd brought an
extra change of clothes, shoes, personal items and

thankfully — an extra field jacket. The spare coat was identical to her ruined one; they'd been on sale and she liked the way it looked. It was her habit of buying extra pairs of clothing. When an item wore out or was damaged, it seemed like she could never find a duplicate later. Her extra cargo pants were light colored, and the ones she was currently wearing were almost black. The tears were small, and she hoped inconspicuous. She donned the jacket and took a quick look in the side view mirror. Her hair was slightly out of place, and an errant piece of branch was stuck in her French braid. She removed the twig, dusted herself off, and headed back to the clearing.

Ania found Ben in the kitchen trailer, conversing with Doctor O'Toole. They were having coffee and talking about where the crosses would be permanently housed.

"Haven't seen you for a bit. Everything okay?" Ben asked, pouring her a cup.

"I wandered around the nearby tree line. Ancient Germanic tribes were known to sometimes leave hieroglyphs, telling of their history. It was a gamble, and it didn't pan out."

Ben handed her the cup, forgetting she didn't like java.

Ania accepted it graciously, using both hands.

Before he could warn her, she took a large pull, and swallowed it like plain water. Ben was alarmed — this pot had just been brewed and true to Teutonic form, was beyond boiling hot. The coffee machine was set to the highest temperature; seemingly hot enough to melt metal. Both he and the doctor had had to wait nearly five minutes before they even considered sipping it.

He'd been distracted by his conversation with O'Toole. He was holding the handle of the mug, and had absentmindedly handed it to Ania. He knew for a fact the cup's surface was impossible to touch. But Ania showed absolutely no reaction when she took it. She took a second sip, still holding it in both hands. The woman looked as if she was searching her own thoughts. He expected her to react at any second, but she maintained her grip—both hands encircling the mug. The unused handle protruded from her fingers. Ben was about to say something, but he wondered if the concept was true that women had a higher threshold for pain. He marveled at her tolerance for the heat.

Doctor O'Toole engaged Ania in a conversation about the hieroglyphs she'd just mentioned. He knew of them, but wasn't as well versed as Ania. She started a brief but detailed explanation of how some ancient Germanic tribes had passed on their history through symbols.

As they talked, Ben took a moment to notice that something about Ania was now different. He couldn't tell if it was from the boiling java she'd just gulped or if something else had heated her blood. She wasn't breathing hard, but there was a rosy redness on her cheeks that usually accompanied physical exertion. She looked as if she'd run a mile at a fast pace. Casually, he made mental notes about Doctor Athania X. Socratatos.

When he'd first met her, he accepted her as the learned and accomplished scholar he knew she was. She looked to be in her late thirties, but she exuded a formidable sense of self that normally seemed exclusive to wisened elders. She was beyond head and shoulders above the average expert on Western civilization. The professor was also exceptionally versed in world history, languages, and her specialty: philosophy. Educational achievements aside, she also came across as being much older than someone in their thirties. If a two-hundred-year-old person could exist, it would be her.

In the short time since he'd first entered her office, a mere four days ago, he felt as if she was changing. The first difference was her face. When they left that morning, he remembered that her eyes had looked different—specifically the iris. They had a natural greenish color that bordered on hazel. There were light-amber flecks sprinkled amongst the green. But this morning, the flecks had been more brilliant, almost golden. He also noticed that upon her entrance to the trailer, her countenance looked younger, and even more vibrant than normal.

Ben mulled over his observations, staring into his cup, as if an answer would materialize in the dark

liquid. He looked back at Ania. As O'Toole veered
into an area of tedious statistics, Ania broke eye
contact with him, and looked at the floor, as if pondering his words. When she looked up, she was no
longer looking at Doctor O'Toole, but rather at Ben.
Her head was angled slightly down, and she peered
up at him. Upon their eyes meeting, Ben was struck
again by Ania's natural beauty. During his years of
international studies, he'd seen thousands of ancient
depictions of beauty. She surpassed anything even
the masters could create. *Thinking* she was beautiful
didn't suffice—she *was* the most beautiful woman
he'd ever seen. For the first time since meeting her,
he experienced something he'd forgotten how to feel:
romantic attraction.

Ania saw the look on Ben's face develop and
slowly broke contact. She looked down at her cup,
then up at Doctor O'Toole. She sensed the meaning of
the look in his eyes.

Ben respected education, and Doctor Athania
Xanthos Socractatos's reputation intimidated him.
He was extremely knowledgeable in his own right,
but her body of work was staggering. Several organizations ranked her among the top one hundred
educators in the world. He had first gone to her as a
student seeking answers. He was so focused on the
information coming from within that he was oblivious to her outward presentation. Before meeting in

person, he'd seen a few photos of her, but they did not do her justice.

Something about her struck a deep chord in him. When he was a teenager, and first noticed the fairer sex, women—actually girls then—radiated some type of energy; a uniquely female power. Different women had varying levels of it. If this force was compared to electricity, most women he'd met were mere static. Ania was akin to touching a live wire. They'd spent time together for a few days, but only at this moment did this register.

The pair were roughly the same age, and neither was married. He didn't think she was dating anyone, and knew nothing of her ever being married or even engaged. A thought flitted across the emotional part of Ben's mind, but he quickly swatted it away. He was working on something important—probably the most important thing in his life. All other concerns would have to wait in line.

Ben, in an attempt to shift mental gears, jumped into the conversation.

"This is typical German coffee—I think the Navy uses it to remove rust."

All three laughed. One of them thought it was funny; the other two laughed to mask growing feelings.

Chapter 23

Discoveries and Revelations

Ben and Ania spent a few more hours at the dig
site, reviewing raw data and examining more crosses.
While they were all new to Ben, Ania was intimately
familiar with each one. For every piece she inspected,
she could picture the pilgrim who'd left it.

The astute professor wondered if Ben could digest
the knowledge of what was in the cave. If anyone on
the planet was capable of dealing with the treasure,
it might be him. His knowledge of history seemed
to rival hers, although his was gleaned from years of
scholarly study, and hers from first-hand experience.
Ania had witnessed things that Ben had only read
about.

In addition to his education, he also had a deep
faith; more so than anyone she knew. Ania believed
in what the crucifixes represented because she'd
actually seen their historical origin. Ben believed as
she did, not because of rote knowledge, but because
of his faith. If he could have an inkling of what was

hidden nearby, the reason why the crosses were there would become clear.

If she led him to the treasure, she would be forced to reveal who and what she was. If he found the cave on his own, he would find the long-hidden object, and might learn of its power. She'd concealed the hiding place so well; only Ania could find it. To guide him to it, her true nature would have to be revealed. Someone like Ben would not understand how someone making a "deal with the devil" could have been the one who guarded something so powerful. She resolved to decide the issue later — hopefully much, much later. The continuing excavation would go on for some time. Long enough, she hoped, for her to figure things out, but not long enough for someone to find the cave.

The late afternoon sun sank in the sky, and as dusk approached, the blustery day turned chilly. They agreed to return to town, get a good night's rest, and start anew even earlier the following day. Ben displayed signs of jet lag, and for appearances, Ania feigned it too. They reasoned that a good sleep would adjust their internal clocks, and give them a clearer perspective when they returned.

Ben told Ania that before turning in, he would make a few online inquiries into the Vatican archives. There was a plethora of information on Charlemagne — facts not know to the general public. He told

Ania that her theory about the ancient ruler's possible connection to the crosses intrigued him.

They left the site as the sun started to hide behind the tree line and drove for some time in silence. Ben was fatigued, and used his remaining energy to focus on his driving. Subsequently, he talked little. Ania was glad for the silence as it gave her time to think. Returning to the cave had ignited many thoughts in her ancient mind, and they were all competing for dominance.

They were within a few miles of the hotel when the sound of a small explosion punctuated the silence. The car fishtailed wildly, forcing Ben to fight the wheel as it tried to twist from his grip. Without so much as a grimace or grunt, he allowed the wheel to oscillate back and forth, until he'd finessed the car to a smooth stop. All was suddenly quiet again.

"I think we ran over something."

He said it casually, as if things like this were an everyday occurrence. Just like the park encounter, Ben maintained inordinate calm in the face of chaos.

They simultaneously opened their doors, and were confronted by an acrid smell; to Ben it was like burnt rubber — to Ania, it was like sulfur.

Ania casually looked around, as if expecting to see something or someone. She was still scanning the trees as Ben knelt down by the rear tire on his side. He had done this while Ania was looking away, and for a second, she couldn't see where he'd gone. She heard the scrape of gravel from the other side of the car and realized where he'd gone. She walked over to his side, and looked at the same shredded tire. It appeared as if a shark had taken a bite out of it. Ben fished a large piece of metal out of the rubber wound.

"Someone's going to have trouble opening their wine bottle tonight." He held up a mangled cork-screw. "Thankfully there was no oncoming traffic." He stood up and removed his jacket, and began to change the tire.

"That's being positive—and thankfully there is still some light." Ania noticed that Ben was always upbeat, regardless of the situation. She enjoyed this rare human quality in him.

Ben popped the trunk ostensibly, looking for the spare. "Glad to see this stuff is all here—I've known people that have flats in rentals, and then find out there's no spare, jack, or even a wrench. Thank good-ness for German preparedness." Ben chuckled.

It was clear to Ania that Ben was always the optimist.

He searched along the underside of the car for a safe place to locate the jack. Unable to find an obvious spot, he went back to the trunk and removed the fiberboard cover that covered the spare tire well. He scanned the instructions that were printed on its underside and returned his attention to the useless wheel. He carefully placed the jack under a small notch, just in front of the wheel.

"Do you remember the good old days when cars had bumper jacks? They were bulky, but there was no hunting for somewhere to place it. They don't call these 'bottle jacks' for nothing." Ben smiled at her, then turned the crank enough to make the top of the lifting device snug into the notch.

Ania never gave much thought to cars and tools, but even she recognized that the diminutive object didn't look substantial enough to raise a car. When she saw the lug wrench Ben was holding, she wondered if something that short could loosen the wheel nuts.

"Don't you need to raise it off the ground first?" Ania commented when Ben placed the wrench on the first lug.

"You loosen the nuts while the tire is in contact with the ground—keeps it from spinning. Once they're no longer torqued down you raise the car high enough to let the tire clear the ground."

Ben did as he'd described; after loosening all the nuts, he cranked the jack enough to raise the car so that the tire was about two inches off the pavement. He easily removed the fasteners from the studs by hand. As he lifted the wheel from the hub, he didn't see that the small jack's crank was pointed toward the axle. He lifted the wheel off the hub, and his left hand slipped; the wheel bounced on the ground and struck the crank, the diminutive jack shifted, and the car began to drop—at the exact moment that Ben fell partially into the wheel well, Ania saw that he was about to be crushed.

"Ben!" Ania yelled, as the car fell. She grabbed his collar with her left arm, pulling him away from the car, but as she did so, she lost her own balance and fell.

As the car struck the ground, Ben was free of danger — but Ania wasn't. There was a sound of scraping metal, coupled with something that sounded like an orange being struck with a mallet. Ben was slightly dizzy, wondering how someone Ania's size could be so strong; she'd thrown him a good five feet from the car. He turned back toward the car and was horrified at what he saw.

Ania's right arm was trapped directly under the car's rear. Blood seeped from where the limb had disappeared under the body.

Moving quickly, Ben ran to her and saw that her right forearm was beneath the end of the axle. She looked calm — too calm. She must have been going into shock. He looked for the flimsy jack, but it, too, was pinched under the car. Racing to the rear bumper, he placed his back against the trunk and grabbed the underside with both hands. Focusing all his strength, he pulled upwards, straining with all his might. The gesture was futile and he knew it, but he was surprised when the rear of the car moved upwards. What he didn't see was that as he was straining to lift, Ania had used her free arm to raise the vehicle herself and pull her other limb free. In his peripheral vision, he saw Ania jerk away from the car and as she did so, his strength appeared to wane and the car dropped back to the ground. Her back was to him, and she was bent over, cradling her arm. Blood dripped onto the pavement from the tattered sleeve of her jacket.

"Stay still, I'll call for help."

He placed his hand on her shoulder and she stiffened up, as if his touch startled her. Ben moved to face her, as he retrieved his phone from his pocket. He looked at her mangled arm, seeing her humerus and ulna protrude from the torn jacket. She was cradling the mangled limb with the other. He looked at her eyes and staggered back. A bright light, glowing green, emanated from her eyes. He stepped further away as she looked directly at him, an expression of resignation on her face.

"What the…"

Ania dropped her mangled arm to her side and stood facing him. Before his own eyes, the blood stopped dripping from her arm. His eyes looked back and forth from her bloody sleeve to the wet ground several times. Before his incredulous eyes, the blood vanished.

"Ben…"

That was all she could say.

In spite of his fear, he reached out to touch her arm, but she withdrew; he stepped forward, but suddenly stopped. His hand hovered about a foot from her rapidly-healing wounds.

"Show me," Ben said calmly in Greek.

Ania remained motionless as Ben reached out and gently took her arm. He could sense nothing wrong with it. He looked at the torn sleeve of her jacket—it was shredded from where it had been pinched between the rear axle and the asphalt. The damage to the sleeve was even on both sides, as if it has been cleaved from both directions. He gently slid the cuff up to her elbow and looked.

There was no injury, no blood, not so much as even a mild scratch. He looked back at the car—there was no blood there, either. Ben looked back to her.

"What in the name of all things are you? I saw what happened, your arm was nearly amputated. I saw blood... What are you?" Ben said quietly, looking hurt.

Ania stepped back, looking into Ben's face. Her eyes were now burning like phosphorous.

"Ben Airaldi, do not fear me—I have no malice within." She whispered to him in Aramaic, as her gaze bore into him.

Ben stepped back a foot and removed something from his pocket. Standing straight up, he began reciting a prayer in Latin. After every line, he repeated it in Aramaic.

Ania averted her eyes from the crucifix Ben was holding in front of him.

"Please—I am not a demon. This is not necessary. I beg you, conceal it from my eyes."

She spoke in an ancient Greek dialect; a version Ben knew had not been used for over a thousand years.

In the Name of the Father,
and of the Son,
and of the Holy Ghost.
Amen.

Most glorious Prince of the Heavenly Armies,
Saint Michael the Archangel,
defend us in "our battle against principalities and powers,
against the rulers of this world of darkness,
against the spirits of wickedness in the high places."

Come to the assistance of men whom God has created to
   His likeness and whom He has redeemed at a great price
   from the tyranny of the devil.

The Holy Church venerates you as her guardian and
   protector; to you, the Lord has entrusted the souls of the
   redeemed to be led into heaven.

Pray therefore the God of Peace to crush Satan beneath our
   feet, that he may no longer retain men captive and do
   injury to the Church.

Offer our prayers to the Most High, that without delay
   they may draw His mercy down upon us;

take hold of "the dragon, the old serpent, which is the devil
and Satan," bind him and cast him into the bottomless
pit "that he may no longer seduce the nations."

In the Name of Jesus Christ,
our God and Lord,
strengthened by the intercession of the Immaculate
Virgin Mary,
Mother of God,
of Blessed Michael the Archangel,
of the Blessed Apostles Peter and Paul
and all the Saints.
and powerful in the holy authority of our ministry,
we confidently undertake to repulse the attacks and deceits
of the devil.

God arises;
His enemies are scattered
and those who hate Him flee before Him.
As smoke is driven away,
so are they driven;
as wax melts before the fire,
so the wicked perish at the presence of God.

V. Behold the Cross of the Lord, flee bands of enemies.
R. The Lion of the tribe of Juda, the offspring of David, hath
conquered.
V. May Thy mercy, Lord, descend upon us.
R. As great as our hope in Thee.

We drive you from us,
whoever you may be,
unclean spirits,
all satanic powers,
all infernal invaders,
all wicked legions,
assemblies and sects.

In the Name and by the power of Our Lord Jesus Christ,
+ may you be snatched away and driven from the Church
  of God and from the souls made to the image and likeness
  of God and redeemed by the Precious Blood of the Divine
  Lamb.

+ Most cunning serpent, you shall no more dare to deceive
  the human race, persecute the Church, torment God's
  elect and sift them as wheat.

+ The Most High God commands you,

+ He with whom, in your great insolence, you still claim
  to be equal. "God who wants all men to be saved and to
  come to the knowledge of the truth."

God the Father commands you.

+ God the Son commands you.

+ God the Holy Ghost commands you.

+ Christ, God's Word made flesh, commands you;

+ He who to save our race outdone through your envy,
  "humbled Himself, becoming obedient even unto death";

*He who has built His Church on the firm rock and declared
that the gates of hell shall not prevail against Her,
because He will dwell with Her "all days even to the end
of the world."*

The sacred Sign of the Cross commands you,

*+ as does also the power of the mysteries of the Christian
Faith.*

*+ The glorious Mother of God, the Virgin Mary, com-
mands you;*

*+ she who by her humility and from the first moment of her
Immaculate Conception crushed your proud head.*

*The faith of the holy Apostles Peter and Paul, and of the
other Apostles commands you.*

*+ The blood of the Martyrs and the pious intercession of all
the Saints command you. +*

*Thus, cursed dragon, and you, diabolical legions, we adjure
you by the living God,*

+ by the true God,

+ by the holy God,

*+ by the God "who so loved the world that He gave up His
only Son, that every soul believing in Him might not
perish but have life everlasting";*

*stop deceiving human creatures and pouring out to them
the poison of eternal damnation; stop harming the Church
and hindering her liberty.*

Begone, Satan, inventor and master of all deceit,
enemy of man's salvation.

Give place to Christ in Whom you have found none of your
works; give place to the One, Holy, Catholic and Apostolic
Church acquired by Christ at the price of His Blood.

Stoop beneath the all-powerful Hand of God; tremble and
flee when we invoke the Holy and terrible Name of Jesus,
this Name which causes hell to tremble,
this Name to which the Virtues, Powers and Dominations
of heaven are humbly submissive, this Name which the
Cherubim and Seraphim praise unceasingly repeating:

Holy, Holy, Holy is the Lord, the God of Hosts.

V. O Lord, hear my prayer.
R. And let my cry come unto Thee.

V. May the Lord be with thee.
R. And with thy spirit.

Let us pray.

God of heaven,
God of earth,
God of Angels,
God of Archangels,
God of Patriarchs,
God of Prophets,
God of Apostles,
God of Martyrs,
God of Confessors,
God of Virgins,

God who has power to give life after death and rest after
work: because there is no other God than Thee and there
can be no other, for Thou art the Creator of all things,
visible and invisible, of Whose reign there shall be no
end, we humbly prostrate ourselves before Thy glorious
Majesty and we beseech Thee to deliver us by Thy power
from all the tyranny of the infernal spirits, from their
snares, their lies and their furious wickedness.

Deign, O Lord, to grant us Thy powerful protection
and to keep us safe and sound.

We beseech Thee through Jesus Christ Our Lord.

Amen.

V. From the snares of the devil,
R. Deliver us, O Lord.

V. That Thy Church may serve Thee in peace and liberty:
R. We beseech Thee to hear us.

V. That Thou may crush down all enemies of Thy Church:
R. We beseech Thee to hear us.

Ben continued the prayer. Ania had not heard this particular one in five hundred years.

"Ben, please!" Ania tried to walk toward him, but some unseen force repelled her.

"If you intend no harm, why do you recoil from Christ's image?" Ben's face was steel.

"I am not fit to look at it. I'm flawed." Her eyes remained averted.

"Why this crucifix? You were able to look upon the hundreds we saw this morning." Ben held the crucifix as if it were a shield.

"I don't know — there is something different about it." She tried to look up at him, and for a moment, Ben saw her eyes had returned to their normal hue. "Maybe it was blessed, or belonged to someone special — I do not know why it halts me."

She was right about the crucifix being special — only he knew that this cross had been blessed by Pope John Paul II. It was one of the final blessings the pontiff had given before his death. This crucifix was Ben's only sacred possession.

A chill came over him. From the first moment he met Ania, he'd sensed something different about her. He initially assumed it was awe. After spending some time with her, he began to feel something toward her that he'd never felt before with anyone else. He didn't know exactly what it was, but it was a feeling that he needed to save her from someone…or something. In his highly rational mind, he knew that there was an explanation for what he'd just seen. *No! This is not rational! This is impossible.* The discovery of the crosses, his meeting her — there was something at play. Since they'd arrived, something was changing in her — he knew he'd seen something different in her eyes earlier, but now…

He looked at her. "Look at me!" he commanded in Aramaic.

She slowly turned and looked at him. Ben said something in the same ancient Greek dialect she'd used moments earlier. Her eyes began to glow again like phosphorous fire. He began to say another prayer, this one solely in Latin.

Ania recognized it as the earliest prayer against a demon. Guilt washed over her. Ben saw the effect it had, and saw her expression darken.

He interrupted the prayer. "Why are you in league with him? He is the Prince of Darkness; all his promises are false!"

Ania replied to Ben in a language he'd never heard before. Though he couldn't understand the words, in his soul he knew what she meant.

Ben resumed the prayer and when he had finished, he simply turned and walked away.

Chapter 24

A Lonely Journey

Ania stood by the car, watching as Ben moved away. As he vanished from view, a hollow feeling swelled within her.

The last time she'd felt this way was in the early years after she was "cursed." The seemingly immortal woman never had surgery, but the sensation was akin to the sudden loss of an internal organ. The newly-vacated space was now filled with pain. In the brief few days since Ben had arrived in her office, an emotional feeling had sparked to life and was growing within her.

The first word that came to mind was "attraction." How that feeling could develop so quickly puzzled her. Yes—he was handsome, but it wasn't his looks that drew her. If a soul still resided within her, that was what was drawn to him. She was not given to infatuation; her mind was far too developed for that, but the force that pulled her to him was overwhelming.

Upon their first meeting, a strange yet comfortable sensation of warmth had enveloped her. She couldn't discern if it was his voice, his smile, or his familiarity with her native language. The dizzying jolt of electricity she felt when he shook her hand... it spun her mind, and caused mild alarm. Most recently she had felt the identical sensation when Ben examined her miraculously-healed arm. She'd come into contact with many persons, yet only he had that effect on her. The only other sensation that felt even remotely similar was the dreaded day she met Bel. She did not remember the details—not because it was so long ago, but because her mind had been shrouded in dark anger when it happened. At that time so long ago, a maelstrom of anger, sadness, anguish, and hunger for revenge swirled within her. At that "young age," she'd never experienced such pure fury, and knew not how to manage it.

The level of hatred surprised her to this day. At the epoch of the raging storm, Bel had materialized— almost as if she'd summoned him. Her mind awash with evil, she'd submitted to him without hesitation. What he actually did to her, she couldn't remember. All she knew was that she wasn't the same after the encounter.

In her short few days with Ben, she had grown very fond of him; this was independent of any seemingly romantic attraction. His sense of optimism was contagious, a feeling she'd not known since childhood.

Outwardly, they were roughly the same age—though in actuality, she was 2,500 years his senior. She had stopped aging after the encounter with Bel. She looked now as she did then. In ancient Greece, a person's age wasn't measured the way it was now. Instead, time was measured by the cycling of the seasons. On that cursed day, she'd counted thirty springs. Her body had stopped growing older, but not her mind—it absorbed knowledge and grew wise. The efficient clarity of her thinking today was unfathomable in her true youth. After the passage of all this time, her mind was almost telepathic. She could process information faster than any computer, and even think on multiple levels. Her acute perspective allowed her to evaluate people deeply, seeing things in them they couldn't even see themselves. She always knew who she could and couldn't trust.

In all these years, she'd known countless people, but never anyone like Ben Airaldi.

Ania's mind returned to current pressing matters, and she pondered returning to the hotel. The walk would have been easy for her, but that would involve abandoning the rental car. She assessed the situation, and decided to act.

The disabled vehicle sat awkwardly; lacking the left rear wheel, the right front corner of the car sat about six inches higher than the others. The nearly-new sedan looked as if a giant had twisted it. Ania knelt by the rear axle — the offending object that had revealed her secret to Ben. The flimsy jack was pinned underneath and useless. After scanning the deserted highway, she clamped a hand on the wheel hub, lifted the car and repositioned the weak bottle jack. There was a gouge in the asphalt where her arm had once been pinned, the only physical evidence that anything had happened. She looked at her torn sleeve and remembered how bad the injury had been. She knew that if she'd been human, the arm would have been amputated.

Ania installed the spare where the flat tire formerly resided, and picked up the lug nuts. She decided to forgo the wrench — it looked as insufficient as the jack. With little effort, her fingers torqued the lug nuts better than any tool. She stood, and looked up and down the desolate road; she was halfway between town and the excavation site. For a moment, she contemplated retreating to the solace of the cave, and waiting for another thousand years or so. Maybe she could start over, and her secret would die with Ben someday. She was certain he would never tell anyone what he'd seen — not because no one would believe him, but because he didn't believe it himself.

For the first time in over two thousand years, she had trouble weighing options. She could return to the cave, wait and re-emerge generations later and start anew; or she could find Ben, and tell her story. He was the only living human who consciously knew of her curse. An old acquaintance, Abraham, had seen her true nature once, but thankfully he was insensibly intoxicated. Bits of his memory emerged years later, and his words were read by thousands. Thankfully, the readers, and Abe, had imagined they were fiction from a fertile imagination. The playwright went to his grave, never knowing he'd met the actual creature of his story.

After setting the sedan squarely on all fours, Ania realized that Ben had taken his set of keys with him — she'd seen him put them in his pocket after opening the trunk. She then remembered there was an extra set in her own pocket. Having the keys was not much of a solution — she didn't know how to drive. Sure, she'd ridden in many cars, as far back as the 1920s. They had changed a lot in almost one hundred years, but they still had a motor and four wheels.

Although she had no experience driving, she was adept at conjuring solutions to pressing problems; she could do this.

Sitting behind the wheel was foreign to her; the presence of the large, round object was reminiscent of a ship's wheel, albeit smaller. The controls, buttons, and everything else in front of her were studied carefully; the wheel controlled direction, the accelerator speed, and the brakes arrested movement. The assortment of buttons, dials, and lights on the dash were indecipherable. As her students were always advised, she started with the instructions. The owner's manual was retrieved from the glove box — it was the size of a small bible. She remembered the first time she'd seen one: a forgetful student had left it in her classroom once; she believed it was the early 1960s. Back then, they had been nothing more than about ten stapled pages of black-and-white print.

What she held now was much larger, and in color. Starting at the beginning, and absorbing every word, she had it memorized inside thirty minutes. The small book accurately described the car and its features, and even told what to do in certain emergencies. What it failed to do was instruct someone how to actually drive.

Ania buckled up, stepped on the brake, turned on the car, and woke the engine. She placed her hands at the ten and two o'clock position as she'd seen Ben do, and then stepped lightly on the gas. The motor revved gently. She released the gas pedal and the RPMs dropped.

After verifying that the road was clear, the selector was put on "Drive." As the brakes were released, the car crept forward. Unassisted, the idling motor moved the vehicle along at a manageable five miles per hour. The gentle movement allowed the nascent driver to acquaint herself with the feel of the wheel. She observed how gentle steering affected the car's direction. The car was slowly weaving all over the empty road for a few minutes, allowing Ania to absorb new sensations of steering. After a mile, she was able to keep the car squarely on the proper side of the road. She tapped the accelerator once, and then rested her foot on the pedal. The speed climbed to ten miles per hour. She now noticed that the steering wheel required less effort to achieve the same amount of control. After another mile, she was up to fifteen, then twenty miles per hour, and she finally settled at thirty. Maintaining this speed, she focused on piloting the car.

She was thankful the road was empty; the last thing she wanted was to put another motorist in jeopardy. For practice, she pressed the brakes with firm and steady pressure; the car eased to a stop. She glanced quickly, and again she was off. The sedan was now moving around thirty-five miles per hour and was still easy to control.

For the first time in many, many years, Doctor Athania X. Socratatos discovered something completely new to her: driving was fun. Within these pleasant feelings, she planned her approach to Ben.

Chapter 25

Back to the Hotel

Ania found Ben sitting on the outside patio of the hotel's restaurant. He was off in a corner by himself, staring at the nearby lake. A full wineglass sat on the table, next to a nearly-full bottle of Chianti. If she didn't know any better, she would have thought Ben had filled the glass, but had yet to drink anything. She sat down in the chair across from him, but did not look at him. She looked at the same tranquil water, wondering what she would say. Ben did not react to her presence.

"Ben, when you first reached out to me, I surmised your request would involve something simple— nothing more than a translation or interpretation. I had no idea that it would, or could, lead to where we find ourselves now. My first impression was that you were merely a historical researcher for the Holy See, seeking some information. After you told me about the find, I feared my secrets would be discovered, but when you first walked into my office, I felt hope.

You are the first person in a long, long time who has seen my true nature. As soon as you invited me on this trip, I prepared myself for the possibility that you would find me out. The intent was not to deceive, but to protect you from vastly incomprehensible and deeply disturbing knowledge. Your faith is deep, but I harbored a fear that you couldn't understand what I was...what I am.

In the last few days, it has dawned on me that you are much more than a mere researcher, but more like an astute warrior. Ben Airaldi—do not fear me. I am not an evil being. Yes—dark forces have marked my soul, but they do not define, nor motivate me. Once you learn the entire truth, my hope is that I may help you understand the source of your faith even more."

There was an almost imperceptible shift in Ben's posture. She'd said something that caused him discomfort. His eyes remained fixed on the water.

"I was once a young, angry girl, and that led me to a horrendous mistake. It's something I've been trying to atone for ever since." Ania took a deep breath and removed something from inside the left lapel of her jacket. She placed it on the center of the wooden table.

Ben's eyes flicked momentarily at it, but otherwise he did not move.

"Ben, if you will look at what that is, something I've guarded for longer than you could ever imagine, it will prove my actions are not driven by evil. I would not...could not have that object if I were." She gently pushed it closer to him. "This may tell what thousands of words will not."

Ben took a deep and slow breath. He picked up the wineglass, swirled the blood-red liquid, sniffed it, and carefully set the glass down, without taking a drink. His fingers remained on the stem for almost a minute. He looked askance at what she'd put down, and his posture straightened slightly, as if he recognized something. His fingers uncurled from the wineglass stem and were drawn toward the object. He was about to touch it, but he appeared hesitant. She knew he sensed something, and that he didn't know if he should handle it.

He raised his left hand to his chest, and Ania could see he was still holding his crucifix. After a moment, he tepidly touched the object, almost as if it might harm him. He took a breath and slowly slid it toward himself. He withdrew his hand and turned in his chair, squaring himself to the table — he did not look up at her. Moving his face to within inches of the object, he studied it closely: it was a metal container, roughly about the size of a desk stapler. It was the color of tarnished copper, and the surfaces were deeply burnished. He'd immediately recognized that the box was ancient. He'd seen this type of work before — it was from the early Bronze Age, most certainly Western Europe. He gently picked it up, and hefted it — the container was weighty, and felt solid. He rolled it to one side, and felt its weight shift slightly, as if something within was moving. Cradling it in both hands, he inspected the exterior, noticing the subtle, yet exquisite scrollwork. He turned it over completely several times, scrutinizing every surface. He felt something shift inside the box as he manipulated it. The last one he'd seen like this was much larger, but empty. This specimen definitely held something.

Ania, was about to tell him how to open it, but she didn't have to; with a series of dexterous moves, Ben released the hidden lock and the cover slid open easily. While the box's exterior dimensions were large, the actual interior was considerably smaller. The container's weight came from the fact that its walls were almost an inch thick. An ancient-looking, purple silk cloth was wrapped around something. Ben set the box down on the table, removed a pen from his pocket, and used it to gently manipulate the material. He exposed what it was concealing. As the cloth parted, he reacted as if something electric pierced his soul. He stood up, causing the chair to scrape on the stone surface. He stepped around to the back of the chair, as if seeking protection from something. He looked at her with serious eyes.

"I was there. That is how it came into my possession. It has not left my sight since." She knew what his question would be before the words formed in his mind.

Ben looked back down at the box, and his eyes became glued on what was within the purple shroud. He stared wordlessly at it for nearly a minute, his eyes never blinking. He gently set the box back on the table and made the Sign of the Cross. He said something quietly in Latin.

"It is what you think it is," said Ania. "From your reaction, I know you have seen the other three. My guess is that they are in Rome. You needn't rely on my words — take that wherever you must and see for yourself. I will return to my room and wait for you. If I do not hear from you in three days, I will return to the States and never trouble you again. I have guarded that with whatever life is within me. I can hardly imagine relinquishing it, but that one should be with the other three."

Ania got up and walked away without looking back.

Ben didn't look up as she left. If at any other time he'd seen this, he would have assumed it to be fake. But after everything that had transpired in the last week, her giving it to him carried a significant amount of weight. Ania was right: the other three of these objects were in Rome — deep within the Vatican's vaults. Only a handful of people knew of their existence. Most thought there were only three — a fourth wasn't something anyone could conceive of. He knew many holy legends, but this one was not even so much as a rumor.

Ben placed his crucifix to his lips and kissed it. He picked up the box and his eyes moistened. With trembling hands, he closed the lid. He remembered the ones in Rome—they were a closely guarded secret, not seen by the outside world since that dark day. History had many questions, but never had anyone thought to ask specifically about the object he now held. Within his hands was something more valuable than any known, or even imagined, relic. If history's despots, dictators, and madmen had even an inkling of this item's existence, they would have sold their souls to have it.

Ben's interest in history had sparked when he was a child, and first learned about World War II. He'd always wondered why the Axis forces had not marched into St. Peter's Square and plundered the holy treasures within. The Wehrmacht juggernaut was relentless as it stormed across Europe, especially when resistance was offered. The Vatican was defenseless, and there would have been no real fight. The British Isle, isolated and alone, at least had a body of water and the determination of the British people to protect it. The Vatican had nothing more than a painted line and humble walls around it, yet the armies of darkness were kept at bay, never setting foot within the sovereign state. It was not until he had joined the Papal Gendarmerie, and been in Rome for two years, that he learned the real reason why evil had not stormed the Basilica. He realized that things — just like the object he now held — had the power to ward off earthly evil. He knew that it wasn't actually the physical objects that repelled SS boots — it was what *made* these objects holy.

Ben opened up the box again and looked inside. The ones in Rome had seemed smaller, but they were sealed behind glass and almost two feet away. As he peered inside, his eyes were no more than six inches away. He held the container in his right hand and looked at the palm of his left. He removed his sacred crucifix from his pocket and looked at the figure of Christ, affixed to the cross. He tried to imagine what the pain might have been like.

Ben left a single bill, more than twice what the tab was, and looked toward the lake.

I have to get to Rome.

Chapter 26

When in Rome

Less than twelve hours after taking possession
of the small bronze vault, Ben passed through the
Vatican gates. He was so eager to get the item to
Rome that he had been tempted to jump into the
rental and drive straight through, but given the
distance, flying was still the best option. The earliest
flight he could book was at six in the morning, and
that would still get him to his destination faster than
by the autobahn and autostrade.

After parting with Ania, he had made a beeline
to a nearby church, and spent several hours in prayer
and deep reflection. If the item he now possessed was
real — and he knew it to be — then the person who
gave it to him was…there was no word for it. She was
not a demon — nothing of evil origin could possess
this most sacred item. A human, even with evil
intent, might have been able to hold it…but Ania was
anything but.

Could she be an angel? he asked himself—but he decided she couldn't be, because the Lord's direct servants did not reveal themselves to humans as she had. His discovery of her nature was made quite by accident. She was something, for sure, but what that was, he had no clue.

From even a young age, Ben knew that there were clearly two sides to humanity: good and evil. Humans could do both, but they were not truly evaluated until the time of judgment, after the immortal soul left its earthly restraints. But Ania was not human, at least from what Ben could see. Her outward appearance was normal, but what he'd seen in her was not possible. The human body had the miraculous ability to heal itself, but not instantaneously. What he had seen was like something in movies. The injuries to her arm were not merely severe—they were grievous. Had she been "normal," only immediate medical intervention could have saved her life. What might have killed any other person affected her as if nothing had happened. The only casualty was her coat. He knew what he saw was real, and not a figment of his imagination. He continued to pray, as the incident replayed itself over and over in his mind.

In addition to the instantaneous healing, her eyes had glowed—actually burned with real light. Pupils did not produce that kind of illumination, not even in reflection. He realized that while the light was blinding, it did not hurt his own eyes — that indicated something to him — something that led him to believe she was…? Nothing in his research or learning had ever prepared him for what he'd witnessed.

By the time he'd left the church, he had decided he would not make any judgment for the time being. All he knew was that someone, or some being, had presented him with the most holy of relics, and it needed to be taken somewhere safe. He would guard it with his life, but he was mortal, and had limitations. The only place truly safe was where he was going at the moment.

Deep within the walls of the hallowed nation-state was the Academy of Sciences. He'd spent many hours in this place of learning, studying subjects and concepts that even the most devout believer could never fathom. In addition to knowledge, this building housed treasures unknown to the outside world — things even many within the city walls did not know of. The outside world knew the Vatican guarded many worldly treasures, but compared to what Ben was about to see, they were relatively worthless. What this building guarded were still products of this world, but given what this particular item was used for, its value could not be judged in human terms. Ben was humbled and honored that he'd been entrusted with the mere knowledge of its existence.

Ben walked down three long flights of stairs from the main floor. This sub-basement was used for file storage, and largely forgotten. It appeared to be four bare walls, reinforced with steel girders. A careful examination, even by an architect or building engineer, would have revealed nothing unusual. Only someone who knew where to look could find it. In a corner of the room, two vertical beams formed a right angle with each other. They appeared to reinforce the stone foundation. They were identical to the other beams, but they were not structural in nature.

Ben retrieved his smartphone from his pocket, and placed it against the surface of the right beam. He opened up a photo file and scrolled through several pictures until finding one depicting a plain stone. He held his index finger in the center of the image and then pressed the power button on the phone. A series of faint chirps emanated from within the solid metal. He removed the phone and waited. After a few seconds, the two beams moved — the one on the left up, the one on the right down. A narrow opening appeared, no wider than two feet. Ben passed through. A set of overhead lights turned on, and ahead of him appeared a long, ancient corridor. The bricks looked hundreds of years old, but were contrasted with modern lighting and bright, stainless steel reinforcements.

Reaching the end, he was confronted by a steel door, identical to one found on a typical bank vault. He touched a glass pane, set to the right side of the door, and a screen lit with a faint-green hue. He held

his palm against the surface, and a series of clicks
and beeps punctuated the silence. The door opened,
revealing a true vault, fifteen feet by fifteen feet. In
the center of the room was a lone armored box, the
size of a copy machine. Its surface was smooth and
it had no external features. To the uninitiated, it
appeared to be nothing more than a large, solid block
of silver metal.

Ben walked up to it, and before touching it, he
knelt. On a wall in front of him was a large crucifix,
made of the same metal as the box. Ben recited a
prayer in Latin and placed both hands on the vertical
surface of the cube, about two feet apart. As he did
so, he intoned a chant. Ben stood up, and then waved
his hand across the top. A steady, electronic hum
emanated from the obelisk, and the entire top portion
opened up like a trapdoor.

Ben stood and looked inside. The interior was
not much larger than a shoebox. The walls of the
small vault were nearly two feet thick. Inside was a
sealed glass container, fitting the internal dimensions
of the box. Within the glass were three oblong spikes,
arranged in a row. They were made of iron, and
glistened blood-red. Two were perfectly straight, but
one of them was bent, nearly to a right angle. Ben
reached into his coat pocket and removed the bronze
container. Sliding open the lid, he moved the purple
cloth with a pen, revealing a nail identical to the two
straight spikes. He reverently placed the bronze box

on top of the glass container. The box was placed so that the nail inside of it now lined up at the end of the three nails. As he did this, he was certain that the red liquid (verified to be blood on the three) became brighter — as if it were fresh. Ben bowed his head and saw drops of clear liquid appear on the top of the glass, next to the bronze box. They were his tears.

Chapter 27

On the Wrong Side

Bella shot upright in the bed, moving so quickly that Seth was almost cast off on his side. Upon opening his eyes, he was surprised to see that Bella was out of the bed, standing upright, and stiff as a board. He blinked several times, and even rubbed his eyes, but his vision of the woman was different than what he'd seen before. If he didn't know any better, it looked as if she cast a red shadow. He'd drunk a lot of Jägermeister the night before, but this was the oddest thing he'd ever seen, sober or intoxicated. He sat up, rubbed his eyes again, and when he looked back at Bella, she was staring back at him.

"Morning, Sunshine!" he said with a grin.

Bella had a look of absolute horror on her face, as if she'd had a night terror.

"What's wrong?" He sat up straighter, studying her darkened face.

"Ah, it's, er, nothing." She looked away from him and out the window.

Seth got out of bed, and walked up behind her. When he placed his arms around her from behind, he was shocked to feel she was ice cold.

"You're freezing—come back to bed where it's warm." He gripped her tighter.

In less than a second, her body became warm, maybe even hot. She turned in his arms and looked up into his eyes. Her expression softened, and her coy smile returned.

"What happened? You rocketed out of bed—did you have a nightmare or something?" He led her back to the tangled mass of sheets.

"Yes—it was a nightmare, something terrible, something out of a horror movie. I hope I never have one like this again." She nuzzled up against him, pulling his arms tighter around her. She then pulled the covers up over their bare bodies.

"Do you want to tell me about it?" Steinbeck whispered gently into her ear.

"Not really, but it was like something had been unleashed into the world and was coming after me." She shivered slightly, and her body turned cold again. The sudden change in her body's temperature startled him yet again.

"Well the sun isn't even up, let's get back to bed." He closed his eyes and held her close to him.

She turned in his arms and looked at him. Her smile told Seth Steinbeck that she wasn't quite ready to go back to sleep.

"Again? Wow, you have an insatiable appetite for 'carnal knowledge.'" He pulled her against him with vigor.

"You are correct—my appetite will never be sated." She writhed against him, initiating the next round.

Chapter 28
Unknown Science

Ben recalled the day he'd first seen the contents of the vault. It had been years earlier, but it seemed just like yesterday. He knew that everyone experienced life-changing events, but Ben doubted that many would say their souls had changed, too.

He'd always wondered about holy relics such as these, but assumed they were either lost to history, or hidden and forgotten. The day he first saw the nails had started uneventfully; he was studying quietly in the library when he was summoned by Bishop Brancaleone. Ben had never met him, but knew his reputation well. At one hundred years old, this cleric was the oldest ordained member of the Church.

They had met alone in a small conference room in the Academy of Sciences building. The elderly man of God had looked all of his age, yet Ben recognized that his intellect was still sharp. After introductions and pleasantries, the bishop had queried Ben about his educational background; he learned about his master's degree in forensic biology — a rarity for someone in the researcher's position. Ben also possessed a master's in Western civilization, with an emphasis on Mediterranean cultures. The combination of these two areas of study gave Ben a unique perspective on the past. He knew about ancient history as well as how to analyze its artifacts with science.

The bishop knew much of Ben's hands-on study of the Shroud of Turin, and had questioned him at length about his experience. Discussing this subject was something Ben loved — and it was clear that the bishop did too. After nearly an hour of lively talk, Ben had been led to the vault, and was shown something he would never forget. The bishop had said nothing as he showed the safe room's contents, but Ben had recognized these holy relics immediately. He had been speechless.

After telling Ben about how the nails were believed to come into the Vatican's possession, he had tasked Ben with transporting them to a Swiss laboratory for analysis. The nature of the trip required complete secrecy and a high level of security. Ben's prior work experience in the States, coupled with his general knowledge level, made him the obvious choice for the task. Ben was honored that he was being trusted with something beyond priceless.

From the moment the nails left the vault, until his arrival in Switzerland, the ancient treasures had never left his possession. It was with great reluctance that he had relinquished control of his charge to the lab techs. Although they were being handled by others, the iron instruments were never out of his sight.

Ben had watched intently as technicians took microscopic samples of the presumed blood from each nail, and subjected them to a battery of tests, among them DNA typing. The initial results were deemed inconclusive — the results were unreadable. The substance may have looked like human blood, but that was the only thing they were sure of.

The second test had produced the same results, and Ben had seen the growing sense of confusion amongst the staff. He'd recognized the testing processes, but not the unexplainable results. By the time the third, fourth, and fifth tests were completed, the lab was abuzz with confused conjecture. One by one, the exam team confirmed that the tests had been done correctly — the blood was the issue in question.

Ben had listened to the chatter among the staff as they tried to rationalize what was occurring. Eventually, the lab supervisor had pulled Ben aside and asked about the nails. He'd explained that the nails came from the Vatican, but gave no explanation as to their origin. Ben knew whose blood was on the nails, but the staff didn't.

Ben and the senior scientist had retreated to his office, and they discussed the results over cups of tea. Ben already knew how the tests were performed, but listened quietly as the man explained the following to him.

"DNA analysis reveals genetic traits from both parents in a single sample. The twisted, helix ladder structure is an equal combination of both parents. The samples under analysis only show the traits of one parent. There is no sign of a second parent. The discernible data reveals it belongs to a female — the X chromosome pattern is clearly from the mother. The Y chromosome, which would...should come from the father, defies logic and science — it should have been present alongside the mother's, but it is not there. The DNA analysis looked at both sides of the double helix, but the 'ladder' was incomplete. The structure they were looking at looked like the ladder had been split longitudinally. The X side of the ladder was visible and strong, yet the Y side is not present. It is scientifically impossible to be seeing what we are seeing. Half a helix structure does not — it cannot exist in nature, yet we are seeing it now. Those samples should not exist on this earth."

The scientist had rubbed his chin and looked at the ceiling.

Ben had been taking notes, as he always did, but his pen had frozen on the paper as he digested what had just been explained. He knew the reason why the father's DNA was missing — it was not of this earth. He had realized that for the first time in history, physical proof existed that the Savior was exactly what all

Christians believed. Ben's faith and education had become one at that moment.

"The only analogy to be made is a flying kite; you see a kite in the sky, but the air is invisible. We know it is air, and that is what makes it logical. Whatever is holding the helix together is as invisible as air — but it is not air." The lab supervisor had looked at Ben.

Ben hated even thinking of the term, but he asked: "Playing devil's advocate — is it possible that the sample has been degraded, and that the DNA has deteriorated to the point that it can't be properly typed?" Ben had masked his excitement at what was stirring in his mind.

"We have analyzed biological samples from Egyptian tombs — those are thousands of years old, yet the DNA structure is always there. A severely degraded sample will show nothing, yet what we have here is truly something — something not possible in the world of science. We understand that the nails belong to the Vatican, but we have not asked what they are presumed to be." The scientist had sat back in his chair and stared off into space.

This particular lab had been chosen for its reputation; not only for the quality of its work, but also for its ability to maintain confidentiality. In addition to providing services to Rome, it had also been on contract with many other nations — countries who required secrecy in their dealings.

"The nails are old, we know that, but their true origin is unknown. I brought them here to determine if the substance on them is human blood. We have no idea in what manner they were used." Ben had been speaking truthfully — factually, the origin of the nails was a mystery, but then so was faith.

"I have been studying DNA and its corollaries for forty years. This is the first time this type of result has ever been seen — or technically 'not seen.' I have never been religious; my faith is in the concrete world of the physical. I'm not an atheist; in fact, religion is a neutral subject to me. The configuration of the nails, and the presence of presumed blood…my guess is that they were used in a Roman crucifixion. Is there a belief these were the actual nails from…" His voice had trailed off as facts became clear in his own mind.

"All we know is that the nails are old, and have been in Rome for many years. We brought them here to seek answers from you. I can't say anything more." Ben's face had remained placid.

"Well, I can tell you this: the Y chromosome from the father may be there, but if it is, it is not organic. You already know that the helix is a 'zipping' together of the mother and father's DNA, as they combine to form a new human. This helix is arranged so, but the father's side of the zipper is not scientifically there. What we have is only one side of the structure. The mother's side of the DNA is there, but it should not be — DNA does not, DNA cannot, do this. My crude opinion is that this sample belongs to someone who is only half-human. The mother is from earth—but the father is not. The father is alien—not necessarily as in UFO, but certainly not of this planet."

Ben had scratched out some more notes. "We can forego a formal, written report, but may I have copies of the raw data?" Ben had already stopped writing.

"Of course—a written report would be nonsensical. If you prefer, we will give you the actual physical results. Would you prefer that we dispose of any duplicates or other evidence that we ever did the analysis? I can assure you our staff will protect the confidentiality of your employer." The man had sat up a little straighter.

"That would be best; I will relay your information to my superiors."

Ben had put away his pen and closed his folio. All evidence of the tests conducted had been left with him. Only the lab director knew that the tests had been done at the behest of Rome.

Ben secured the vault, taking the bronze box with him. He would deal with this new discovery after the situation in Germany was resolved. The nail itself would remain here, safe within the Vatican's ancient walls. There was no reason to take it back. When Ania had given it to him, the implication was that she was only safeguarding it. She had known that this blessed relic needed to be with its brethren. For the second time in his life, Ben was in possession of actual, physical evidence that the Son of God had walked the earth.

With a deep breath, and new resolve, he walked partway down the hall, and stopped in front of a heavily-armored door. Like the container in the vault, it too was made of smooth metal. The brushed-steel finish contrasted with the surrounding, rough-hewn brick. There were no features to the door; not even so much as hinges. Unlike the vault though, this entrance was not hidden, but it still looked formidable.

Ben entered a code on the numeric keypad on the wall aside the door. A soft "clunk" signaled the unlocking and he walked inside. Overhead lights came on automatically, illuminating the plain, non-descript room. The only feature in the space was a wall composed of an evenly-spaced row of small doors, resembling bank safe-deposit boxes. He removed a key from his pocket and unlocked one of the miniature vaults. This particular mini-vault was exclusively for his use. He never used it, and thus it was empty. He slid out a long drawer, opened the lid, and gently placed the bronze box inside. He paused, picked the container back up, and opened it. He stared for a while at the nail, digesting what its significance was to his faith, as well as history. He knew it to be real, even though the circumstances surrounding it seemed unreal. He took a deep breath, closed the lid, and resecured it. The newly-found relic would be safe here.

Ben pondered as to how he would introduce what Ania had given him to his superiors. How would he explain that a beautiful woman—a renowned university professor, with super-human abilities—had been in possession of the fourth nail of the Crucifixion...*the Crucifixion*. No tests had been done on this nail, but he knew it was authentic. There were some that might need to be convinced, however that would introduce Ania, whatever she was, into the equation.

His initial thought was that she was a demon sent to tempt him, to lead him astray from his mission to discover the truth of the crosses. These items, long buried by time and covered with undetonated bombs, presented many questions—questions that he was tasked with answering. He would try to make sense of all that later, after he met up with Ania in Aachen. The mere fact that she possessed the true fourth nail precluded her being evil.

He knew she was not an angel either. *Purgatorium*? Ben said to himself. It came from somewhere in his heart.

Purgatorium, the Latin for "purgatory." This concept was a disputed belief among many denominations of Christianity. Ben knew that Church teaching described it as a place for those who die in a state of grace; a "way station" on the way to heaven; a spiritual state in which a soul that is still imperfect may be purified of its sins. Ben wondered if Ania was in this state, somehow atoning for her sin. Maybe her supernatural healing was connected to it.

He remembered reading some Greek texts describing a place to be "tested." Ben wondered about being tested. While he was ready to accept anything required of him, he wondered what those trials might be. As the idea of fire developed in his mind, he instinctively rubbed his arm. He would be willing to endure pain and injury again; he would endure anything in the fight against evil. His first "test of fire" many years ago had changed not only the course of his life, but also the very way in which he thought.

A twinge of regret pierced his heart, even though he knew he'd been justified in his actions. What he'd done was not a sin — that fact had been confirmed by the priest who counseled him in the following weeks. Logically, even he knew that what he'd done that day was right, but something about it still haunted him. Ben was humble, always willing to turn the other cheek. He forgave freely, but he was absolutely fierce in protecting the external elements of his faith. While he was meek before his Lord, he was the opposite with anything or anyone that posed a threat to the faithful. That fateful day, he'd protected an innocent, but at a great cost.

Ben Airaldi was grateful for his many gifts and abilities; he knew they were things to be held close, to be used as tools for good, not things to boast about or flaunt. Memories of the day they were called to action was figuratively burned into his being. He gently drew his left hand across the top of his right arm. He remembered the pain in his body and his spirit. Everyone had judged that what he had done was just. Even the bishop had assured him that he'd done what duty required of him. The senior cleric had even refused to acknowledge Ben's confession that what he did was a mortal sin. Bishop Matthew was the wisest and most learned person he'd ever met. He was Ben's inspiration for doing what he did now. Bishop Matthew had talked to Ben for hours and calmed his troubled mind. Everyone else had cheered him as a hero, but deep down, it still felt wrong—he had done something irreversible, something that could not be undone on this earth.

What he had done had also halted an evil juggernaut. His one act had prevented several other acts, acts by which someone else would affect many lives. Ben wanted to purge himself of that day. Rationally, he knew his acts were just, his decision correct, but guilt remained on his mind. There were no significant, negative consequences of what he'd done that day. He hoped that somehow God would forgive him for destroying something He, the Lord, had created.

Ben left the anteroom and proceeded back down the hall. On the walls were many paintings, some as old as a thousand years. The artwork depicted the history of the Church, from the day of His birth through His life, death, resurrection, and legacy. He'd seen the pictures many times over the years, but not in this particular state of mind.

He went to one that depicted the Crucifixion; it showed Christ on the cross, flanked by the two thieves. This depiction of Golgotha, the "place of the skull," was judged to be the most accurate.

The site of the Crucifixion was not only a place of death but also a depository for bones, especially skulls. After an execution was carried out, it was generally up to the family of the deceased to remove the body for burial. Those of the Jewish faith were buried in accordance with the customs of the day. Those who were pagan were mostly left where they were; their bodies were allowed to remain on the crosses until they deteriorated and dropped to the ground. Eventually the bones were carried away by animals, or kicked aside by the Romans.

The heads remained, as if to serve as a warning. In the painting, several skulls were around the bases of the thieves' crosses. As he looked at the two robbers, whose crosses flanked Christ's, Ben noticed something he never had before. In the background was a far-off hill, resembling a stone cliff. Looking closely, he saw a small object; if he didn't know any better, he would have described it as a cloaked figure, seemingly watching the event. The more he stared at it, the more his mind convinced him that it was a figure. He thought about the person—or entity— waiting for him in Aachen.

He made haste to return as quickly as possible.

Chapter 29

After Rome

The sun was well into its afternoon descent when Ben arrived at the hotel. He headed straight for Ania's room, not even stopping to drop off his luggage at his own. When he knocked on her door there was no response, so he returned to his own room to think things through. His first move was to leave her a voicemail. That accomplished, a sudden bout of fatigue from the quick, turnaround trip overcame him. His body craved sleep, but his mind was eager to find Ania—sleep would take up too much time. He compromised with a hot shower, hoping it would revive him. That, and it would clean off the grit of two airport experiences.

The falling water calmed his busy brain; the high-pressure blast on his head was successful in dislodging impediments in his thought stream. As the nearly-scalding water soothed his body, he considered two major facts he'd learned in the last few days: first, before Ben's own eyes, Ania had

displayed superhuman abilities. This simple observation pushed him toward the concept that she was
an immortal demon, or a mortal human possessed
by something demonic. He'd studied possessions in
Rome, and that included exorcisms. The prayer he'd
recited in front of her was a short version, accepted as
the standard of exorcisms. While he'd never witnessed an actual exorcism, let alone seen a possessed
person, historical accounts told of seemingly miraculous healing abilities. Her extraordinary language
abilities seemed consistent with the possessed.

The leaning of his mind toward demonism was
halted by the issue of the fourth nail: nothing evil
could have possessed it as she did. If he stipulated
that the relic was authentic, then her being of evil
origin was impossible. Evil could linger near true,
holy relics, but were repelled from coming too close —
let alone touching them.

As he shut off the water and opened the shower
door, a cloud of steam escaped and filled the bathroom. No sooner did the vapor vanish then chatter
intruded into his recently-calmed thoughts. As
concepts echoed inside his head, he realized that his
emotions were running high, and moving his reasoning in too many directions. There were answers to be
found, but they would not emerge right now. If he
was going to get those answers, he needed to focus.
This current situation was something he feared would
distort his long-held beliefs. He was both faithful and

logical, and they used to exist in harmony for him. At this moment, it seemed that the two were colliding, creating great confusion for him.

After drying himself off, Ben closed his eyes and stood before the mirror. Steam had fogged over the glass, and the only thing Ben could see of his reflection was a shapeless mass. He focused on this form, acknowledging it was himself, and closed his eyes. As he breathed deeply, he relaxed and allowed his mind to return to a time years before, when he was employed in his original occupation: an accomplished investigator. As he remembered his favorite fictional thinkers, images of Holmes and Spock came into his thoughts. He had used this technique before and been quite successful.

The nail's existence was real—only another lab test would confirm that the blood on Ania's specimen possessed the same qualities as that of the other three. The test was not necessary—when the fourth was placed near the others, the blood on all four had glowed with equal luminosity. As when he had first seen the original three spikes, several years prior, the blood had been wet, and was still so to this day. It had never dried. On this fourth nail the blood glistened with life, as if it were freshly drawn.

He knew why the blood on all the nails was fresh: it was truly alive, as its Owner was, too. The owner was not a mere mortal…He was the Prince of Peace.

The blood of the Savior would always be alive—living blood did not dry.

As he opened his eyes, Ben saw himself clearly in the looking glass. While he'd been meditating, the steam dissipated and the mirror reflected his true form. He had more answers now than when he'd first begun.

He would meditate some more. Looking upon the clear-blue lake would bring more answers than the bathroom mirror.

Ben returned to the hotel's outdoor dining area, and found an unoccupied table by the overlook. He hadn't eaten in twelve hours, but wasn't hungry. A bottle of Chianti would allow him to stake out the table for a while if need be. Regardless of how long he remained, he would not drink more than a few ounces. He never drank more than a glass at any one sitting, but he liked seeing the bottle nearby. Something about a wine carafe sitting on a table appealed to him. Many a server was surprised to see Ben leave a nearly-full bottle and generous tip.

Ben was seated at the same table from just a few days before, looking at the same tranquil body of water. The waning sunlight cast a warm glow over the lake's smooth surface. Lost in thought, he was unaware of being watched. A faint noise behind him released him from his thoughts and he sensed Ania's presence. Knowing it was her, he motioned with his head for her to come over and join him.

When she came into view, Ben forgot for a moment about the accident and the nail. Something in her face had changed, he couldn't say what, but he experienced a sudden sensation of internal warmth. She was dressed in a simple outfit: a black turtleneck sweater and slacks. Her reddish-brown hair was pulled into a loose ponytail, revealing her complete face. She looked as if she were younger than when he last saw her. He wondered if sharing her secret with him had removed a burden from her shoulders, allowing her to finally relax. Ben didn't quite smile at her, but his expression clearly said that he was glad to see her. He motioned for her to sit and she took the seat across from him.

She perched gently on the front portion of her chair, sitting not quite fully on it. She was on the edge, her back straight and her feet flat on the ground.

"Ben, what can I say? It saddens me that this secret was imposed upon you, but how could I reveal myself to you...or anyone else?"

He looked out at the lake, and took a deep breath. "You were right—that was the fourth nail, it is identical to the other three. The only difference is that the travels of the other three are a mystery. The one you have—if what you say is true—has a provenance which the others don't." His face became placid, as if he was becoming comfortable with Ania, whatever she might be.

He knew this woman before him was different; she was no ordinary human. He cleared his mind, and focused his thoughts. He'd seen her injuries heal before his eyes; he'd seen her blood disappear; she had the fourth nail. Internally, he shifted from scholar and historian to his foundational occupation: investigator.

"Tell me everything from the start of your life to this moment right now...everything."

Ania summoned the waiter. She ordered a bottle of Riesling for herself. Wine did nothing for her, but she reasoned she'd need to put on appearances to others. They would be there for hours.

She turned to Ben, moving her chair so that she faced him from directly across the table. He'd already turned to face her. His demeanor had changed imperceptibly; a serious look was on his face, different from any she'd seen before.

In an ancient, regional Greek dialect, one Ben was familiar with, yet had never heard spoken aloud, Ania declared: "Ben Airaldi, servant of the Lord, my original name was Athanasia. My mother was Xanthippe... My father's name was Socrates."

Chapter 30

Ania's Story

Ben cleared his mind of all thoughts and images. He'd need considerable space for Ania's story to unfold. Suspending all logic would be the only way he could absorb her words. He convinced himself that he was about to hear a fantastic tale. But no matter what she said, he would let every word paint its own picture, no matter how fanciful it might become. Once he had a clear picture, he would square it — or at least try to — with the facts. For now, he was going to allow Ania's voice to pour in through his ears and fill his empty mind. He would do nothing other than listen.

Ania prepared to reveal her innermost secrets to someone she had only recently come to know — yet felt she could trust. Over the years, bits and pieces of her story had spilled out — some voluntary and some not. These specks of information never provided the complete story. Now, right here, right at this moment, all would be revealed and nothing would be held back. Ania had never planned to tell all her secrets, especially to one person — but Ben was well on his way to figuring things out all for himself. She felt he deserved to know the full and accurate account of her long life.

"Father was nearing his fiftieth year of life at the era of my birth. During that same time, his public oratories and philosophies were quickly falling out of favor with the powers that be. He knew his time was at hand, and protecting his youngest child was his highest priority. As a result of the prevailing jeopardy he found himself in, my mother's pregnancy and my birth were kept secret. To the outside world, I was the child of a servant, but in the home, I was the child of Socrates and Xanthippe." She looked dreamily off into the distance, remembering happier times.

The rational side of Ben's mind cleared its throat as it prepared to speak. *Not yet,* he told it. He recalled knowledge of the ancient Greek philosopher. In addition to history, Ben was well versed in Greek philosophy and history, particularly with regards to Ania's purported father. He recalled seeing various sculptures of Socrates, but could not see any resemblance to the woman now speaking to him. Reality tugged at Ben's sleeve, but he brushed it away, actually swiping at his arm. He would hear the entire story from start to finish before he'd allow any judgments to register.

Ania released the nostalgic images and looked back at Ben — his face was passive and relaxed, but his alert eyes clearly showed that he was listening.

"My father's philosophy vexed those in power, and he was admonished to attenuate his outspokenness. He would not, however, concede, even knowing that harm was imminent. I feared for him, beseeching him to bury his thoughts, but he would not be swayed or silenced. His continued public oratories eventually led to his arrest and a sham trial. Even after being convicted and sentenced to death… he accepted the punishment, well-knowing he was innocent. He had many chances to escape, yet he refused to flee. His stubborn adherence to his philosophy forced him to submit to the authority over him. Even knowing he was to die, he refused the label of 'martyr.' He revered the system of law — even one that was twisted and intent on silencing him. Up to the moment of his end, he remained stoic and accepted the situation as it was." Ania looked down at the table, a shadow of anger clouding her face.

Ben recalled the account of Socrates' trial and death — it was based upon the accusation of three Athenian officials — they alleged the renowned philosopher of treason. The "crime" he was accused of was simply advocating that people think for themselves and question all they heard and saw. That manner of thought was frowned upon not only then, but even to this day in some places. Some feared people thinking for themselves would foster a revolution. Ben looked at Ania until she returned her eyes to him.

The flames of Ania's anger lessened in intensity, but still glowed. "A daughter stood by and watched helplessly as her father was murdered at the hands of the corrupt 'leaders' who claimed 'enlightenment.' I felt weak and powerless—unable to save his life, and it stirred something dark in me. Frustration and grief grew wild within me, and this morphed into a deep anger and hatred. I'd been willful my entire life, but never prone to uncontrolled emotions. Father taught me about the virtue of patience, reflection, and peacefulness—especially in times of strife. My mind fought itself, even as he took his last breath.

"When his heart beat no more, darkness enveloped me and something broke open wide with rage. A storm of feelings—feelings I'd never thought possible—danced in my mind. It felt as though every cell in my body was afire. If it was possible to see, I knew my blood was boiling. Eventually, tears eroded my external restraint and I considered doing horrible things to the men who killed him. The word 'fury' does not begin to describe what was about to be released upon Athens."

While her overall demeanor was calm, Ben saw her eyes change—actual flames were flickering within them. If Ben didn't know any better, he would swear they radiated heat.

"During those 'enlightened' times, we still believed in the mythical gods, and I prayed to those marble idols for vengeance. The stone figures offered no help, but something else did. My angry pleas became incarnate, and suddenly there he was: a being in physical form. He looked human, but there was an immortal energy about him — I could actually see it. His sudden appearance scared me, but he soothed me with words and offered his services — he said he'd heard my prayers. He wouldn't tell me if he was a god, but something about his ways convinced me he was. He radiated unlimited power, and simply being near him calmed my rage and infused my spirit with possibilities. As he spoke, his words soothed the painful burn of my uncontrolled anger. He told me he was a 'friend" from far away, yet knew well of my situation. While he appeared mortal, he was unlike anything my eyes had ever beheld. His features were striking: hair blacker than night, and eyes bluer than the Aegean. I could not take my eyes from him. His radiant energy seduced me and drew me in. He offered to share his power — telling me it would allow me to avenge my father's death. This was exactly what I was praying for. If someone else had said this I would have dismissed it as absurd, but his words touched something within. In my blind anguish, I submitted my entire self and spirit to his control. He promised me the power of a 'god on earth' and I accepted without question. That decision — the act of a grieving daughter — is the sole reason I sit before you now." She gently rubbed the area over her heart with her right hand, as if it hurt.

Ben watched sadness shroud her face. He knew exactly of whom she spoke, and the image appearing in his mind chilled his core. Through his shirt, he felt for the crucifix that John Paul II had given him. It was a source of strength and protection for Ben; he anticipated needing it now more than ever.

Ania took a deep breath and her face suddenly turned confident. "My physical strength became immense—I did feel like a god. I was also invincible and nothing could permanently harm me."

She picked up a metal, mechanical corkscrew from the table and held it in her palm for him to see. She closed her hand, and the sound of crunching metal echoed in Ben's ears. He looked up momentarily at her face—the confident look remained. Slowly, she turned her hand over and dropped what was left of the sturdy bronze implement. Ben looked down and despite the noise he'd heard, was still surprised to see the debris of the formerly well-made tool, which now looked as if it had been run over by a steamroller. Ben gripped his cross firmly as the sight of it registered in his mind.

With his free hand, Ben moved his glass slightly aside and sifted through the metallic shards with a pen. No piece was larger than a pea. He looked at her hand and she turned it upwards. The flesh was torn and bloody. Without any reaction, she plucked the spiraled spike of the corkscrew from the web of her hand. It had pierced the skin on the palm side and

protruded out the back. Blood dripped to the tablecloth and he looked back and forth quickly between
her hand and the white material. Within seconds, the
blood began to vanish, and the jagged flesh mended
itself. His eyes darted to her face and her eyes were
still aflame. As he watched, her pupils eventually
returned to their dark green hue. He looked back to
her hand and saw that it was completed healed. The
spilled blood had vanished. With his own hand, he
picked up the broken fragments, examining each
carefully. He put the pieces down and looked back up
at her, trying to conceal his astonishment.

"This new-found power," she went on, "fueled
the fire of my anger and a beast awoke inside me. In
addition to the strength, my other physical abilities
reached tremendous heights. Had I been allowed to
participate in the games of Olympus, I could have
won any event with ease."

As Ben watched, Ania reached into a nearby
planter and picked up a stone about the size of a golf
ball. She looked around, and saw that no one was
watching. Without even standing up, Ania threw
the rock toward the lake. Ben watched for several
seconds, until he saw a small splash in the water—
over one hundred yards away.

When Ben looked back at her, she saw that his
face was still relaxed, but his eyes were darting from
her hand, to the broken bottle opener, to the lake,
and then back to her face. He had said nothing so far,

nor displayed any overt reactions. She'd never had someone listen that intently before. It was something not even her best students had ever done.

"When I realized what these powers would allow me to do, I set out to act against those who'd murdered my father. Even after their demise, the anger and rage remained. I had hoped that once the murderers were destroyed, my fury would be quenched and satisfaction would develop. In reality it saddened me. By ending those who had murdered him, I became no better than they. My father had many chances to escape, but his beliefs had required that he acquiesce. I'd betrayed his legacy."

Something within Ben did change when he realized Ania had taken human lives. It saddened him that she'd felt the need to exact the ultimate revenge on those who'd taken her father's life. All human life was sacred, and he of all people knew just how much so. As the information sank in, Ben realized he believed her story—he wouldn't have reacted to the killings in this way if he didn't.

Ania saw Ben's subtle look of disappointment when she admitted what she'd done. Long dormant feelings of guilt resurfaced. She pressed on:

"Because of what I'd done, I abandoned everything and fled Athens. I wandered around Greece for years. I learned that friends and family aged and died—yet I remained as I was. How you see me at this moment is the same as I was then."

Ben studied her face. She was Greek, but rather than looking like a modern Mediterranean woman, she seemed reminiscent of ancient Hellenic statuary and even Renaissance paintings. In his many years of study, he'd seen the countenances of many women — women who had lived over a thousand years in the past. He had always found them beautiful, and now, one sat before him. He knew why she was so unique: she was a time traveler from the past. He forgot for a second who she really was and allowed his attraction toward her to surface. His face must have shown something, because she looked quizzically at him. He reset the expression on his face and she followed suit.

"My solitude seemed permanent, and the wandering endless. I stopped marking time after several decades, believing a curse had descended upon me, and that I was to wander the earth alone for eternity. There was no purpose to my life and I felt inhuman."

Ania picked up her wineglass, sniffed it, and took a small sip. The wine meant nothing to her, yet she used it as a pause. What she was about to tell her confessor was something which she feared even he might not be able to accept.

"Shall I continue?" she asked, as she set down her wine.

Ben said nothing, simply making a gesture for her to go on.

"Countless years later, I was in the area of Neapolis, close to the Sea of Crete. Night fell and an inky darkness enveloped the land. There was no moon, and the stars were hiding. I was staring at the water, seeking answers from beneath the surface. I considered praying, but to what being those pleas should have been directed was something I did not know. I hung my head and asked for forgiveness from whatever great and true deity existed — the one I knew must have created the world and all things in it. I eventually lifted my gaze, just enough for something in the water to catch my eye; there was a tremendous brightness, shimmering on the surface — it looked as if the water was aglow. I thought the moon had suddenly appeared, casting its light upon the sea, yet when I looked up, it was not the moon that was glowing with hope."

Ania paused, and an expression of serenity appeared on her face. She looked upwards and closed her eyes. She was now smiling — re-living something momentous.

Ben did not know what to make of her silence. A timeline materialized in his mind, beginning with the presumed death of Socrates, around 400 BC. Doing some crude math in his head, his mind suddenly struck something, and his entire being shuddered. The thought was so strong, and so powerful, that he felt the urge to break his silence and ask her the question she was about to answer. He focused on her eyes and saw that she was already looking into his — she knew exactly what he'd just realized.

"Yes, Ben, it was a star — a glimmering star. It was the largest and brightest celestial being I'd ever seen. And yes, it was four hundred years after my father's passing."

Ania and Ben looked at each other, motionless. She watched as the gravity of what she'd just told him settled in his mind. For the first time, a tense expression appeared on his face. He remained motionless for almost a minute, as if a "pause" button had been pressed. When he finally moved, his sole act was to reach for his full glass of wine. As he picked it up, a small series of ripples traversed the liquid's surface. Ben's hand was imperceptibly shaking. He must have realized this, for he set the glass back down without taking a sip.

"I was unable to take my gaze from this star; not only was it bright and beautiful, but it pulled me toward it. After hundreds of years of aimless and hopeless wandering, something was now drawing me toward it. I crossed the sea, and made my way to the Holy Land. Even as daybreak came, the star was still visible, and had remained still, regardless of how much the earth had moved. The beacon was fixed in position, leading me to a specific place. As darkness fell again, I arrived in the town of Bethlehem. Although the star was high in the sky, it seemed to point to a specific location. Something was about to happen, an event unlike anything the world had ever seen."

Ben's mind was trying to keep up with what he was hearing. He knew what she was about to tell him. While he knew the event had happened, his mind came to a screeching, logical stop. His reason stood up and yelled to his brain that this person was not—could not—have been there on that night. This was all impossible. Up to now, all he'd seen her do were physical acts. She'd had the nail—but what did that mean? There was no other proof that she was over two thousand years old.

"I need to take a walk. I will return momentarily," Ben said, as he abruptly stood up, the chair nearly falling over backward.

Ania began to stand, but Ben stilled her with an outstretched hand. "I need to be alone for a while."

He walked off toward the front of the hotel.

Chapter 31

Steinbeck and Bella Talk

At the end of his campaign, it was all gone. Other than faint whispers about the "New Dark Age," no one discussed anything but reality and that which was tangible and concrete. All their stone buildings had been destroyed and the locations were now green parks. Not even their written materials had survived; no books, articles, stories or even websites existed anymore. The statues, icons, monuments, and shrines were ground into gravel, which was then used to build roads. When people died, their bodies were turned into a biodegradable substance using an environmentally-neutral process, and the residue was released into the sewer. Burial grounds were dug up, bodies liquidated, and the empty land turned into places of "reason" or "logic."

With no religion, organized or otherwise, the world had become tranquil and civilized. With no more wars, there was peace, lives were saved, and little blood was shed. With the lack of death, the world population was stabilized by birth control, terminating unborn lives, forced sterilization, and medically-assisted suicides. With no religiously-influenced thought, morality was not necessary: "logic" and "reason" prevailed. Natural selection was allowed to work as it should; non-productive beings ceased to exist and no longer wasted precious resources. If a pregnancy was not going to produce a functional member of society, it would be terminated. If elderly people couldn't fend for themselves, they were allowed to simply wither and die. If people were injured or became ill, no resources were used to heal them. Medical intervention would only be used if it could economically restore someone to able-bodied productivity.

Evolution provided for survival of the fittest— that is how the animal world worked, and since humans were merely sentient beasts, the same should do for them. By looking at things scientifically and practically, less time, effort, and resources would be used on medicine, and more on technology. Diseases and injuries were nature's way of "thinning the herd." If humans were culled by the same process as animals, most hereditary diseases and defects would literally and figuratively die off. Beloved Margaret's dreams would finally be fulfilled.

With no fantasy-based moral guidance, eugenics would work as it should, the world's population would diminish, and the earth could recover from the strain of overpopulation. The impact of man would diminish.

The world would finally be at peace, and humans might someday evolve further, and the possibilities were endless.

Seth Steinbeck's dream continued, seemingly on its own. He did not know that someone lying next to him was watching his dream, enjoying it immensely.

Chapter 32

Ben Ponders

Ben walked past the front of the hotel and into a park across the street. His mind was reeling and he needed somewhere quiet to settle it down. A full-blown conflict raged inside his head — seemingly opposite, yet equal forces fought for control of his thoughts. Skepticism and belief traded repeated blows, with neither showing signs of relenting. This kind of conflict was a new experience for Ben Airaldi. He sat down on a wood bench and took some deep breaths.

Fictions were easy to suspend belief for — one knew from the outset that they were made up. Any story, even those above and beyond any threshold of reality, could be digested because one knew from the start that they were not true. Told in a story, tale, or fable, Ania's background and abilities would have made for great entertainment. Told at length, they would make a best-selling book. A cinematic telling

would be a blockbuster. The problem was that what
Ben had just heard and seen was presented as fact.

If not for the extraordinary things he'd seen in the
last few days, he would have concluded that Doctor
Athania X. Socratatos had lost her mind. She was
renowned as a brilliant professor, but Ben knew well
that no mind was immune to fantasies and delusions;
he'd met many "educated" people in various intellectual settings, yet some of the things they spouted
were pure lunacy. Some of the world's greatest
thinkers, writers, inventors and respected leaders
occasionally veered off the road of rational thought
and into the ruts of insanity. Brilliance and "bonkers"
were on each side of the same coin.

Ben opened a file on his phone, and pulled up a
photo of Ania. He'd saved it from a website that he'd
visited shortly before first meeting her. He wasn't
sure why he'd saved her image—in fact he didn't
remember consciously doing it. The picture was
from the university's website, and looked recent—at
least, from what he could guess, seeing as she herself
supposedly didn't age. Ania's smile was serene and
relaxed, atypical of most posed photos. Looking at her
eyes, he wondered if they really were the windows
into her soul. He shut the phone and closed his eyes.
He deepened his breaths, and worked at clearing his
mind. As he meditated, the image of a plain white
piece of paper appeared. A heading materialized on
it which read "Publications." Beneath that appeared

a paragraph listing her substantial body of written
work. He'd read nearly all of it in the last few years,
focusing on anything connected to the Church. After
a few minutes, the blank page he envisioned filled up
with titles of books, articles, and treatises written by
this enigmatic woman. Additional pages filled with
synopsis after synopsis of her work. Rereading the
words he visioned, he recognized no evidence or patterns that she was imbalanced, or even slightly "off."
Every word was used properly, and every paragraph
read smoothly. In the end, the only conclusion to be
reached was that she was brilliant. She was the best
writer he'd ever encountered.

Ben opened his eyes and absorbed the solace.
He was the only person in the small park and was
glad for it. Closing his lids once again, he resumed
his meditation and a new blank sheet materialized.
The heading "Personal Life" appeared at the top
of the imaginary page. Unlike the previous surface,
words emerged more slowly, and the facts were
sparse. He realized there was a dearth of information with regards to her personal details. In the days
before their first meeting, Ben had looked up her
biographical information, hoping they would be able
to "connect." He'd always tried to learn in advance
something about people he was about to meet for the
first time—it was a habit picked up as an investigator.
Whether it was a victim, witness, or even a perpe-
trator, knowing something about them allowed the

interview to progress smoothly. Not only that—Ben simply wanted to know who he was about to meet.

Returning his thoughts to Doctor Socratatos, he remembered having discovered little about her social or personal life. Her academic pedigree was well-documented and substantial, but there was little about her as an individual. He'd read about her emigration from Greece decades earlier, and how she'd spent all her time since learning, teaching, and writing. He had found no mention of her life on the Agean—not even so much as a blip. Other than the school's website, there was little to be found anywhere else. Many sites referenced her publications and literary reviews, but nothing more. She had no Internet "footprint," and he had found nothing about her on social media. Her relative anonymity was not uncommon—some people had no desire to broadcast every detail of their personal lives or inner thoughts to the world. Other than two e-mail accounts, Ben himself wasn't much for electronic communication. His preference was for face-to-face interaction, and when that was not possible, he relied on printed words.

Ben opened his eyes once more, and saw that he was still alone. He closed them once again and deep breathing resumed. A third blank page appeared in his mind and the word "Observations" quickly materialized on it. It noted that Ania presented herself as reserved, even a little shy. Nothing about her behavior gave any hint that she was "off." He replayed

everything that had transpired up until the incident
with the flat tire, but nothing remarkable came to
mind. He recalled every word she'd said and every
expression she'd made — still nothing.

Ben could coax nothing that was remotely strange
about her into his memory before the roadside
accident. Until the breakdown, Ben had observed
no irregularities in her persona. He recalled his first
impressions of her, and nothing was out of the ordinary. There were a few odd phrases she'd used, but
since English was not her native language, he gave it
little consideration. Suppressing any images since the
accident, a sudden memory pierced the veil his mind
was holding: there was a character from an old TV
series Ben used to watch as a kid — an eminent archaeologist, who spent years studying ancient Egypt —
was struck on the head by a falling rock during an
archeological expedition. After regaining consciousness, the highly-accomplished scholar believed he
was King Amun-Ra. Ben wondered if it was possible
that something similar had happened to Ania. She
had spent many years studying ancient Greece…that
was a stretch, he thought.

Shifting gears, he did remember that her
demeanor had changed slightly once they'd arrived
in Germany — she had become even more reserved.
He'd chalked it up to the fact that she was more
of a thinker than a talker, and now that they were
"in-country," she was "all business." Coming to

Germany was the first step in seeking answers to a historical puzzle. Someone like her would be extremely on-task, considering what was at hand. Ania's being more silent and introspective may simply have been a way to prepare herself for the upcoming task. He himself did tend to quiet down when he was focused. The situation reminded him of a saying his father had once shared with him: "Those who don't know talk. Those who know don't talk."

If that was the case, then Ania knew even more than Ben had imagined.

Chapter 33

Seth and Bella Talk

"You must have had a great dream last night…"
Bella waved her celery stalk like a magic wand as she
spoke, then took a greedy bite.

"Do I talk in my sleep?" Seth set down his cup and
wiped his mouth with a napkin. He noticed a mischie-
vous gleam in his paramour's eyes.

"Not that I can tell. You slept like the dead. I know
I do when my dreams are pleasant." Bella seductively
chewed on the green stump.

"It was one of my 'What a Wonderful World'
dreams." Seth sang the words as his eyes closed
dreamily.

"Let me guess: a world free of religion and all its
useless trappings." She washed her garnish's rema-
nats down with a long pull of her Bloody Mary.

"Good guess. It's a wonderful daydream: no
religion, no fanciful beliefs, no chicanery…a world at
peace."

"So a simple, efficient planet, no fluff. I've had that dream too. Only I think it's a tangible possibility. It's just a matter of getting the right people in power. Things in the last five years or so appear to be slowly heading that way." Bella speared a piece of her steak tartare and twirled it for emphasis.

Seth didn't consciously see it, but his traveling companion had a taste for nearly-raw meat and red-colored liquids.

"Things have improved considerably since about 1964," he said. "It's been slow, but thankfully, every new decade brings more clarity of thought to the world. Maybe in our lifetimes we may see it come to fruition. You know, 'I may not get there with you, but...'" He knew that she knew where the words came from.

Bella knew it was improbable Seth would see that dream come true in his lifetime. She knew that he had only another thirty-three years left to live. Since her time left was unlimited, she knew she'd see it. It was ironic that he'd used a phrase from Martin Luther King's speech. She was directly involved in ensuring that King had not seen the things he'd dreamt of.

Chapter 34

Ben Ponders More

Ben was lost in thought—the concept of time eluded him. The sun's position told him an hour had passed. His mind was much quieter than earlier—the conflict still remained, but the two combatants within him were resting in their respective corners. No conclusion had yet been reached. Before ringing the bell and restarting the mental bout, something dawned on him: he'd not asked for guidance.

With clasped hands and bowed head, Ben prayed. After reciting the Our Father and Hail Mary, he initiated a series of reflective prayers, asking for guidance and wisdom. Whenever he was in doubt or indecision, Ben gave his thoughts over to the Lord and waited patiently for the light of revelation.

He prayed for almost thirty minutes, then opened his eyes and realized that his senses seemed sharper and his mind clearer. The idea that Ania was delusional presented itself gently once again. A mental illness might address her claims that she was the daughter of the philosopher Socrates. However, that did not explain her strength and miraculous healing ability. He'd seen two separate instances where her body healed itself of serious injuries in mere seconds. These were not magic tricks or illusions, and his mind was not playing any tricks. He'd studied human anatomy and biology extensively, and knew the human body could not do what he'd seen hers do. He thought of what she'd done to the bottle opener earlier. She was inordinately strong. The bodily repairs and strength were real events. Where did she get them from, he wondered? Suddenly a new answer to the question startled him:

Demonic possession?

His mind wandered to the possibility that she was a malevolent entity: evil incarnate, sent to lead him astray.

He knew more about exorcisms than most clergy. Father Candido was to be thanked for that. He'd never seen extraordinary healing abilities such as hers, but the experienced exorcist had told him of seeing them. This elderly man of God had told Ben of instances where a possessed person's actual physiology changed, right before his eyes. Wounds suddenly appeared, and disappeared just as quickly. Eyes changed colors, skin developed new textures, and limbs twisted themselves into pretzel-like shapes.

The things he'd seen in Ania were consistent with symptoms of a possession. He would guess that it

really was a demonic influence, but countering that
was the fact that she had the fourth nail: one of the
many tortures Christ was forced to endure. This
unknown, holy relic was only mentioned briefly in an
ancient text, written at the time of the Apostles. Only
Ben and a handful of other living people knew of the
legend of this nail. If she was trying to trick him, why
of all things would she have presented that particular
item as proof of her *bona fides*? She could not know
that the other three nails were in Rome, and that he'd
personally overseen their scientific analysis. Of course
evil beings knew inner secrets, and used them as
needed. Of all the things he'd had to debate, the nails'
authenticity was not one of them. He had no doubt
that what she'd presented him was real. In addition
to not only having the iron device, it also had fresh
blood on it, blood that glowed when brought into the
vicinity of the other three. If her evidence was counterfeit, it would not have reacted as it did.

Ben picked up a small stick and poked the center
of his palm until it hurt. He imagined what a piece of
cruel metal might feel like.

His mind may have wavered, but his mental steps
were even and consistent. He focused on what he'd
seen of her abilities, and nothing else. How could
a human have the healing ability and strength she
demonstrated?

His mind drifted back in the thought that she
was possessed, or even a demon in human form. Ben

knew that evil existed, but unlike many fellow believers, he also knew that there was a "living" entity known as Satan. Other Christians had faint notions of an evil being, but it was an abstract thought. Ben knew that the Prince of Darkness was an active, scheming, and energetic being. The devil was everywhere, and always active.

Ben knew that his brethren believed in the Lord Christ, God the Father, and the Holy Spirit, but many were unable to grasp that there was a real devil: Lucifer, in all his malevolent and prideful glory.

Ben's extensive study of history clearly showed how the Evil One had shaped world history. When he was young, evil was an intangible concept, even to someone like himself. When he began his work in Rome, he'd had first-hand encounters with demons. He'd been present during several exorcisms, and what he saw was evil in the flesh. These were not simply people with mental illnesses—they were truly possessed by Satan, or one of his demons. He remembered that even small children, possessed by diabolical forces, were capable of tremendous strength. That inhuman power was one of the symptoms of a possession. He'd been present during an exorcism of a ten-year-old girl, who was thrashing about on her bed. Four strong men had tried to restrain her and prevent her from gouging her own face off. He'd been beside Father Candido, merely as an observer. When the girl flung two men off her and against the wall, Ben had sprung into action and grabbed one of her arms: it felt as if an elephant's trunk was whipping him about. The girl was no more than fifty pounds, yet she swung Ben around like a rag doll. The closest thing he could compare it to was when he'd been talked into riding a mechanical bull in college. He'd lasted about five seconds on the whirling contraption before being violently cast off. Yet the afflicted girl had had three times the force of that electro-mechanical steer. Although he could maintain a grip on the girl's skinny limb, he'd been swung against all four walls of the small room, the ceiling, and the floor. After several minutes, Ben's and the other men's strength had started to fade. Thankfully the exorcist's prayers took effect and the girl had calmed down. He never actually saw the demon leave, but he knew it had gone when the girl's beastly strength dissipated and he could easily control her arm. He'd never forgotten that day.

Was Ania a demon? But how could she have been in possession of the nail? Demons could be in any place: churches, convents, monasteries, holy places, anywhere. There was no physical barrier to their movement. However, they could not possess holy relics: such objects were their "Kryptonite." No demon could have been so close to it, let alone have it on them.

What was she then? If not a demon, was she a test? Could the Lord be testing him, similar to the

Story of Job? In Job's case, the trial was clear: would he still praise the Lord, even during the worst of afflictions?

But what was Ben's test? Ania had asked nothing of him — on the contrary, she'd given him the holiest of relics: an actual iron spike that was used during the Crucifixion. The Crucifixion! Was she about to ask something of him? Was her presence in his life now, her presence in the mystery of the crosses, leading to something?

He was finding himself drawn to her. She was beautiful. He had entertained fleeting thoughts of seeing her socially after their work was done — it was only natural. But was he attracted to her as a person, an individual? Or was she using her wiles, the way Jezebel and Delilah had? Was she trying to lure him astray? He had knowledge of and access to things and places within Rome that no one could ever dream of. Was she after the other nails? Was she after the spear? Was she after the Vatican? These questions ran circles in his mind.

Upon walking to the other side of the park, he discovered that his prayers had led him somewhere significant. He looked up at a figure on a nearby roof's apex and made the Sign of the Cross. He thought for a moment. Then he decided that if he was being tested, he was going to go through it willingly, and pray for the strength to get endure it.

Ben turned around and walked quickly back to the hotel. Whatever Ania was, he was going to find out. Regardless of what she offered or told him, he would use his faith to guide him. Whether she was a lost soul, an angel, a demon, or something undefined, Ben Airaldi was going to find out and if need be... he'd act.

Chapter 35

On Holy Ground

Standing in the vestibule, Ben watched Ania's slow yet steady approach come to an abrupt halt. It was as if an invisible barrier had suddenly materialized in front of her. Backlit by the sun, her profile reminded him of a Victorian silhouette. If he accepted her story as true, then the owner of this silhouette preceded the birth of England's Queen Victoria by eighteen hundred years.

The juxtaposition of her dark outline against the bright light caused the words "angel" and "lost" to waft through his mind. Her eyes were cast downward, hinting at residual shame.

Ben's working theory was that this enigmatic woman was perched on a fence between two realities: "evil" and "good." Her reluctance to enter the church might have tipped his belief in the former, but her look of utter humility gently nudged it back. A third possibility emerged: she was trapped between two worlds, and the fence upon which she balanced was

her limbo. With a warm smile, and a gentle wave, he
beckoned her inside the church. Her response was
a short, cautious step, moving barely an inch. Her
subsequent movements were hesitant, reminiscent of
a baby learning to walk. She stopped at the threshold
and took a deep breath...with a shudder, and no
further prodding, she slowly crossed over.

"I do not belong here," she said, her eyes glued to
the vestibule's gleaming marble floor.

"Why do you say that? How can you say that?
You know more of Him than anyone living today.
This is *His* house—all are welcome." Ben peered
through the glass windows in the doors between the
vestibule and the church's interior.

"I do not know. When He was born, I...I thought
things would change...they did—but not for me.
When He died, my condition remained as it is today.
My horrible transgressions may be unforgivable. I've
been this way for so long, it appears it is permanent."
Ania's eyes flicked briefly up to his, then quickly back
down.

Ben gently cupped her elbow and was surprised
when she yielded; five minutes earlier, when they
were a hundred feet from the church, she'd stopped
dead in her tracks, realizing where he was taking her.
She had planted her feet in the middle of the sidewalk, and refused to move. He'd softly touched her
arm and she felt like a statue: immovable and just as
solid. His hand loosely encircled her wrist—there had

been no movement whatsoever. He was half a foot taller and had about eighty pounds on her, but that made no difference. The smaller woman could not be moved. This had reminded Ben of his first occupation, many years earlier. Back then he'd wrestled many a time with passively-resistive people, some bigger and some smaller than he. Regardless of the size, even a three-hundred-pound giant could be moved with the right touch. But at this moment, Ben would have had a better chance moving a granite block than Ania Socratatos.

After entering the vestibule, Ania allowed him to walk her right up to the inner doors, but she stopped again, her feet stuck to the ground.

"Please, I can't." She turned her upper body away slightly.

"You can — your sins are not unforgivable — that is why He gave His life for us." Ben opened the door and she reluctantly allowed him to draw her inside.

With Ben by her side, Ania walked awkwardly, as if her feet were sticking to the floor. She allowed herself to focus on images projected onto the ground by the stained-glass windows. Ten steps in, she stopped once again, and noticed that Ben was no longer by her side. From her peripheral vision, she saw him dip his hand in a font of holy water and bless himself. He walked up to her.

"Let us sit," he said, pointing to a pew. He knelt on one knee, blessed himself again, and sat down on the well-worn seat.

Hesitantly, she did the same, and as she did, a tingling sensation kissed her knee and radiated into her body. Although the floor looked cool and hard, the sensation felt by her kneecap was pure softness and warmth. It was as if she'd genuflected on a bed of sun-warmed straw. Something was suddenly different.

Ania still refused to look up at the altar, but she allowed herself to settle back against the bench. Ben watched her for a moment, then knelt on the thinly-padded kneeler and began to pray silently.

Although Ben believed pure evil had marked her permanently, the things that had transpired since the car incident had replaced feelings of fear and revulsion with empathy and sorrow. Even though her eyes remained downcast, she was here with him, and that told him there was a profound struggle within her. Ben surmised that her refusal to look up at the altar was borne of shame, and not repulsion.

Ania followed Ben's lead and knelt by him. He quietly recited the Our Father, just loud enough for her to hear. As he prayed, he sensed that some of her tension evaporate. As he progressed to the Hail Mary, his mind concurrently replayed the things he'd seen, heard, and felt since first meeting her. The image of the nail she had given him came to the forefront of his thoughts.

An image of the Holy Grail appeared alongside that of the nail in his mind. The existence of the cup of Christ was a well-known legend, and not only to believers. The earliest stories of the Grail had surfaced several centuries after the Crucifixion and continued to the present day. The story of the nail predated that, surfacing as early as the immediate days after the Crucifixion, but mention of it was no longer referenced so much as a year afterwards. Ben Airaldi was one of the few people who were able to read and understand one of the oldest of ancient texts that told the story of the nail. He'd only seen the texts when they were discovered a decade earlier and had surprised his colleagues by translating them with ease.

Ben looked over at his companion—she appeared to be praying. He had an idea and reached into his pocket.

"Open your hand...please," he said quietly.

She did as he requested, knowing what he was about to do. With closed eyes, she felt him place it in her palm. The sensation initially felt like a burn, but in actuality, it was intense warmth.

Ben clasped her hand and closed her fingers around the cross. The contact with his hand caused dizziness to return to her. Her belief was that he was righteous and that she was the opposite, which made his touch like an antiseptic to her curse. She gripped the cross tightly and Ben removed his hand. Tingling developed from the warmth, and went from her hand and up her arm. A firm, yet painless jolt went right to her heart, causing her to straighten up. With closed eyes, she turned her head toward the altar.

Ben watched her. He could see that something was changing within her. Where fear and confusion had occupied his thoughts earlier, something in him was drawing his thoughts to her. Her eyes still closed, he studied her face; she looked to be enveloped in complete serenity. He studied the contours of her chin, tracing them to her cheeks, and then her eyes. Her countenance was like nothing he'd seen before. Remembering the sculptures and paintings he'd studied during his lifetime, it dawned on him that he actually *had* seen her face somewhere before. In a fantastical reach, he wondered if maybe she'd been used as a model for an ancient Greek artwork. He'd seen thousands of Hellenic statues over the years, and something about her appearance kept sending his mind in that direction.

Looking toward the altar and closing his eyes, he visualized her in the flowing dress of an Athenian. He allowed his mind to wander and drift, and after fifteen minutes, his focus returned to the present. He opened his eyes and looked at her. Her eyes were open too, but her eyelids fluttered as if she was being exposed to bright light. There was a new glow in them; it looked as if she were watching a flickering candle. As she kept her eyes open longer, the glow in them intensified. She was looking directly at the crucifix above the altar. There was a look of sadness on her face, as if she was present once more at the Crucifixion.

"Why were His enemies after the fourth nail? It shouldn't have held any significance for them," Ben asked, looking up at the altar.

"They had no concern for the nail, something that small couldn't be used as a symbol." She looked down at the floor in front of the altar.

"You told me that when you picked up the nail, the centurion thought you were a demon—because of your eyes." Something in Ben's mind tried to get his attention.

"He was actually the one who had the nail. He gave it to me later. He thought I was a demon because I was able to lift the…"

She never finished, because Ben suddenly looked as if he'd been struck by lightning. His eyes shot up to the cross; the statue of Christ's body was life-size, and the cross upon which it was hanging was also of life-size proportions.

In the span of several moments, his mind flashed images of countless paintings, statues, and carvings. He remembered the depictions in movies of Christ moving slowly toward the place where he would die.

Athania saw the puzzlement in Ben's eyes, and realized he had not known, up to that moment, what she'd actually taken from the "place of the skull."

Ben remembered his studies of history — that of Western civilization, and the Church itself. He thought of Constantine's mother, and what she'd found. He wondered if it was possible that…

"Athania Socratatos," Ben whispered to her in the original Greek dialect. "Where is it?!"

Unable to take her eyes off the altar, she knew that this was the time. "It is closer than you could imagine."

Another jolt struck Ben. He remembered what he'd seen at the dig and all the photos of the bombs.

Ben stood and placed his hand on her shoulder. He looked down into her still glowing eyes. "Please Ania, take me to it."

She looked up at him and saw something in his eyes that she'd not seen in two millennia: understanding.

Chapter 36

Revelation

Ania and Ben's drive back to the dig was much different from their first. Whereas that one was relaxed and calm, this one was anything but.

Ben maneuvered the car in his typical, careful manner, but his focus was clearly not on his driving. Ania could feel a wave of tension radiating from him, and it was affecting her. He was anticipating a life-changing revelation. He was about to see something no other living human had seen in two thousand years.

Ania's unease was from the knowledge that she was revealing the location of something she'd kept hidden for so long.

Ben parked the rental on the outskirts of the dig's activity, hiding it behind a row of trailers. He wished to avoid the attention of Doctor O'Toole. The eminent historian and archeologist was an astute observer, and would most certainly sense something. On top of that, Ben did not want to be stopped by the good professor's verbosity, which could delay them for hours. The affable scientist could talk all day if given the chance.

"Show me," was Ben's first utterance in thirty minutes.

Ania led Ben into the tree line opposite the west side of the dig. Nothing was spoken, but the understanding between them was clear. As they hiked purposefully in silence, a soft fog of serenity suddenly enveloped Ben. He'd been angst-ridden from the moment they left the church, but all that vanished the moment his feet touched this ground. During the ride from the chapel, he'd searched his memory, recalling everything he thought he knew and believed. The events of the last week had flooded his mind with volumes of information, and that data created even more questions for him. His knowledge and beliefs had lived in harmony for his entire life, and recent events were upsetting that balance. The picture unfolding in his mind would have been too much for anyone to absorb, but Ben Airaldi was no ordinary person. His deep and abiding faith gave him a rare mental strength, which kept the facts of the blossoming situation from overwhelming him.

While Ben prepared himself for what he was about to see, Ania was consumed by a whirlwind of sensations. She remembered that Marcus of Capernaum was the only other human who'd ever been in the cave, let alone knew what was hidden within. He'd been gone for almost two millennia, and Ania was the only one alive who knew about the ensconcement and its contents. She trusted Ben, but she didn't know what would happen after he'd seen the contents. The treasure was not hers, but she considered herself its protector. What was happening at this moment caused her to question her qualities as the object's lone guardian. Ania was prepared to wait as long as it took for Him to return, and reclaim what was rightfully His. Ben's discovery of her true nature, and what she'd protected all these years, was not something she'd anticipated. But it had happened, and she would have to deal with it. She likened her situation to that of old Pandora. The difference was that the ancient Greek character had let something out into the world that could not be controlled. In this particular case, Ania was about to let an uncontrollable world into her special refuge.

Ben followed Ania along the invisible path into the rolling green hills. He was quiet, lost in deep thought.

"We are close."

Her words pulled his attention back to the outside world. He looked ahead and saw a rock ridge in the distance.

She knew they were quickly approaching a point of no return — once Ben knew the location of the cave, the rest of the world might know it too.

As they continued along the gradually-changing terrain, Ania remembered being alone with the treasure; its mere presence nourished and sustained something within her that she didn't know she had — faith. When Marcus left her, Ania had secluded herself in the cave, prepared to wait as long as needed. Being in the stone shelter, alone with the actual object that had given hope to humanity, was an experience she'd never wanted to end. She would have stayed for eternity, if that would have redeemed her cursed soul. The only reason she'd left the cave when she did was due to an earthquake that had seemed to stretch the cave in multiple directions. The hollow had remained intact, but the violence of the movement made her think the earth had shattered. While the cave had survived, the entrance to it had been partially buried. The change was fortuitous, as it had created additional rock barriers between the outside entrance and the ravine. The cavern was well-hidden before the quake, and afterwards, it was all but invisible.

Making their way down the cliffs, Ben could feel it; pure energy emanated from the ground, and it seemed to pull him toward it. He was eager to reach the site, but that eagerness was tempered by the realization that what he expected to see had not been seen by human eyes for two millennia. He remembered attending catechism classes as a child and wondering why the Ark of the Covenant and the Grail seemed to be a focus of history, while other more significant things were not. He thought back to several hours earlier, when it had dawned on him that the nail wasn't the only thing she'd taken from Golgotha, the "place of the skull."

At the bottom of the ravine, the air was becoming electric. Not a word had been said during the descent, but it became clear to both of them that a threshold was about to crossed. Ben looked at the face of the rock wall, and a dark circle appeared before him. Ania parted a growth of vegetation, exposing an opening. When his eyes adjusted, he saw the shape of a natural entrance in the rock. The light was dim, but enough was present to make the interior of a small cave discernable. They stepped in, but there seemed to be nowhere further to go. He was about to speak, but stayed silent as Ania began pulling herself up a wall by small cracks in the stone. He followed her.

Although Ben was strong and fit, scaling the wall with his finger and toe tips taxed his body. After what seemed like an eternity, Ben looked down to see that he was almost fifteen feet up. Looking higher, he did not see Ania, until she peered over at him from a ledge another five feet up. Ben struggled up another foot when Ania offered her hand. He was about to reach up when she took a firm grip of his wrist; he was quickly, yet gently, lifted up and deposited on the flat surface next to her. Though she was smaller than he, she had picked Ben up as if he were a child's doll.

His eyes adjusted further, and even though the light from outside was twenty feet below, he could see better than he'd thought possible. He realized that they were on a ledge, about ten-feet wide and five-feet deep. The rock surrounding them had no further openings. When he looked at Ania, she sensed his question, and answered it by stepping over to the vertical stone surface at the inner end of the ledge. She placed her hands flat against the rock, and pushed. After a second, a loud scraping sound echoed in the stone chamber. He watched in awe as she moved what looked to be a large portion of granite wall. It was a truck-sized rock that she shifted several feet, and a gap appeared between the rock and the wall.

Ben was about to reach into his pocket for his pen-light, but when he looked up at Ania, he dropped it; her eyes were glowing as bright as burning phosphorous, and they cast a warm blue light wherever she looked. He'd seen them aglow earlier, but that was nothing compared to what he saw now. He replaced the light in his pocket. It was clear that they needed no artificial illumination.

Ania turned, and her light revealed a passageway directly ahead. She moved forward, and he instinctively followed.

As they walked, her eyes illuminated the passageway as if she were holding a torch. He was about to ponder this, when suddenly his energy level swelled; he was close to something powerful, and it was affecting him in ways he'd never experienced before. Whatever he was getting close to was radiating a force that he felt as "peace." The only thing that was even remotely similar was when he was deep in prayer — something he could do for hours when time permitted.

After about ten minutes, Ania stopped and turned to Ben; the light in her eyes no longer blinded him, and he could see her pupils.

"We are here." She motioned behind her.

A faint outline appeared in the dark where she was gesturing, and Ben recognized it immediately. He fell to his knees and then forward, flat on the ground, affected to his very core.

Chapter 37

Bella Tells Steinbeck about the Treasure

Their eyes were locked, held fast by a mutual trance. No words passed between them, but the message he received was clear: she was hiding something, but wanted desperately to reveal it. Seth Steinbeck had only known Bella a short while, but he was good at reading people's non-verbal "tells." Thinking she was just like any other human, he was sure she'd be easy to read.

He was thinking about how to broach the subject, but she moved first.

"How did you do that trick with the balls during the seminar?" she asked, with a cock of her head.

He forgot everything he was about to ask and chuckled. The "bouncing ball" trick was his favorite — he always laughed inwardly at what he could pull off. He'd never told anyone how it was done — the only other person who knew the secret was his assistant. Many had asked, yet it was the one thing he kept to himself, a magical secret that would haunt people to their dying day. Anyway, magicians weren't allowed to reveal their secrets.

"Would you believe I'm psychic?" He raised an eyebrow.

"Up until a week ago, I might have believed it, but having gotten to know you, it is clear that you do not believe in psychic abilities." She smiled.

"I guess there's no use keeping up the pretense. It was a simple parlor trick." He smiled back.

"I know that—but how did you do it?" she prodded.

"You have no theories? But your level of wisdom and intelligence is rare." He smirked.

"There were too many people involved for it to have been staged. My guess is that electronics was involved."

"Well if I could ever be accused of having a 'religion,' then technology would be it. I worship all things digital and wireless." He absentmindedly fingered his smartphone. He was a prolific user of his device, constantly communicating his thoughts and ideas via social media. But whenever he was with this sultry woman, the phone never left his pocket.

"I think you used wireless cameras, but you were not looking at a monitor. How the information made its way into your labyrinthical mind puzzles me. Even with all the tech in the world, there's no way you did it by yourself." She steepled her fingers, as if in deep thought.

"Well, Moses had Aaron, that Carpenter had the Apostles, Elijah had Muhammad, Buddha had…" Seth trailed off with another wiggle of his brows.

"You're driving me nuts, just spill it!" she said in mock exasperation.

"Simple. When we were setting up the day before, I hid a network of wireless cameras in the ceiling tiles, directly over the seats. When the game went 'hot,' my assistant was backstage, closely watching monitors. I had a tiny Bluetooth earpiece in my ear—just like that candidate used in the last debate. My assistant simply watched what the person wrote on their note pad, then told me via my earbud." Steinbeck sat back and folded his arms in satisfaction.

"Ingenious. I would have figured for the camera angle, but your showmanship made it look like you could really read minds." She reached over and squeezed his forearm.

"It was rather simple; the only issue was making sure the victim—I mean participant—wrote the numbers legibly on their note pads. The cameras were great, but a few times, a participant was holding the pad in a way the camera couldn't view."

"How did you get around that?" she asked.

"My assistant would tell me she couldn't read the number, so I'd play the target, feed their ego, and tell them their mind was complex and nearly impenetrable. I'd ask them to write the number larger, and focus harder. The flattery angle always worked and once the numbers were big, my confederate could see it." He smiled.

"Brilliant. Do you think they believe you to be psychic?" She looked at him admiringly.

"The smart ones knew it was a trick. The rubes thought I really had ESP." He smirked once more.

She laughed with a bright face, then clouded with seriousness.

"My beloved Seth, I must share something with you, something you may not want to hear. I debated whether to tell you, but for the sake of possibly all humankind, it was clear to me that you of all people would know what to do." Bella looked deep into his eyes, into his soul.

He felt something pierce his brain.

"I knew you were hiding something." He looked calm, yet his insides were roiling with anticipation.

"I am not one to blow things out of proportion—I've seen much in my years of study, and this possible event causes me to fear for humanity." She suddenly looked pained.

Seth was logical, almost to a fault. He mentally processed what she'd told him so far. Perhaps she was about to tell him that she was married or possibly bisexual. He could easily deal with personal matters like that, but the word "humanity" told him that she was talking of something much greater. He, too, was afraid for humanity — fearing that all religions might gain in strength in the coming years.

"Bella, there is something about you that I've been unable to pin down in my mind. You know, I don't even know your last name…"

She cut him off.

"My last name is Deville, Anabella Lucifa. I thought you knew it. I've always thought my full name revealed too much, especially to strangers. Bella is what I prefer." She smiled shyly.

"Anabella Lucifa Deville — it's beautiful, you should use it boldly — sounds regal and exalted." He said her name as if with pride.

"When I first started out, my name was something I was highly proud of. It did make me feel regal, like royalty, above all my peers. In fact, I once made a crown out of branches and considered myself the greatest ruler of all. I had a fun time until…" Bella trailed off, looking wistfully at the sky.

Seth was amused. He too had liked to imagine that he was the emperor of the world; he would then have been able to impose his thoughts and beliefs on everyone. Those that followed him would be rewarded; those that didn't, well…

"It sounds like this is something serious," he said. "Please tell me."

"I went to your seminar that day, hoping to find someone to share this with, someone who might know what to do, and succeed at it. When I saw you up there speaking, well, that moment made me certain I had come to the right place. Of course the idea of 'seduction' never came to my mind." She cast her eyes downward, as if she thought he'd seduced her. The opposite was what had actually occurred.

Seth did feel as if he'd seduced her. She was alluring and mysterious, but he knew that he was the one truly in charge and that he'd planned on bedding her the night he met her. He succeeded. He wasn't much of a player; his calling kept him too busy for that. Inevitably, every seminar offered a selection of naïve women, and all he needed to do was regale them with his personal philosophy and to have them hanging on every word. Most of the sexual experiences were pleasurable, but he considered them a victory if the woman was religious—especially if she was Christian. "Please, if you've put your faith in me, I do want to help."

She looked up at him—a look of sadness and worry lined the smooth skin of her face.

"The background story about how this came to be is not important—it started long ago, longer than anyone living might remember. The real issue is what's going on now, at this moment. I was on the periphery of the plan; my original intent was to stop this scheme from ever getting off the ground. It started with a bang, but quickly ended with the proverbial death and burial of the idea. Unfortunately, the still-active grifter dug the idea back up and it has continued in earnest. My original idea was that I could reason with the author of the plot, talk him out of doing it, but he was so…firm a believer in what he was doing. The authorities knew what he was doing, but didn't act in time, and the idea lifted off and reached the heavens. Very soon, this fanatical plan may explode and flourish. You are the one rational being that can save the world from the greatest con ever played." She looked up at him, imploring him with her eyes.

As Seth's pride swelled like a balloon filling rapidly with water, he was certain he would be the one to help her, take charge of things, and deal with this unknown situation. "What is it? I may be a mere mortal, but I will be your champion — I will vanquish your dragon."

Bella looked at him with tears in her eyes, not of sadness, but of joy. She proceeded to tell him what was going on at the outskirts of the German town of Aachen. She knew that he would be the one to get her task done. He was not psychic, but she relished the fact that she had a power much greater than the ability to read minds: she could read souls.

Chapter 38

The Search

Ben and Athania walked away from the ravine in silence. Deep shadows penetrated the rock formations, revealing the fact that many hours had passed while they were inside. The concept of time held no significance for her, but Ben could mentally track minutes like a clock. The half day they'd been with the treasure had passed like seconds to him, revealing a profound change that had occurred in his life. The Ben Airaldi who had just left the stone sanctuary was not the same one who went in.

Ben was eerily silent, but given what he'd just seen, it was no surprise to Ania; there was much to digest. She'd had many years to do so, while he had only had hours. Thinking back to when he first saw the object, she had seen Ben collapse on the ground; her first thought was that he'd passed out, and she hurried toward him. But the soft words of an old Latin prayer froze her movement. If she'd harbored concerns that Ben might not believe what he was seeing, they rapidly vanished. His reverent recitations made it clear that this bright and learned scholar recognized what stood before him — no other confirmation was needed. As he continued praying, Ania had gingerly stepped back and sat noiselessly on a small boulder. Just before closing her eyes in meditation, she saw that Ben's diminutive flashlight had fallen next to him. The fob-sized light had bathed the object in an aura of pure, white light. Its illumination gave the object the appearance of levitating. What she saw at that moment was vastly different from what she remembered from her first time here. The first mortal who came with her had used firelight to guide his way. The light cast about now was the result of modern technology. As her mind drifted to a quiet place, she debated whether the same science that brought this new light to the cave was any indication of the world's readiness for what might be revealed.

Athania remembered the time so long ago, when she had initially retreated into the rock fortress. The only other human being who'd been here with her was Marcus, and, sadly, he was long dead. Ania held a fervent hope that the young Capernian had done well and thrived. Although she wondered where he'd gone after leaving her, Ania Socratatos knew for an absolute fact that his life was not ordinary. The young boy had only been alive when they met because of his father's faith. The righteous centurion believed in something he couldn't see yet knew to be true. Yes,

Marcus's father, considered a lowly pagan by the "learned elders," had demonstrated more faith and humility than they ever had...or would. The Roman's deep convictions had saved his adopted son from the throes of death. From that point forward, Marcus Capernas was a member of a small, yet gifted group of people: those touched by God's healing hand.

Walking quietly alongside Ania, Ben's mind raced, attempting to process all he'd heard and experienced in the last few days. Although his eyes stung from what they'd just seen, strangely, his soul felt a comfort that overwhelmed any physical pain his pupils may have suffered. He thought that pain was not the right word for what his eyes felt — the exact word eluded him, but he likened it to what an infant must feel after having been born. Eyes closed since conception were now opened to a new and strange world outside the womb. While he couldn't remember his infancy, it's what he felt to be an apt comparison.

As they walked, his thoughts of what she was were changing. There was no evil in her — that was impossible, considering what she'd just revealed. He surmised that she was merely an agent, sent to deliver a message. The word "angel" returned to his thoughts, but he knew they were not the only beings who bore words of faith. In questioning everything he'd seen and heard up to this point, he now believed that between the realms of good and evil there was a wide spectrum of existence. She was no angel, but she was no demon either. He would, from that moment onward, consider her to be a simple messenger and nothing else. Their meeting was not by chance; it was something that was destined to happen. His duty now was to take heed of what he'd been shown, and decide what to do next.

His first idea was to return to the cave, and contemplate the secret it held, but he stopped abruptly, turned to Ania and pronounced: "We must return to the dig!"

She barely had time to nod as Ben's pace quickened into a run.

Chapter 39

Ready to Erase

Seth Steinbeck's mind was awash in a flood of anger. He'd been upset countless times before, but this feeling was different—and dramatically new. His emotions were a mixture of rage, hatred, loathing, and every other negative feeling a human could experience. Concurrently, he realized that the angrier he became, the stronger he felt. For the first time in his life, he felt cognitive turmoil to be a good thing. He prized his mind as the sole source of who he was and what drove him: this energy coursing through his gray matter felt spectacular. Because he did not believe in the existence of a soul, he saw the human brain—especially his—as the source of all conscious thought and physical movement. He knew he was highly intelligent—this elevated his status among all men. Physical prowess was useless and did not interest him; everything could be accomplished by using brains, not brawn. This moment, however, he'd never felt so able-bodied, strong, and virile.

For the first time in Steinbeck's life, he was invincible…unstoppable. Whatever this dark energy was, its high-octane fuel fed his muscles and pushed his movements with increasing vigor. He would destroy what he now saw as the paramount obstacle to the furtherance of his message of logic and reason. This time, there would be no intellectual approach to defeat the unfolding papist plot.

The only thoughts he had now were focused on each step he was taking as he stormed along. There would be no blogging, no seminars, and no information trees through social media — there was no time. The only way to stop this elaborate fraud would be to become a wild animal, and tear the enemy apart. So focused on his newfound abilities was he that Bella's nearby presence no longer registered. He stormed on, and her trailing footsteps fell on deaf ears. His blood was rushing so fast and his heart pounding so hard that all he heard were thumps and breaths. A snorting, charging bull would cower if it encountered Seth at this moment.

Bella purposely kept out of view, not wanting her puppet to see that she was holding his strings. She was rapidly whispering words that only his subconscious could perceive. Like sound frequencies heard only by a beast, Bella's strange utterances provided encouragement to his animal brain, which was now controlling his actions. Seth's lower mind readily absorbed the chants, and the more she whispered, the angrier he became. As his fury rose, so did her sense of elation. A victory over the half-mortal Carpenter and His Father had never been this close before. If she'd been human, the feeling was akin to arousal.

As Seth stampeded across the ground, he was unaware that a smoky-black haze enshrouded him. Bella had seen this before, but never had it been so dense. She was beyond pleased—she was ecstatic at the results of her efforts. There was little doubt that she was getting better every century. The dark cloud that enveloped her companion was invisible to mortal eyes—only something of Bella's ilk could see the product her evil engendered. Hellish beings thrived in the company of the black fog of pure, unadulterated hatred. Throughout history, this dark-haired being had witnessed the similar results of her diabolic influence. Her previous efforts had produced endless waves of death, destruction, and despair. History proved there was no limit to what she could incite.

Demons were generally forbidden from manually altering human history, however nothing prevented them from making suggestions to receptive minds. Sinister words, spoken at the right time, were more effective than curses, spells, and possessions. While Seth Steinbeck thought his mind was an impenetrable fortress of logic, the true reality was that it was literally and figuratively made of tissue. Bella had shadowed his life since birth, and although he didn't remember, they'd crossed paths many times before.

Their prior encounters were seemingly innocuous, but on a few occasions, Bella's efforts were direct. As a child, she'd been the little girl he met and played with in the park. During his pre-adolescence, she was his school teacher. After that, a high school classmate. In college, she'd been his study partner. Currently, she was his lover — or so he thought. She had no affection for him — it was strictly an encounter of opportunity.

Bella had played the amorous object before, but she reserved this guise only for grand schemes. Physical contact with humans, especially sexual, repulsed her. *He'd* created the act to propagate life, and that disgusted her. The true thrill was in the ensnarement of suggestible beings. Those she successfully seduced went on to destroy lives, families, communities, and even entire societies. While her immediate goal was not quite "global" in nature, its completion would sting the Father and Son in a "personal" way. Two millennia prior, she'd had forty days to "turn" the Carpenter, but failed miserably. The wound of that loss still ached and she owed them both an insult as payback. Lighting Seth's fuse would be the ultimate revenge.

Seth considered himself an above-average atheist; he dwelt in pure logic and reason, and he knew what he was doing. He'd succeeded many times before, and was confident he would again. His blind spot, though, was that in focusing on the denial of the true

God before him, he was oblivious to the fact that
Satan was behind him.

⸳ ⸳ ⸳ ⸳ ⸳ ⸳ ⸳

As they neared the dig, a quick, yet painful
sensation rattled Ben's spine—as if a jackhammer was
suddenly pounding his bones. The last time this had
happened was when he was present at an exorcism.
A decade had passed, but there was no mistaking the
feeling: something truly evil was nearby. For some
inexplicable reason, a line from Macbeth pierced his
mind: "…with the pricking of my thumbs, something
wicked this way comes."

⸳ ⸳ ⸳ ⸳ ⸳ ⸳ ⸳

The security checkpoint forced Seth and Bella
to park two miles away, necessitating an arduous
trek through the forest. The inconvenience mildly
annoyed Seth; something foreign, yet welcome,
propelled him forward. Erroneously, he believed the
newfound power came from within himself—the
reality was that it was supplied by his raven-haired
companion. The terrain was rugged, but with his
newfound strength, he could have ascended Mount
Everest.

⸳ ⸳ ⸳ ⸳ ⸳ ⸳ ⸳

Ben and Ania arrived back at the dig and proceeded directly to the encampment's main tent. The
walk to the cave had taken an hour—the return trip
less than thirty minutes. Thankfully, the talkative and

affable Doctor O'Toole was nowhere to be found, and other than a silent guard outside, they were all alone.

"How were these buried?"

Without replying, Ania walked away from Ben, and stopped fifty feet down the main aisle.

"This was first."

She pointed to a miniscule stone crucifix, no bigger than a golf ball. The object was roughly hewn, and its intended shape barely recognizable.

"We'd arrived here about one calendar year after He died. We didn't mark the passage of time as we do now, but by counting the sun's cycles, it was over three hundred days. This area was devoid of any civilization, and the last village we'd passed was a fortnight's walk back. Something told me this was the right place to stop."

She used two gentle fingers to pick up the small object and place it in her palm. With closed eyes her mind went back in time:

"I found the cave a few days later and we hid the cross there. My precious companion, Marcus, kept guard and I regularly returned here to ensure we weren't followed. During one of my forays, someone approached, and I hid amongst the trees. A single, bedraggled traveler came through; he was seeking something, and I presumed it was us. He wandered in circles, then suddenly walked to the exact center of where the excavation site is. He reacted as you did in the cave and was motionless for nearly an hour.

When he finally stirred, he placed something on the ground and then he prayed. After a few moments, he left quickly. When the man was safely out of sight, I went to look, and found this."

She offered the relic to Ben, gently placing it in his hand. He pondered it for a few moments, then returned it to the table.

Ania walked to another table and pointed to another cross, this one of dark wood. She walked a few feet beyond it and pointed to a third one made of bronze. "These were left the following year. It was an elderly couple. Their actions were nearly identical — they dropped to their knees on the exact same spot as the first visitor. They prayed longer — for hours — and left these."

"Didn't they see the first cross that had been left?" Ben asked, not taking his eyes off the table.

"No, my fear had been that if anyone saw what the first pilgrim left, our presence might be detected. His enemies were most surely still looking for us. If word spread that someone had already been here..." She did not finish.

"What did you do?" Ben knew what the answer was, but needed to hear it.

"I didn't want to move the crosses from where they were, but they had to be concealed. I put them in the ground, deep enough that they wouldn't be found." She saw a quizzical look in Ben's eyes.

In a wordless answer, Ania knelt on the ground where she stood; a heavy, industrial-looking rubber mat covered it. She pulled the covering aside, revealing trampled grass.

Effortlessly, she drove her fist directly into the soil, and her arm disappeared above her elbow. Ben had already seen her unworldly abilities, but its demonstration still astonished him. She looked up at him as she withdrew her arm. With the same dirt-encrusted hand, she smoothed over the hole, replaced the mat, and stood up. She raised her hand upward, as if reaching for heaven. The symbolism of her gesture was not lost on him. Lowering her arm, she used the other to brush moist soil from her skin.

There was a long gash along the back of her wrist, and the veins underneath were clearly visible between the edges of her torn flesh. A jagged cut had been made by a sharp stone that was embedded in the soil. As she'd pierced the ground with her hand, the rock tore the skin going in. Coming out, the same hard edge tore in the other direction. A thick stream of blood trailed down her arm and dripped from her bicep. As Ben watched impassively, the wound closed itself and the red flow stopped. After a minute, the injury was completely healed, and the blood had vanished. Ben was not shocked as he had been before—after what she'd shown him in the cave, he thought he understood what she might actually be. Ania felt his stare, lowered her arm, and self-consciously rubbed it with her clean hand.

She walked to yet another table, provided a brief description of the crucifix's donor, then moved on to another. After an hour, she'd pointed out over fifty crosses and relayed details about each one. The seemingly-inanimate objects began to take on life as their origins were revealed. A question was forming at the back of Ben's mind and he finally asked gently: "Did you talk to any of them?"

"No. I knew the reason they came—even though they didn't. To them, an unidentified, invisible force pulled them here." Her reply was just as soft.

Another faint question he'd had a moment earlier came out. "How did you bury them all so deep? Your arm isn't that long."

Ben didn't realize he'd said something humorous, but the new smile on Ania's face made him glad he had. He also realized he'd never seen her truly grin before. Everything else aside, Ben knew she was certainly the most beautiful woman he'd ever met.

Ania recognized what Ben was feeling, and it embarrassed her. No one had looked at her that way before—even before she'd been cursed. Feeling like an unholy monster for so long, it was hard to believe that someone—especially someone like him—saw something pleasant in her. Trying to distract him, she interrupted the silence:

"I believe it was sometime around AD 300 when there was a tremendous earthquake. The cave rocked and rotated, yet not a single pebble fell. I was alone by then—Marcus was long gone. Returning here to see what had happened, I saw that the earth beneath the crosses had collapsed about fifty feet. There must have been an air pocket between the surface and the cave below—this was fortuitous since it drew what was already buried much deeper. As a precaution, I filled in the hole with soil." Ania looked at the ground.

"It must have been a big hole—there are thousands here." He gestured to the collection of recovered relics.

Ania's smile became a gentle laugh. Ben had said yet another unintentionally funny statement. He liked to see her laugh.

"There were only a few hundred hidden by then. The rest came in waves. Oddly, about every few hundred years, another huge earthquake occurred, and the ground opened once again, and what had been near the surface dropped many feet. If I knew no better, it was as if the cave was pulling the crosses closer. Every time a chasm opened up, all that needed to be done was to fill in more dirt." Ania gestured with her hands as if smoothing an imaginary hole.

"How did you move all that..." Ben knew the answer before the words left his mouth: she'd done it handful by handful. It was clear that in addition to

her super-human strength, she possessed an immea-
surable amount of stamina and patience. Thinking
about the depth of the excavation, he quickly calculated that she'd moved several hundred cubic tons
of soil all by herself. That fact alone clearly demonstrated just how long she'd been here. Lots could
be accomplished in two thousand years. He shifted
mental gears as he remembered what had brought
them here in the first place

"The bombs — why here?" He spread his hands
wide.

"I left this place at the end of the nineteenth
century. I never knew of the presence of the bombs,
but upon reflection, it appears the Reich sensed something important was here and they tried to obliterate
it."

"Why would they try to destroy this place? They
didn't know about the cave — it is as if they were
trying to destroy something they couldn't see, but
knew was nearby." He was still processing his
thoughts as she answered.

"The evil that took over this area in the early 1900s
was not something new. Europe has been in constant
turmoil since man first set foot here; plagues, wars,
famine, pestilence, genocide, disasters…it has never
stopped. This perpetual state of chaos is what drew
me to the study of Western civilization. I wanted to
know if it was possible that my presence here had

brought misfortune upon the land." A look of mild exasperation clouded her face.

"Europe does not have the sole claim to evil and turmoil. The world has been turning itself inside out ever since the fall of man." Ben believed he knew why she was always so serious: she carried considerable guilt, not only over what she'd done, but also for much of what had happened here.

"During the industrial revolution, disorder and death gained efficiency by way of technology," she went on. "This place is sacred and it radiates some-thing that evil cannot abide. They thought they could drop bombs on this place and destroy it. What they failed to realize is that man-made objects cannot destroy things created in heaven."

"How was it possible that none of the bombs exploded?" Ben looked around at the tables, then thought of the mounds of explosives that had lain close to them.

"With all the years I have spent learning and studying, many things are clear — but why none of those things detonated is something I've pondered since we first met. The answer still eludes me." Ania gently shook her head.

* * * * * * *

Seth and Bella were about a mile into their trek when the angry atheist stumbled over a log and fell hard. He tried to stand, but felt an excruciating pain in his left ankle.

"Damn it! It's sprained!" he said through gritted teeth. He slumped down hard on the log that had just injured him.

Bella, faking concern, knelt beside him. There was no way any mortal issue would hinder her grand plans. She looked at his rapidly-swelling joint and placed her hands over it. "This won't hurt a bit."

Steinbeck was about to recoil in pain, but something in her eyes reassured him. He believed in her. He slid off the log and onto the ground. He closed his eyes and lay flat. "Do your magic, my queen." He tried to ignore the throbbing pain. With his eyes closed, he did not see the smirk on Bella's face when he referred to her with a term of royalty. He was now truly hers.

Chapter 40

Bella and Seth Reach the Cave

Whatever Bella had done, it did more than just heal Seth's injury — it poured more energy into his very soul. The moment she'd laid hands on him, not only did the pain in his ankle disappear — every other ache he had also vanished. The electric jolt from her fingers shot him up and placed his feet squarely on the ground. He'd used the occasional drug before, but even the most potent stimulant paled in comparison. This new, altered state felt good — very good.

Upon reaching the ravine's edge, Bella halted. "I can't go down there?"

Her regular confident affectation was gone, something he'd never seen before.

"What's wrong? We're almost there! We can't stop!" Seth was breathing heavily as if he was spent, but his energy level was off the charts.

Bella's legs wobbled, and Seth grabbed her by both arms to keep her from falling. He led her to a nearby tree stump with exasperation, and sat her down. "What's wrong?" he asked again, as he looked down at her ashen and clammy face.

"I'm claustrophobic…even being near enclosed spaces affects me greatly. That place is suffocating!" Bella ran the back of her hand across her forehead, smearing the beads of cold sweat.

"You don't look good, but we need to get down there. How far away is it?" Seth hopped from foot to foot, unable to stand still.

"The entrance is close — I've…there are markers for you to follow. The place you seek — it's at the bottom." Bella swooned, and leaned forward, plopping her forehead on her knees. She weakly muttered that she was going to be sick.

"I'll go it alone — you'll be alright here." Seth was already moving in the direction of the small valley.

Without lifting her head, Bella half-heartedly waved him off. Seth was already gone by the time she'd finished the gesture.

* * * * * * *

Ben stood at the edge of the pit, his eyes focused on the screen of a GPS device. Based on the data he'd collected in the cave, the cell phone-sized gadget confirmed that the center of the excavation was directly over it. Adjusting for elevation differences, he calculated that the cave was almost 2,000 feet below. Ben believed that even if every bomb had exploded, they would not have breached the impenetrable layer of bedrock. Reflectively, he gazed off in the distance. He knew that evil was powerful—not stronger than good, but certainly more cunning, devious, and deceitful.

Yes, Satan knew what and where the holy object was, but would never be able to use its power. If he couldn't wield it, he would want it to be destroyed. Hell's monarch couldn't directly touch earthly things but was more than capable of manipulating the weak-minded to do his dirty work. The twisted cabal of the Third Reich was tailor-made for this purpose and had once had open ears to the whispers of evil. Not satisfied with the mere atrocities of the war, the destruction of this—Ania's refuge—and its contents had received higher priority than genocide. The death of millions was nowhere near the prize of this treasure's destruction.

Ben had no answer as to why it had taken two millennia to set the wheels in motion. The Prince of Darkness knew of the object from the moment it was created—he'd been its architect, and supervised its builders. Similar instruments had been used for years, but this specimen had been destined for Him. The only reason Ben could fathom for the delay was technology: mass destruction had only reached a high-water mark in the 1940s. Finding the cave would have been simple enough, and almost any sinister force could have done so and claimed the prize. He wondered what would have happened if the Reich had discovered it. Would they have blindly followed orders and destroyed it, or would its presence have pierced the fog of hatred and healed their hearts? Blindly dropping bombs from the sky didn't have the effect that evil itself had hoped for.

·······

Once Seth was out of sight, Bella regained her composure. While she was anything but claustrophobic, she was still incapable of moving any closer to the cave. As Lucifer's earthly agent, she had full access to anywhere on the planet—except for the cave. There was no explanation for it, but regardless of her form, some unseen force presented a barrier and repelled her. She knew what was hidden nearby, and hated it with all her might. Had she reached it herself, it would have been destroyed long ago. But because of Him, the only thing she could do was use her influence. There was no doubt Seth would succeed—he was the most pliable puppet she'd ever owned. It would all be over soon.

·······

Ania looked around her and realized that this was the first time she'd seen all the crosses en masse. The first time she'd seen them, it was in trickles and then waves. She knew she'd been busy all those years, but standing amidst the rows of tables, she allowed herself to acknowledge her labors. It must have been something good. Ania Socratatos believed herself to be unredeemable, but she hoped her actions had pleased Him.

Something drew Ben's gaze down into the pit,
and an ill sensation came over him. Something was
wrong. The air around him turned stale and felt like
death. He looked up and the sky suddenly darkened —
evil was nearby. Before his mind realized what was
happening, he was running toward the ravine.

At the same moment, Ania, too, felt that something was wrong. Darting out of the tent, she scanned
the area. There was no sign of Ben.

"The cave!"

Her words were left in the wind as she ran
toward the ravine.

● ● ● ● ● ● ● ●

Something guided Seth Steinbeck's movements,
even though nothing was visible to the naked eye.
The compelling energy Bella's touch had given him
was drawing him forward. As he reached the ravine's
bottom, something in the rocks caught his attention.
What's that doing down here? he asked himself, as he
moved closer to it. The yellow glow transfixed his
gaze and he reached down to grab it.

● ● ● ● ● ● ● ●

Rounding a bend in the trail, the sight of her
ahead was that of true dread. Ania stopped so quickly
that her own cloud of dust trailed ahead of her.

"Why are you here?" she demanded angrily.

Bel got up from the tree stump, straightening
his tie. "I'd heard of this place — all those worthless

trinkets. How did those simpletons find their way here?" He motioned with his head toward the excavation site.

"You know full well those 'trinkets,' as you call them, represent something more powerful than your whispers. Not all of them are susceptible to your influence." Ania was angry that Bel was so close to the cross; even though he could do nothing to it, his proximity to what she held so dear was troubling.

"Even with all my eyes have seen, I still get curious." A self-satisfied smirk crossed his face.

"Those you refer to as 'simple minded' were anything but. They were humble pilgrims, whose minds were not clouded by greed or ambition. They felt the power of His grace." She motioned with her arm for emphasis.

"You of all people know how mortals love graven images—especially you. The statues of Zeus, Venus, Aphrodite...I could go on for hours. You and your ancestors prayed incessantly to those empty marble objects. The crosses are no different. At least your statues bordered on art." He sneered.

"No one ever saw the Greek 'gods,' but I saw Him—He is real, and everything He told is truth. I know it and so do you." She moved toward him.

"He was a charlatan, skilled with sleight of hand. Nothing he did was real. Water to wine? Healing the blind? Raising Lazarus? Those were nothing more than acts of deception. Only His death finally put an

end to His games." A look of gladness crossed his
face.

"What about the earthquake? That was no coin-
cidence. Actually — it was more than an earthquake —
the earth almost cracked in half!" She looked around
at the landscape.

"Come now! You know that just because something follows an event, it does not mean the event
caused it. The ground was going to shake, even had
he not taken his last ragged, lying breath." Bel ruefully shook his head.

"What about this?" She pulled her blouse a few
inches off her shoulder to reveal a deep red mark on
her right shoulder.

Bel looked askance at the long red mark; he knew
what it was, but would not acknowledge it to her.

"Interesting — but it's nothing more than a birthmark." He looked truly puzzled.

"This is no birthmark, it is *His* mark." She gently
placed her left hand over the dark skin on her shoulder, and a sense of warmth permeated her hand.
"Whatever this is, it has always been my sole sense
of solace and hope. It proves He is what He said He
is." She reset her blouse and reverently smoothed the
fabric over what she'd just displayed.

"Your 'curse' as you call it may make you immortal, but that doesn't mean your physical being is
incapable of change." He shrugged. "Whatever that is,
it's nothing more than another trick."

Ania moved closer, and leaned toward him. She pulled her blouse away again, re-exposing the mark. "Then prove it." She tugged the fabric even further, inadvertently revealing her bosom to Bel.

"That is tempting. We've not had physical contact since the day you were given the 'gift.' I fear that the feel of your soft flesh would inflame my passions and what happens afterwards...well that is beyond even my control." He had a lustful look in his eyes, but it was marbled with fear.

Bel reached out, and Ania saw her chance—she pulled his left hand directly onto the mark. His eyes opened in pained fury and he recoiled back. He tried to pull his hand from the mark, but Ania held it firm. His arm was locked and he could not move. Brilliant blue flames engulfed his left hand, and for the first time since Creation, he was in actual pain. Before Ania's eyes, Bel's image changed from his normally handsome self into a striking, raven-haired woman. The sudden change startled Ania, but she became even angrier when she recognized the face. "You!" she shouted.

Bella smirked beneath the pain. She knew Ania remembered her from that night. As Judas Iscariot walked through the town, counting his silver, Bella had approached him. Congratulations were in order. Ania remembered passing them, but at the time did not know who either of them were. Only later, when she saw his lifeless body, did Ania realize she was looking at the betrayer himself.

The former Bel, now Bella, was able to extricate her hand from Ania's grasp — nothing like this had ever happened before — whether she was Bel or Bella, she was still a god; this Greek expatriate was still a lesser being. Bella knew it should not have been possible for the ancient Athenian to overpower the Baron of Darkness.

"What is this! How dare you trick me!" Bella held up her hand and saw it was now aflame, emitting acrid smoke as the flesh burned. This had never happened either. For the first time, the earthly demon had been wounded.

"Yes, I have no power over you, but He does. You've touched His mark and it hurt you! There is your proof; a mark made by His blood truly destroys evil." Ania felt the red stain's warmth return.

"Deceit! How could you, after all that I've done for you?" Bella watched as the flame eventually subsided, leaving a smoldering stump. After a few moments, and with much pain, her hand regenerated itself.

Ania had expected some type of reaction, but not what she'd just seen. In "mortal" form, he was invincible. While her own injuries healed before her eyes, she'd never seen anyone else do this. Bel's hand had burned and he was in actual, physical discomfort.

"His blood is poison to you — like antiseptic on a festering wound." She covered up her shoulder.

"Trickery! I am Lucifer's servant—the most exalted of all beings. You were born a mortal and will die a mortal." Bella pointed the newly-grown hand at her. "I too can give pain… 'the Lord, my Lord' taketh and you know the rest…!"

A blood-red beam of lava erupted from her (his) hand and shot toward Athania. She braced herself, but when it came close, it harmlessly diverted around her, like river water around a boulder. The glowing stream dissipated a few feet behind her. It was unclear to both what happened, but Ania realized it first.

"You cannot hurt me. His blood has marked me and I am His. While I carry this 'original sin'—having believed you once, your power over me is gone." She stepped forward as Bella recoiled back.

Ania grabbed Bel/Bella around the neck and flipped him/her behind her, easily, as if he was a doll. When the toggling form of Bel/Bella stopped rolling and stood up, Ania saw that the demon was truly afraid. As she watched, the figure's appearance changed. The person who had transformed from Bel to Bella changed yet again; now the form of a twisted, distorted demon materialized. The sight of Bel's real essence startled her. What had stood before her was a conglomeration of every nightmare monster she could remember. After a few moments, something reminded Ania why she had originally come in this direction. Bel's presence may have been planned— something to distract her.

Ania raced past the grotesque figure and it smiled as she passed it. "It is too late!"

Ania ignored it, and did not see it simply vanish when she'd passed by.

Chapter 41

The Cave Confrontation

Breathing heavily, Ben finally reached the ravine's bottom. Nothing initially looked out of place, but he knew someone had recently been here within the last hour. As he caught his breath, he scanned the area for any signs of an interloper. With every new inhalation, a faint odor of sulfur assaulted his nostrils. To anyone else, the smell would have simply meant that a book of matches were burnt. Ben knew the true source.

He knew evil was near, and the cross was in danger — if that was possible.

• • • • • • • •

As Seth moved through the rock tunnel, a feeling of inner warmth developed. What seemed odd was that the heat was coming from somewhere unknown to him, almost as if he had a soul. He knew he did not have one, but the sensation was coming from where he would have estimated it to be. After a moment, he reasoned that the air in the deep passage was causing delusions. All kinds of odd gases emanated from natural formations, and considering he was so deep underground, it seemed like a reasonable conclusion.

* * * * * * * *

Ben reached the opening behind the foliage — it was clear someone had been through here recently. When he and Ania had left a few hours earlier, they'd carefully replaced the thorny branches, erasing their tracks. Now, it looked as if someone had hacked through the green curtain with much vigor. His feeling of dread was overwhelming.

* * * * * * * *

After a few more minutes, the passageway opened into a clearly-defined cave. It was a natural formation, but the symmetry of the stone formation seemed unreal. There were no tool or explosive marks, but Seth knew someone or something had made the enclosure. He'd studied geology, and knew caves were formed from random air pockets and stone fissures. What he had just walked into was a natural occurrence, but it was as if the earth made this place with precision during the fury of the planet's birth.

* * * * * * * *

Ben had no light with him, but something led him through the passage, as if he were on rails. Every blind step was secure, and it even allowed him to run when possible. While his eyes registered nothing, something within allowed him to "see" where he was going.

* * * * * * * *

Shining the light around the cave, the beam reflected off something. Turning to his right, it suddenly appeared before him: a large cross, almost ten feet high and seven feet across. The entire vertical section was covered in what appeared to be fresh blood. He stood transfixed, staring at it. He traced the beam to the top and saw a rectangular piece of wood, affixed to the top. He'd seen the letters before — INRI — but never like this.

"They're going to claim this is the cross. They're going to 'reveal it to the world' and millions will buy into it," he shouted. The excavation was a farce. The presence of the small crosses was a "warm up" to this. The true scientific community would prove this to be a counterfeit, but the gullible people — there would be millions. He knew what must be done.

He set down the light and removed his backpack.

Seth Steinbeck set the ax and the container on the ground. The gold-colored hatchet and gas can had been waiting for him when he'd descended to the bottom of the ravine. The tool's gleaming blade had caught his eye, and when he leaned down to retrieve it, he'd seen the container of fuel next to it. The gasoline was odd enough, but the ax was like nothing he'd ever seen; the blade looked to be made of pure gold. It shone and glittered like a piece of costume jewelry. He felt the blade and it was hard, very hard. If this had been pure gold, the metal might have felt slightly malleable. The handle was no doubt constructed of wood, but the grain and finish was also something his eyes had never seen before. The entire affair looked like something out of a science-fantasy quest game. The role-playing of "Serpents and Sagas" from his youth came to mind. During that game, certain weapons were capable of piercing stone and metal. This exact item is what he used to visualize.

* * * * * * *

Far ahead of him, Ben thought he saw a flicker of light. The passage and cave were normally completely devoid of any source of illumination, but here was something foreign. He picked up his pace as best he could. He heard shouts coming from his intended destination—someone was already there. Ben moved even faster than humanly possible.

* * * * * * *

Seth was repeatedly drawing the ax up, then lowering it. He looked at the can of gas, and wondered if burning the cross would be easier. All he had to do was douse the false icon, light it up, then walk away before the smoke filled the rock enclosure.

"This is personal! My hands will destroy this quickly, not leaving this to some slow-burning chemical reaction!"

The ax was swung up and over his back, and he coiled like a spring.

* * * * * * *

Ania was halfway down the passage and moving fast. She heard shouting far ahead, and could see artificial light coming from the same place. She'd moved fast before, but something within her spooled up. Her steps covered yards, and the distance was covered in mere seconds.

Ben reached the mouth of the cave and saw Seth in a baseball batter's stance. The golden glow of the ax was unmistakable—whoever this was, he had evil in mind.

Seth closed his eyes and swung the ax at the cross with all his angry might. He was so focused on putting all his effort into the swing that he didn't hear Ben coming into the cave. As the ax made contact, the feeling wasn't what he expected—it wasn't like chopping wood. What he felt was more like the ax had struck a heavy blanket. When his lids rose, he was staring directly into Ben's wide eyes.

Chapter 42

A Saintly Act

Ania reached the cave the moment Seth Steinbeck realized what he'd done. The image before her was frozen in time; a movie that had been paused. Her eyes met Ben's. As she watched, something seemed to escape his pupils.

Seth looked down from Ben's face to the ax. The handle was visible, but the wood ended at the juncture with the metal. The thing that puzzled him was that the blade was not visible. His first thought was that the intruder had blocked the ax, and snapped off the golden chunk of metal. He was partly right.

Ania saw Seth draw back, and attempt to take the ax with him. He moved back, but the weapon did not. Looking at Ben, she saw that the wood handle appeared to be sticking out of Ben's front. With anger and horror, she realized the tool's head was embedded *in* his chest.

Seth, now aware of Ania, looked at her and reeled back in horror — the woman's eyes were glowing with

a red flame. He stumbled backward, against a wall.
The sick feeling of what he'd just done was entangled
with the fear of what the woman was about to do to
him; her look told him he was about to die.

Ania had not felt this level of anger since the
death of her father. Her initial instinct was to descend
upon Steinbeck, and do to him what she'd done to
those who killed her father. Before she could take
a step, Ben collapsed to the floor; he landed on his
back and the formerly horizontal orientation of the
ax handle was now vertical. She forgot Ben's attacker
and rushed to her companion's side. Ania knelt and
cradled Ben's head in her hands. His face was ashen
and he was not breathing. A flow of blood streamed
in pulses from the grievous wound. After a few
seconds, the pulsing stopped and the blood simply
trickled. Ben Airaldi was dead.

Seth fell prostrate to the ground. His fear of death
at Ania's hands was replaced by the realization that
he'd murdered a complete stranger. He'd never given
much thought to the concept of a human life, and
death had never troubled him. His belief was that
when someone died, they ceased to exist, as there was
no soul to carry on. As he sobbed, a strange, strong
stabbing sensation pierced the very soul he suddenly
realized he'd always had.

Still ignoring Ben's assailant, Ania sat back and
drew him onto her lap; she felt his heart trying to
escape his chest cavity through the gaping hole. His

body was completely slack, and she knew life had left him. Gently, she grasped the ax handle and withdrew it from Ben's chest. There was a scraping sound as the blade moved across the severed sternum bone. As the metal appeared, the yellow gold of the ax head shone beneath the coating of blood. A flash of anger went through Ania and she flung the instrument of Ben's death at a far wall. The metal fractured into large chunks and the wood handle splintered into shards. Both Ania and Seth heard a demonic howl as the tool broke into so many pieces. Ania didn't see it, but Seth saw the ax's remnants vanish before his weeping eyes.

Ania looked down on her new friend's gray face, and any anger she felt changed to sorrow. She realized she'd fallen in love with him. This was the first time she'd felt this way in her entire, long life.

Seth Steinbeck watched as the dark-red-haired woman stroked the dead man's face. The scene reminded him of a famous sculpture he'd seen years earlier. The desire to kill himself became strong, so much so that he wished the ax was still there—he would brain himself. He looked around for a heavy rock to drop on his own skull, hoping it would end the piercing pain within him.

An electric sound suddenly filled the cave, causing Ania and Seth to look up. At first, there was no source to be seen, but the sound became louder, and as it did, a brilliant-white luminescence filled the room. The dark cave was now glowing with blinding light. Seth shielded his eyes, confounded by what was happening. He was temporarily blinded. He shut his lids in pain and covered his face with both hands.

Ania remembered this light; he was here.

"What saddens you, my sister?" a gently-resonant voice asked from somewhere within the room.

Ania looked up at the figure that now stood before her. The last time she'd seen it, the face was stern with warning. Now, a look of comfort was radiating from the magnificent being.

"I didn't save Him then and I failed to save another." She looked up at the figure, then at the cross, and then down at Ben.

"I admonished you then that it was not your duty to save Him. It was as it was meant to be. He chose to save you." The figure looked down at Ben.

As Ania stared at Ben's whitening face, she whispered, "I have failed three times; when I submitted to Belial, when I took my vengeance, and now this. I am now truly lost—my curse is permanent."

"Cursed? Sister, cursed you are not. Young and naïve were you when my brother used your time of sorrow to his benefit. In your grief, you were vulnerable and receptive to his temptations. Things will be made clear in the passage of time. Just remember, temptation is my fallen brother's weapon and lure. Your refusal to give in to his further beguilements, and your guardianship of His symbol, have led to your redemption. The time of your trial is over." The figure motioned to the cross; as he did so, something inside Ania stirred.

Seth watched in wide-eyed amazement as the being spoke to the woman; he'd always denied everything spiritual and ethereal. But he'd seen depictions of angels before—and one now stood before him.

Seth cried out, "I will take my punishment—whatever you intend to do to me, I accept it. I have been blind and conniving my whole life. That has led me to this. Banish me to hell—I deserve it." Seth lowered his head, and waited for his end.

The figure turned to the prostrate Steinbeck. A massive hand gently lifted his chin and Seth looked at the smiling face of the heavenly emissary.

"My brother, you are not damned—you were deceived by those who should have known better. A child knows nothing, and those who mislead them do so at their own peril. You have seen this, and it will be your responsibility to use this new knowledge for His glory."

"But I've murdered this man in cold blood; surely my soul is forfeited. I know of the Commandments, and this is one of them." Seth tried to avert his eyes from the figure, but something kept gently drawing his gaze back.

"Dear brother, you are not condemned. He sees what is in your heart and your contrition has provided your absolution. What you do hereon will be your chance to share His truth to others. Everything will be made clear to you as your journey begins. Go forward, my dear brother, and use your abilities to spread His message."

The figure motioned to the cave's entrance. A bright light came forth and drew Seth back toward the outside world. As he looked toward it, the cold, sick feeling of guilt was replaced by something warm and comforting. Without another word, Seth Steinbeck, former atheist, left the cave.

Chapter 43

Waking

Oblivious to the exchange between the angel and Seth Steinbeck, Ben's body was the only thing Ania cared about. As she looked down at the lifeless form, a storm ignited in her soul. At first, it was a sprinkling of tears, but quickly grew to a torrential flood of emotions. Before she realized it, Ania was sobbing uncontrollably, and could barely see Ben's face. As she rocked and wailed, it felt as if a weight was lifting from her shoulders. The more Ania wept, the lighter her spirit felt, for some inexplicable reason. She'd grieved the loss of her father, but it was tinged with rage and anger. This new loss possessed no rancor—just emptiness. For the first time in centuries, Athania Socratatos had felt a connection to another being, but now it had been broken.

She'd only been weeping for a few minutes, but her voluminous tears completely drenched Ben's chest. The huge quantity of liquid began to wash the blood from his fatal wound.

In all her emotional torrent, a feeling of solace came to the forefront of her mind. Instinctively, she looked up at the brilliant being, and saw that he was smiling at her. While he spoke no words, his countenance radiated reassurance to her aching heart.

As the ethereal being continued to smile, Ania realized she had not cried since her father died. It dawned on her that no tears had fallen from her eyes for over two thousand years. With much effort, she looked away from the angel, and looked down at her wet hands. But there was no blood on them. Moments earlier, both hands had been drenched in Ben's life source. Looking around, she could see no red anywhere.

Ania looked up at the angel in astonishment. "Do my eyes deceive me?"

Saint Michael smiled, then went and stood before the cross. He bowed his head reverently and dropped to one knee. The gentle clank of his bright armor echoed within the cave. With his head still bowed, the mighty archangel gently touched the cross. As his fingertips rested lightly on the blood-stained wood, a light enveloped his hand. With more clanking, he stood up, and turned toward Ania and Ben. Still smiling, he extended his arm toward them.

The beaming light from his outstretched hand shown brighter than the sun.

"This is the light of truth…His truth. Consider your heart, Athanasia Socratatos! You protected and

sheltered this treasure as your self-imposed penance.
When I told you to 'bear your own cross,' you mis-
understood my meaning. Your actions, however, in
protecting His legacy, were the source of your solace
for all those years."

Ania looked up at the crucifix and remembered
her time with it. It had been her sole companion for
two millennia, and it was truly her only source of
comfort during her voluntary exile.

The mighty angel walked to Ania and Ben, and
gently laid a massive hand on her shoulder, right over
the mark.

"You have always known what caused this. He
bore this cross for mankind's children, and once its
destiny was fulfilled, your faith caused you to take it
up as your own. The mark you bear here will be proof
of that."

Ania felt the warmth from her shoulder radiating
throughout her entire body. "Proof?" She looked
quizzically up at the massive figure.

"Yes—there will be a time and place that it will
be made known, but until then, keep the knowledge
of its origin to yourself." Michael gently pressed his
fingers on her shoulder in emphasis. "Your duty here
is done. The test you willingly accepted has been
passed sevenfold. The time of your current existence
is over."

Ania realized that her ultimate end was at hand. She'd pondered death, and readied herself for what she thought was about to happen.

"I am ready," Ania said, as she bowed her head. She thought the mighty being would strike her with the massive sword slung across his broad shoulders.

Saint Michael leaned forward and gently raised her chin with the tips of his fingers. "My sister, you are not going to die—remember, this cross is what He used to defeat it; death will never prevail. Your life, as you have known it for these longs years, is over, but not your time here on this world."

Ania looked up at the angel's face. When she looked at him, all she could feel was hope and tranquility.

He smiled broadly and continued. "Go with this servant, the gift's heir, and live your lives as you would. Your work together is not done. By bringing your talents together, you will bring great good to your brothers and sisters."

"His heir? Whose?" she asked with much confusion.

"Do you not recognize the son of Marcus? It surprises me that even you did not see it." The angel nodded at Ben's body.

"His child? But that was many lifetimes ago. How can that...?" She looked down at his face and compared it with a mental image.

"Perhaps 'progeny' is the most appropriate term." Saint Michael's look confirmed her sudden hypothesis.

"Ben is related to Marcus?" She looked from the ashen face to the angel's.

"Related? You are all related, but Ben Airaldi is the one hundredth son of Marcus, a direct descendant of the centurion's adopted son. The passage of generations has changed much, but Marcus's blood lives within this brave servant. Have you wondered why his touch startles you? Christ healed Marcus through his father's faith; Marcus and his descendants carry the power of His love forward."

Ania looked down at the motionless Ben. "But he is dead."

"No, sister — he only sleeps. Remember: death can't win, and this treasure is the proof. This man only rests — he has labored much." Saint Michael gestured back to the cross. "All my fallen brother's efforts were in vain; he is free to influence the weak-minded, but Lucifer cannot provide anything other than suggestions. The weapon he left for brother Seth was not of earthly origin. Things forged from the ore of hell's fires may not harm God's children."

Ania allowed her mind to digest all that she'd just heard. She was about to ask another question when she sensed a stirring.

The angel spoke once more, and it diverted Ania's attention momentarily. "Together, you will protect and strengthen each other. This warrior loves you as you love him. It was not by chance that you met; you both chose the path of righteousness and that is what brought you together. His newborn love for you is pure and selfless, and his eternal heart drew him to you. If you both choose, your love will grow and be fruitful."

Ania realized that Ben was moving. When she looked down, there was no evidence he'd ever been hurt. Color had suddenly returned to his face.

"My sister, one thing more." Saint Michael's face turned serious.

Ania looked up at him as Ben started to wake.

The angel continued: "Your meeting with this servant was a gift to you both. His lineage carries His healing touch. Your lineage will carry the strength you gained from your journey. My fallen brother's efforts are ceaseless—he will continue to whisper to those who know no better. You resisted his direct charms and influence; your wise father's lessons inured you against his evils; be ready, for someday you may be called upon. This battle will rage, but always know that one of us will walk with you. Be strong and remember my words."

Ania felt a mild tingle in her spine, and a jolt of warmth electrified her body.

Ben sat up and looked at her.

"What happened?" He shook his head to clear the cobwebs.

"We're okay. I have much to tell you."

Ben jumped up and felt his chest. The wound was gone. He looked toward the cross and saw a translucent image of something with wings. As the image faded away, he saw a smile on the angel's face. He looked back at Ania.

"I will tell you later," she said as she steadied him.

Ben woozily swayed and Ania moved quickly to support him, accidentally drawing the back of her hand across a jagged stone protrusion. A fresh cut on her hand bled gently. She watched for several seconds as a small trickle ran down to her wrist. To her astonishment, the wound did not heal.

She picked up a small stone and squeezed with all her might. All she felt was solid resistance. For the first time in over two thousand years, she was a mere mortal. Belial's curse was gone.

Athania Socratatos now felt something she'd never experienced before: serenity.

Epilogue

The solitary figure sat on a rock, looking reflectively off to the west. His posture appeared relaxed, although his eyes were never still—they constantly scanned the area in a smooth sweep. The most appropriate word for this activity was "vigil." The sight before him presented a picturesque landscape of rolling meadows, framed by a fence of green trees. If captured properly in a painting, it would have rivaled any artist's masterpiece. Natural greens and golds accented a pale-blue sky, which defined the horizon in sharp focus. To any tepid believer, the beauty of the setting could prove that the Lord was an artist.

Punctuating the scene was a single geometric shape, about a mile away. The lone man-made object resembled a tall triangle affixed to a broad, rectangular base. Its glimmering spire reached optimistically to the heavens with glass and bright-steel fingers. Its brown and red stone-brick base contrasted well the rolling fields with earthy hues.

At this distance, the edifice looked like a simple crown set atop the undulating land. The tip of its glimmering extension stopped at the horizon, with only a single projection piercing the sky. Closer inspection revealed that the church's pinnacle (for it was a church) was a plain wooden cross. With the right lighting, which was usually at late afternoon, the edifice itself blended into the background, and the universal symbol of Christianity appeared to float in the air, above the earth.

The accomplished warrior had not moved from this spot for two years. In fact, he'd not slept, eaten, spoken, rested, nor even taken his eyes off Saint Michael the Protector's. Prior to the archangel's arrival and "changing of the guard," an army of lesser angels had encircled the area, forming an impenetrable sphere around the newly-built church and what was hidden nearly a half-mile under it. The heavenly servants had originally assembled at Golgotha, two millennia prior, and had maintained their watch, even after Christ's body was removed and placed in the tomb. In Christ's absence from the hill, the seraphim had watched over the instrument of his death, which would eventually become the universal symbol of His sacrifice. They had known of Athania Socratatos's role in the course of history, but were still somewhat awed at the power she'd possessed. They had watched as she reverently approached the cross and first attempted to remove it. The sudden appearance of the centurion, and his sword attack on her, was something to see; thinking her to be a thief, he had drawn his sword and run her through.

Her lack of reaction, and failure to succumb to the fatal injury, had startled and frightened the seasoned warrior. The confrontation turned into a stalemate. The battle-hardened soldier then came to understand her true nature and decided to help her. After the arrival of his son—the servant healed by Christ—the angels surrounded and protected them as they made their way to the west. All but two angels had gone with them; these two had a special task. They remained with the centurion, for the soldier had his own task to accomplish, and the two guardians would ensure his safety.

From Jerusalem to Aachen, Athania and Marcus were never alone. Although their battalion of heavenly guardians was not visible to them, any potential threat to her, Marcus, and the cross was kept at bay. Human predators, usually robbers and thieves, were easily dealt with by the unassuming woman. The true threats—demons—were kept far away from the three. Upon realizing that Christ had defeated Satan and death, these hellish creatures had pursued what they thought to be the next best thing to overcome: Christ's eternal symbol. Lucifer's minions, unable to attack the cross and its protectors directly, used the Third Reich. A series of whispers to the Wehrmacht had ignited World War II. When the Luftwaffe started their annual bombing campaign over the cave, the angels went to work: as each bomb fell, they had caught the explosive ones and gently set them where the dig would one day exist.

To this day, the archeologists and scientists do not know why there were no detonations. But the answer was clear to the faithful: they knew that the protective force of heavenly beings had prevented harm from coming to the place where His cross lay. The angels had been inordinately busy, but being trusted servants of the Lord, their powers had no limits.

There was a new presence suddenly, but the hyper-vigilant archangel knew of it, even before it spoke:

"This victory is yours — for now."

This statement was uttered defiantly, but Saint Michael sensed the underlying resignation.

"This was not my victory — it was His." Michael did not turn to the voice, but his hand moved deftly toward his weapon.

The intruder approached the mighty angel's back, and a swift metallic sound punctured the air as his sword was unsheathed. The blur of speed surprised even the ancient demon. Although he considered himself the superior being, the Prince of Darkness was eternally jealous of his estranged brother's abilities.

If the scene had been visible to naked eyes, the meeting of the two adversaries might have looked like a melding of a painting by the artists Raphael and Bosch.

The archangel was surrounded by brilliant colors of light; Lucifer was shrouded in fury and disturbing shapes.

Still somewhat fearful of the Lord's commanding warrior, Satan remained still and raised his deformed hands in a show of surrender. "My brother…I come in what you still like to call 'peace.'"

"That word has no meaning to you. I know you better than any except the Father. You do not materialize on earth unless there is a scheme to be spawned. This area is forbidden to you—now, and always." The mighty archangel set the tip of his sword on the top of his armored sandal, and gently rested his hands on the hilt. He looked relaxed, but in reality, he was ready for anything the Evil One might attempt.

"That? Another crude monument to the Father's illegitimate son? If the talking monkeys wish to waste their efforts on these useless tributes, that is all the better. They pose us no threat." The devil waved a single talon dismissively.

"If the Son was what you say, why do the children here still worship Him as they do? Why did you tempt Him while He was here?" Michael's grip tightened around his weapon's grip.

"Worship? Even a dog will blindly follow anyone who feeds him. These upright beasts are no different." Lucifer sniffed.

"You used the correct word for once. He does feed them…but not with food. It is that thing you always seek. His nourishment is what protects their souls from your grasp. Also, He does not feed them to control — it is out of love, His and the Father's." Saint Michael knew he'd made a rare point with his estranged brother.

"Loves them? Why did He even waste the effort to create them? They do nothing but rebel and curse His name. Just look at this place! If they obeyed Him, the wars that scar the land would never have come to pass. We were His true children! And we did not seek to destroy our own home as these creatures do." Satan grimaced, remembering how he'd felt when learning of the Lord's plan.

"The damage you did to heaven made all this seem like nothing. You started the first 'Great War,' and anything ill that followed was your doing." Saint Michael's words were full of force, but they were not said with anger.

"That war was not initiated by me! I was the Father's favorite, even more so than you! I did nothing other than counsel Him against creating simple-minded beings and He would not listen. Out of spite and fear, He set you against me. I could have remained with you all, and there would have been order. I was above you all, and so you were jealous. You turned my other brothers against me and banished me from my true home. They may call you an 'archangel,' but I was *'the angel.'* You were the most powerful warrior, but that is only because you failed to think for yourself, and He rewarded you with your abilities. Do not forget,

Michael, that I was your better; the Father was number 'one,' I number 'two,' and you were down there with Raphael and Gabriel—three, four, and five."

Lucifer still thought he was the greatest being, even though he was long gone from heaven.

Saint Michael smiled, seeing how his fallen brother's pride had not waned. "Lucifer, this talk is pointless—what brings you here? You will not be able to destroy it. You may have designed it, and even helped with its construction, but it belongs to Him now." Saint Michael allowed a quick glance at the cross that sat atop the church.

"Yes—I did create its shape, and I even steadied the builder's hands. Those meaningless pieces of wood mean nothing to me. That 'son' of his can have it. But let me ask you: if it is now His, why is it still in that cave? They went to all the trouble to build that shanty over there, and put a bad replica of it on top. Why not show it to the world? Would that not be the proof they all want? Oh...wait—that thing in the cave is a forgery. But you already knew that. Does she? Is she aware that she spent centuries, guarding something that was not what she thought it was?" Lucifer thought of that shape—the one thing that still forced him to avert his gaze.

"Does it matter? She thought the cross she had protected for two millennia was the actual one. It might not be the actual cross He died upon, but its origin is not what anyone other than our Father knew. Even I was unaware." Saint Michael relaxed his grip somewhat.

"How would she feel, though, if she found out she'd spent her life keeping company with a fake? It might change her view on things," Lucifer sneered.

"How do you know she doesn't already? You underestimate her wisdom — she knows more than your minions, let alone you. She passed the test, but her work for Him is not finished. She may be mortal once again, but her gifts and talents are still immense." Michael looked off at the church.

"She may have passed the test — but you know how these primates are — they fall — they always fall. Maybe she could still be of use to me yet." The prince of evil raised a deformed eyebrow.

"You are mistaken if you think she is as she was when your nephew first tempted her. She has taken her sacraments now — that, and she knows of you and your brethren. Also, do not forget that she has our protection." Michael retightened his grip ever so slightly.

"Of course — you and your ilk can protect them from 'direct' action, but we are always free to whisper and suggest." He grinned. "I think it's called 'freedom of speech.'"

"For all your criticism of these 'creatures,' as you call them, Athania proved Father's point, almost as well as Job." Michael did not know which lost wager had stung hell's ruler more. He continued: "He told you, that given a choice, His thinking children would make the correct decision, even if they did not know of His existence." The mighty angel relaxed once more.

"While she refused my ultimate gift, she almost stayed Pilate's hand—had you not stopped her, she might have changed history." Satan regretted not being able to tempt Christ any longer, but he was hopeful that Ania's misguided efforts might thwart destiny.

"That was not part of the wage. True, she wanted to save Him, but she'd never heard His direct words. Ania did not know that His death was ordained. I merely admonished her that she was not to interfere," Michael replied.

"She only partially obeyed your warning; you told her to 'take up her own cross,' and what did she do? She picked up a wooden toy and dragged it from Jerusalem to here. Her efforts resulted in nothing. All she did was preserve that poor counterfeit." Satan was dismissive, although he knew that Athania had indeed done something substantial.

"If the cross was a useless fake, why did you enlist your nephew to have it destroyed? Belial spent considerable effort to induce Seth Steinbeck to try to do what he did," Saint Michael replied.

"My faithful servant was doing what he thought best. Any cross is an insult to us all. He tries to keep himself occupied," Satan said.

Saint Michael knew just how busy Lucifer's minions had been; history was proof of that. The existence, though, of Christ's actual instrument of death, or what was thought to be the actual one, was something Lucifer could not bear. Destroying it would have accomplished nothing, even if doing so was possible. While the cross was originally of earthly origin, its anointing with Christ's blood had inured it to any threat, earthly or otherwise. While Ania's efforts may have seemed superfluous to Lucifer, Saint Michael knew that their true purpose was to redeem her. While he was the Lord's trusted servant, even he did not know the course of all the Father's plans. All he knew was that she had thought she was guarding the true cross, when in reality it was an annointed decoy. The true cross had been taken away shortly before Ania had returned that night. The cross she had taken…only the Father knew its origin. Her true duty was the act of protecting the cross which she thought to be the true instrument of Christ's death and future symbol of hope. It was a duty she had completed superbly.

"Be gone! This place is off-limits to you and your demons." Saint Michael's words had the force of law to his fallen brother. Without responding, Satan vanished.

Michael resumed his watch and wondered with a glad heart at what Ania might accomplish next.

* * * * * * * * *

The speaker approached the podium and assessed the large crowd. He'd talked before large groups, but this was something much more. The seminars of his "dark days" were becoming a distant memory. Also, those crowds had always seemed to possess a negative energy, and were always scowling. Those about to hear his new words were different; they smiled, and out of real joy. He sipped some water and smiled himself.

"Greetings to you all here now. We've come from far-off places, but our faith is universal. Let me introduce myself; my name is Seth Steinbeck, and I am a recovering atheist."

The crowd collectively chuckled at the statement. The words may have seemed like a joke, but many were themselves recovering from the same illness. He stepped from behind the podium, showing that he did not need something to lean on or prop himself up against. He turned serious and pronounced:

"There is a God, and I can prove it!"

• • • • • • •

The giggling toddler stumbled playfully after a butterfly. His parents reveled in the innocent glee of their child, pleased to see his simple joy in trying to catch the beautiful creature. The colorful insect, sensing the grasping hands, quickly flew up and out of reach. Realizing the folly of the chase, the child stopped, placed his hands on his fleshy hips, and pursed his lips defiantly. His young, inquisitive mind pondered his next move. Reflexively, he looked over at his mother and father, and upon seeing their beckoning smiles, was overcome by joy and wobbled toward them. Upon reaching the picnic blanket, he playfully collapsed across their laps, closed his eyes, and feigned exhaustion.

Athania leaned over her son and brushed his rosy cheeks with the ends of her hair. Feeling the tickle, the boy scrunched his tiny nose and gently pushed aside her locks. Inadvertently, he grabbed a small handful of her locks, and tried to use them to pull himself up. Ben assisted his son, and gently loosened his fingers, taking the strain off his wife's hair. He playfully nibbled them, making the child giggle. Then he stood him up — the child was now at eye level. Waving his hands for balance, several strands of hair wafted from his grasp.

Athania X. Airaldi looked down and was puzzled by what she saw.

"Looks like a faint hint of gray — I've never seen that before," she said, incredulously.

"Are you sad?" Ben asked, running his fingers across her back, and settling on her favorite shoulder. They both felt the warmth from the mark under her blouse.

"Quite the opposite. The level of bliss I feel is higher than Mount Olympus." The doting mother playfully tugged their son toward them.

The child placed his hand upon his father's, which was still resting on top of his mother's shoulder. A serene smile came over his face and he suddenly became inordinately calm. He looked up, and then at his parents. With a little effort, he uttered his first word.

"Did Michael just say what I think he did?" Ben looked quickly from his son to his wife.

"He did — and in perfect Greek. His grandparents would be pleased." Ania looked directly at Ben and their eyes locked.

They then looked to their son, who repeated the words.

"Iesous...Iesous," the bright child uttered as he gently patted his father's hand. His first word was the Greek pronunciation of "Iesous," which, in English, meant "Jesus."

As they embraced the child, a delicate wreath, fashioned from previously-picked flowers, fell from Ania's head, and landed on Ben's lap. Her husband picked it up, and was about to replace it. As he did so, his expression changed, clearly indicating that an idea had been sparked within his mind. Ania, so synced with him, knew the question before he could ask, and said, "I wondered when you would ask."

Ben's eyes widened and he nodded eagerly for her to continue.

"Yes — I know where that is too...but that must be another story for another time."

THE END

 **About Leonine Publishers**

Leonine Publishers LLC makes fine Catholic literature available to Catholics throughout the English-speaking world. Leonine Publishers offers an innovative "hybrid" approach to book publication that helps authors as well as readers. Please visit our web site at www.leoninepublishers.com to learn more about us. Browse our online bookstore to find more solid Catholic titles to uplift, challenge, and inspire.

Our patron and namesake is Pope Leo XIII, a prudent, yet uncompromising pope during the stormy years at the close of the 19th century. Please join us as we ask his intercession for our family of readers and authors.

www.leoninepublishers.com